Lonely Hearts

By

Amanda Stephan

Lonely Hearts
By Amanda Stephan

©2011 by Amanda Stephan

Cover Design: Linda Boulanger
   www.TellTaleBookCovers.weebly.com
Interior Design: Linda Boulanger and Amanda Stephan

Published by: TreasureLine Publishing
   www.TreasureLinePublishing.com

ISBN: 978-1-61752-112-6

Also available in eBook publication

www.BooksByAmanda.com

The following is a work of fiction. Names, characters, places, and incidents are fictitious or used fictitiously. Any resemblance to real persons, living or dead, to factual events or to businesses is coincidental and unintentional.

Printed in the United States of America

For John, my loving husband. You are the hero in all of my novels. So, don't be mean to me, or I'll have to kill you off in my next book…but seriously. *I love you*. I love your sense of humor and the witty, romantic emails you send me. My favorite ~

"Roses are red. Violets are blue.
Should I order one pizza, or make it two?"

Mom and Dad, Brenna & JD ~ thank you for listening to yet another long, drawn out book conversation. I know I have bored you all to tears, but you were so good as to hide the glazed looks. I appreciate it and love you.

To my peeps ~ you know who you are…I am blessed to have such friends as you! Yes, that means you, April Crawford, Aunt Bea, Nell Abel, Tricia Delk, Jane Paul, Tina Torrez, April McKinnon, and Judi Bostwick…thank you for spreading the news and being a great source of encouragement.

Special Thanks ~ Karin Kaufman, Aileen Stewart, Hazel Nelson, Ursula Gorman, Kelly Hagen, and Darlene Shortridge ~ Thank you for your patience in helping me with proofreading and for sharing your thoughts as you read through this book. I appreciate each of you.

Linda Boulanger ~ you have been so patient and kind to me, I'm grateful to not only call you my publisher, but my friend.

The John 3:16 Marketing Network ~ a family, brought together by one woman's dream ~ thank you for sharing it with us, Lorilyn Roberts. You are an inspiration.

My Saviour ~ You are teaching me every day that with You, all things are possible. I love you.

What others are saying about Lonely Hearts

This story was a delight to read and one I had a hard time putting down until I finished it. This is the second book by Amanda Stephan that I have read and she is quickly becoming one of my favorite authors. A 'thrilled' fan.

~ *Judy Glidden, blogger of good Christian fiction*

Lonely Hearts … tugged at my heart and made me laugh and cry. I hated putting it down and wished it had continued… a beautifully written story of love, family, friendship, struggle and faith. Amanda does a wonderful job of pulling the reader into the story.

~ *Ursula Gorman, Author of Old Acquaintances*

Author Amanda Stephan does it again! She has a wonderful way of weaving faith in the Lord, everyday life, heartache and romance into terrific stories. Lonely Hearts is uplifting and full of adventure.

~ *Kelly Hagen, author of Jake & Jesus*

Beautifully written story about second chances at love and life. The characters were genuine and seemed real to life. I was captivated at page one of the book, and read it in only one day! This was a clean, uplifting story that was not overly mushy like some romance stories can be. Amanda Stephan did an amazing job pulling me into the story so I was sitting on the edge of my seat as it unfolded. I will recommend this book to my friends and family.

~ *Anastasia W., avid reader and crafter*

I LOVED this story. From beginning to end it kept me totally enthralled and wondering how it would all work out. Loaded with zippy dialog and great characters made for a fun and very satisfying tale. I felt happy, sad, excited, angry, and frustrated. You know a story is good when it has that effect. The theme running though our story is 'things may not always be as they appear'. It's a great reminder that man looks on the outside but God looks on the heart. If you enjoy an easy-to-read, fun and entertaining story with a great message, I highly recommend Lonely Hearts.

~ *Sherry Kuhn ~ Avid reader and Reviewer*

Amanda Stephan addresses an issue that too few authors write about—second chance at love. This book will capture your heart and like Becky's kids, your heart will flip-flop as you embrace one bachelor then the other for Becky. Who will win Becky's heart and how will the others handle her decision? This book is full of hope, anticipation, optimism, faith, and possibilities. If you have lost a love, this book will restore your faith that the possibility of true love has not withered as a flower in the hot summer sun. Amanda will capture your heart from the first page with this delightful story.

~ Theresa Franklin, author of Journey to Fulfillment

You'll find yourself nodding with delight at Becky's courageous reactions, cheering her on and sighing with her during her ups and downs of life. But even in the fresh humor that sprinkles through her experiences, you'll admire her rare quality to uphold what's important. Although romance wasn't a priority, God's ways usher Becky to unforeseen encounter with what often is inevitable when you trust in God's lead, hold on to your convictions and are deliciously surprised in the end.

~ Janet Perez Eckles, author of Amazon #1 bestselling, Simply Salsa: Dancing Without Fear at God's Fiesta, Judson Press, 2011

Just when I thought I had the story figured out, Ms. Stephan would throw in an unexpected twist, tossing a monkey wrench into her characters' lives--and a rather large monkey wrench near the end of the story. If you like romance, a touch of sweet humor, and characters who face life head-on, this is the perfect book to curl up with!

~ Karin Kaufman, author of The Witch Tree

Once again Amanda Stephan has kept my interest (a very hard thing) while reading Lonely Hearts. For all you who love romance and a bit of humor Lonely Hearts is definitely for you!

~ Brenna, avid reader and book reviewer

Lonely Hearts
Apple Pie Recipe

provided by
Darlene Shortridge
author of
"Until Forever"

Lonely Hearts Apple Pie Recipe

Pie Crust –
4 c. flour
1 Tbs sugar
2 tsp salt
1 ½ c. shortening
1 egg
1 Tbs vinegar
½ c. water

Mix flour, sugar and salt in a bowl. Cut in shortening till crumbs are the size of peas. Beat egg, vinegar and water. Sprinkle over flour mixture. Mix well with a fork. Divide dough into four equal parts and roll out on a lightly floured surface. Makes two double crusts.

Apple Pie Filling –
2 Granny Smith apples
2 Jonathon apples
2 Jonagold apples
½ c. sugar
½ c. dark brown sugar
2 tsp flour
½ tsp nutmeg
½ tsp cinnamon
2 Tbs butter

Prepare crust. Preheat oven to 375 degrees. Peel, core and thinly slice apples and combine in a bowl. In another bowl, combine sugars, flour and spices. Sprinkle half of sugar mixture into the pastry lined pie pan. Sprinkle the rest of the sugar mixture over the apples and mix well. Mound apples in pie pan and dot with butter. Fold the top crust under the edges of the bottom crust. Pinch to seal. Vent top crust by making decorative slits. Beat one egg white. Brush over top crust and sprinkle with cinnamon-sugar. Bake 50 to 60 minutes until lightly browned.

Chapter 1

Becky Callis was new in town, and she felt her intrusion.

A bearded man outside the hardware store stopped sweeping, broom held in mid-air and watched them narrowly as they drove past, perhaps wondering if she were the type to plunder and loot his shop. A couple of older women that had been chatting outside a tiny florist shop suddenly turned to stone, their mouths gaping open, snickering about what kind of woman would be caught dead in such an old pick-up truck. Becky even imagined one of their tongues hung out. She repressed a giggle and waved, receiving an incredulous half-wave from one of the women, and no acknowledgement from the others.

She hated being stared at, and tried to keep a somewhat pleasant smile pasted on her freckled face as she drove through. She could feel her fair skin literally burning with embarrassment.

Her thirteen year old daughter, Jen, gave her a twisted frown. "Mom, what is wrong with these people?" Her pixie face turned dark red as a teenage boy waved at her. "They act like they've never seen strangers before."

Becky's grin grew larger and more realistic as she gave a two-finger salute to the policeman leaning on his squad car with arms crossed as if daring her to go faster than the posted thirty mile an hour sign. Obediently, she stopped at the one red light the town could boast of and waited for it to turn green.

"I guess," she said with a shrug, watching an old man sitting outside a diner pretend to read a newspaper. He spit tobacco juice into a jar and set it down next to his chair, his bushy eyebrows making it very clear he was looking at them. "They don't get too many newcomers here."

Jen grimaced and pushed her sleeping brother's head off her shoulder onto the vinyl headrest instead. "Well that's fine, but they don't have to stare. Makes me feel like we're pets in a pet shop."

"Or beef at a cattle auction." Becky laughed at her discomfort, noticing that the green light flickered faintly before going completely out. She drove on at the urging of the honking car behind her before she spoke. "Oh don't worry, they'll get used to us and I'm pretty sure you're going to like it here. Just think," she said brightly, turning onto a dirt road the ratty map indicated. "We're celebrities!"

Jen laughed and looked out the window, taking in the country scene before her, the nosy townsfolk left behind. Large open fields of tall grass, trees lining the road, and mountains off in the distance made it a lovely scene she couldn't find fault with.

Becky smiled a sad, wistful smile, thankful she had her kids. In the nine lonely years following Frank's death, she often found herself wondering how she was supposed to cope and go on as she desperately missed her 'better half.'

At least I'll never forget what Frank looked like, she thought a little morosely to herself as she glanced over at Jeff.

Tall for his eleven years, he liked his dark hair short so he wouldn't have to mess with it, and his cherubic face hid a wealth of mischievousness and humor that always brightened her day. Especially when he looked at her with his guilty dark brown eyes as if to say he were extremely sorry for some prank he was about to pull or had pulled. Just like his father. Her heart wrenched with sadness, and she quickly turned her thoughts to another source of comfort. Jen.

When she looked at her daughter, it was like she was looking into a mirror. Petite, sassy copper hair that loved being just a tad on the unmanageable side, her hazel eyes full of compassion and loyalty, quick to laugh and quick to cry, she promised to be a beauty when she got older. Like her mother.

That's what Frank had always said, Becky fought against the lump that insisted on forming in her throat as more memories of her dead husband flooded in.

Just in time to stop a tirade of reminiscent thoughts that would have pushed her into a melancholy spirit, Jeff let out a tremendous snore and wetly smacked his lips, making them erupt into giggles as his head lolled once again onto his sister's shoulder. She rolled her eyes, but didn't move him.

A few minutes later, Becky pulled into what looked like a tractor path instead of a driveway and stopped abruptly when a home came into view. "Jen, would you please check the address and see if this is the right place?" She asked solemnly, studying the old, dilapidated farm house, complete with thigh-high weeds for a lawn.

Brittle shutters hung on by sheer will-power next to dusty, grimy windows that hadn't seen a washcloth in years. A huge, antique antenna had fallen off the roof and now hung dejectedly by a thin wire as if for dear life and swung endlessly against the side of the house, knocking off peeling paint with every slight breeze. A rustic lean-to that served as a shed, as well as termite dessert, stood forlornly off to one side of the drive. She tried to stifle a laugh and ended up snorting instead.

"Mom," Jen answered doubtfully, looking at the paper in her hand. "This is the right place," she wrinkled her nose, "but I don't think the guy you're renting it from told you the truth. Didn't he say it was nice?"

They looked over at each other and burst out laughing, waking Jeffrey out of a terrific snore storm.

He bolted upright and rubbed his eyes, looking out the window. "Huh? What? What are you guys laughing at? Why are we stopped here?"

"Welcome home kids," Becky said, grinning as she pulled up alongside the drooping porch and turned off the truck.

Jen opened her door and glanced down at the weeds. Becky could almost see her thinking about ticks and bugs getting on her. "Oh my word," she muttered as she looked around, a dismal frown on her face. "How are we supposed to get in? Is he going to meet us here or something?"

Jeff, always ready for an adventure, hopped out of the truck and ran to the porch. "He said he would leave the key under the mat by the front door. Come on," he said as he ran, wanting to be there before his more cautious sister.

Always in a hurry, he yanked on the handle of the screen door, causing the whole thing to fall right off the frame on top of him.

"Uh, mom?" He hung his head in shame, embarrassed that he'd already broken something. "I think we're going to need a new screen door."

"I'm pretty sure that's not the only thing we're going to have to work on." Jen laughed, thankful that it had happened to him, and not her.

"Noted," Becky answered good-naturedly, giving him a thumbs-up. She unlatched the tailgate and smacked her hands across her jeans in an effort to erase the dust she'd accrued during their long hours of driving with the windows down.

"Hey mom! You should see the beehive up here." He pointed to a gigantic paper wasp hive in the corner of the porch ceiling.

Jen jumped off the porch, squealing as Jeff picked up a stick to poke at the hive. "Jeffrey Allen! Don't you dare!"

"Did you find the key?" Becky called, trying to distract Jeff from the beehive.

"You don't need it," he said, innocently trying to hide the stick behind his back. "The door's open."

"Leave it alone," warned Becky just as he was about to give the hive a good whack.

"Aww," mumbled Jeff, dropping the stick and shuffling with his hands in his pockets. "Do you have eyes in the back of your head or something?" He grumbled, stepping up next to her as she pulled some boxes toward the edge of the tailgate of her old beat-up Chevy.

"Here," she said, handing him a smaller box. "Why don't you two help me and take some of these boxes in the house. And no, I don't have eyes in the back of my head. I just know you awfully well." She smiled indulgently at him, ruffling his thick hair.

Jen grabbed a box and started hauling it to the porch. "Too bad we sold our mower. Maybe we should get a cow!" Hopefully, she looked back at her mother.

"What's the matter? Don't you like the grass?" Becky laughed as she pushed more boxes near the end of the truck making it easier for the kids to grab them.

"Grass?" Jeff asked dubiously, struggling with his load. "If it were any taller, it would be over my head!"

Sensing an opportunity to pick on her brother, Jen blurted, "What do you mean, 'would be'? It already is." Somewhat sensitive about his size, he glared ferociously at her and she stifled any more comments she might have had.

"Come on," Becky said repressing a grin as she slapped him on the back. "Let's all get along now. We've got a lot of work to do, and I'm going to need lots of help. Here," she handed a box of cleaning supplies to Jen, and a broom and mop to Jeff. "Please take these into the kitchen."

They did as they were told, quietly quarreling amongst themselves as they left her to stack things on the porch. Becky was just setting down another load when she heard a loud crash and screams coming from the kitchen. Immediately dropping everything and with her heart in her throat, she raced into the house expecting something terrible. A large box of pots and pans lay ominously in the middle of the tiny kitchen and several lids had rolled over toward the antique refrigerator. This had obviously been the loud crash she had heard outside. Nudging the upset box with her toe, she wondered momentarily if a large poisonous spider had hitched a ride from their previous home and had scared them.

Looking wildly around the kitchen, she was surprised to see both kids standing on the chipped white Formica counter, their faces white with terror. "What is it?"

Jen pointed to the small utility closet at the end of the room while she clutched Jeff's arm with the other. "There's an animal in there!" She said, shuddering with horror. "I think it's a huge rat."

"Of all the things we have to have in the house, it's got to be a *rat.*" Becky said shuddering convulsively, her lips stretched in a thin line. She hated rats and mice more than anything, and was always disgusted whenever she had to deal with them for some reason or other.

Cautiously, she grabbed a broom and tiptoed to the door,

listening intently for any sound inside. Jeff shrugged off his sister's hand and lightly jumped down off the counter, interested in seeing for himself what was in the closet.

"Do you hear anything?" he whispered.

Becky shook her head and gently twisted the knob, ready to use the broom as a weapon and squash whatever it was. Slowly, she pulled the creaky door open. Taking a deep breath, she peeped inside and caught sight of tiny brown eyes looking back at her. Opening the door all the way, she found to her surprise and immense relief, a pair of baby raccoons.

"Oh look," she said, motioning for Jen to come down from her perch and look.

"They're so cute," Jeff said, poking his head inside the door so he wouldn't miss a chance to see what had caused all the fuss. "Can we keep them?" he asked, looking up hopefully.

"No way," Jen said, finally getting up the nerve to climb down. "That thing scared me to death."

"I wonder how they got in," Becky mumbled, looking around the closet.

"Maybe through there," Jeff said, pointing to the broken floor register. When he stepped in to get a closer look, one of the raccoons backed up to the wall and hissed menacingly at him.

"I think we're not going to get to keep either of these little critters," Becky said, pulling him out of the closet by the back of his shirt. "Go open the front door and I'll try to sweep them out. Jen, get the mop and head them off if they try to escape." Obediently, Jen grabbed the mop as Becky started sweeping both hissing and angry raccoons out the door. Finally, after three mishaps with one of the raccoons almost getting away and Jen re-climbing onto the counter while screaming, they managed to sweep them both to freedom. Laughing, they hurriedly shut the door before the coons could come back in.

"Jeff," Becky said, turning to him. "Get the tool box out of the front of the truck and see if you can try to fix that register so they can't get back in that way." Jeff's face lit up, happy to have a 'man's job' to do.

6

"We don't have much more to do," Becky sighed, as she and Jen went outside to finish unpacking the truck.

Her face red with exertion, Jen swept a few strands of hair back and stood erect, trying to unkink her back after lugging a large box into the front room. "I sure am glad we decided to have those yard sales before we moved."

Becky puffed and tried to navigate around the room with her vision blocked by the load of boxes in her arms. "Oh come on, don't you think it would have been interesting for you, Jeff, and me to carry in a couch?" She laughed as she and Jen slid down the wall and finally slumped to the floor, relaxing.

With an air of delight and pride, Jeff came in and joined them, his grin splitting his face in half. "I tried to fix that register the best I could. I don't think they'll be back. Duct tape fixes everything."

Becky clapped him on the back. "Thanks. And thank you too Jen. I appreciate both of your help." She leaned back and closed her eyes, drained.

Contentedly, they sat for a few minutes, hoping this could be the last move.

"Mom," Jen said, her alarmed voice breaking the silence. "Someone's here." Groaning, Becky stood up and arched her back just in time to see an old flat bed farm truck coming up the rutted drive.

"It could be the guy we're renting from." Quickly, she tucked a few stray hairs behind her ears and dusted off her jeans, trying to look presentable to whoever it was. As it neared the house, the truck turned off the driveway to park in the long grass right in front of their door.

A bent over old man in greasy overalls managed to get out and limp up the steps, chewing on a weed. He spat it out and knocked before he entered the room, uninvited. Alarmed, Becky stood with her hands on her hips, ready to push the fragile looking man out the door if necessary.

"Howdy," he drawled, eyeing her and the two kids. "Name's Pickles." He stuck out a grubby, calloused hand her way, obviously intending to shake.

Becky took his hand and gave it a light squeeze and a gentle shake, afraid she would hurt him. "You're the landlord?" She asked, looking over his shoulder at her open-mouthed kids.

He ran his hands up and down his overalls straps, amused. "Yup," he said, glancing around at all the boxes. "This all ya got?"

"Yup," Jeff mimicked humorously before Becky could answer. She shot him a warning look, her scowl deepening as he shrugged his shoulders and smiled like a Cheshire cat.

"That's my kind of boy," the old man grinned, scratching his bald head. "Ya got a year lease and yer rent is due the first of the month," he said, getting right to the point. "I live right down the road to the left if ya be needin' anything, just give me a holler. Glad ya made it," he stuck his hand out again.

Liking his simple, country ways, Becky found herself pumping his hand up and down a little more enthusiastically this time. "There is one thing we need, if you wouldn't mind. I don't have a lawnmower." She hinted with raised eyebrows as she walked him out to the porch.

A look of pure astonishment passed across his weathered features as he scratched his head again. He thought a moment before answering. "Well ya ain't got to worry about the grass. It'll die in a few weeks."

Becky followed him to his truck, not quite ready to give up. "You don't have one? We'd really like to cut the grass."

Jen snorted, close at her mother's heels. She hated being left out of conversations. "Yeah, we can't find Jeff if he steps off the path." Becky nudged her in the ribs, making her squeak.

"Sure I got one," he said, climbing into his truck. "Bye." He waved as he put the old truck in gear and drove off, another long weed clutched between his teeth.

Stunned, they watched him leave, a trail of dust clouds hanging in the air. "I think that means he'll bring it tomorrow," Jeff said after a moment, joining them on the porch. Amused, they burst into laughter at their neighbor's odd ways.

Becky ran a hand over her face, her eyes twinkling merrily. "Who's hungry?"

Always anxious to eat, Jeff gave a loud whoop as he jumped in the air. "I'm starving! What're we going to have?"

She shrugged, looking from one happy child to the other. "I thought we'd just go out for something tonight, what do you think?" Grinning at their exuberant 'yes', she clapped Jeff on his shoulder and grabbed her purse. "Let's go!"

Chapter 2

Their hunger being the deciding factor for their visit to the curious town, they didn't notice when everyone stopped what they were doing to stare at them as they entered the quaint diner. Almost.

After an awkward silence that seemed to last more than the five seconds it actually was, a pretty young waitress escorted them to a booth toward the back of the room. She set a few menus down on the red and white checked vinyl cloth, and asked, "Can I get you something?"

Her face flushed with embarrassment, Becky gave her the best smile she could muster under so much scrutiny. "Could we get three cokes please?" Bravely, she locked gazes with no less than three different diners as the waitress went to fulfill their drink order.

Jeff, not in the least bit shy, smiled and waved at several people, earning a few friendly waves in return while Jen looked through her menu with purpose and dedication, her face brick red.

He turned his attention back to his own table. "Mom? Can I go check out the hobby shop next door really quick? I just want a hamburger."

She looked over the top of the menu and grinned, both eyebrows raised. "I don't know if you can. Are you asking permission?"

He rolled his eyes in response, hating it when she corrected his grammar. "*May* I please go check out the hobby shop?"

"I don't mind, but only if Jen goes with you. Do you mind?"

Jen set her menu down on the table with a dramatic sigh. "I don't mind," she said grudgingly as she scooted out of the seat after a very bouncy Jeff. She glared at him. "But you owe me one. I just want a burger too, please."

"Don't be long," she said quietly as they walked past. She

watched as they walked the few steps to the adjoining shop and peered into the glass. Jen lifted a hand to cut the glare on the window as Jeff excitedly pointed something out, his face wreathed in smiles.

After giving their order to the waitress a moment later, Becky once again felt she was being stared at. She gave a cursory glance around the well-kept diner. A tall, nice looking cowboy standing by the counter with some friends gave her a crooked grin when their eyes locked. Embarrassed, she gave him a quick smile and looked away, the tips of her ears burning. Nervously, she fidgeted with her napkin, grateful that the kids were returning to the diner as he sauntered toward her.

"Excuse me," he said politely, standing a little to the side so Jeff and Jen could slide into the seat. "I couldn't help noticing that you're not from around here."

Shaking her head, she fought against the nervousness that washed over her. "We just moved in today." She looked up into his friendly blue eyes and tried to relax.

He twisted the rim of his cowboy hat around, winking at Jen and Jeff as they stared at him. "Today must be my lucky day then."

Confusion flooded her face. "Pardon?"

His crooked smile grew bigger as his eyes twinkled merrily. "I figure it's my lucky day because I'm the first to meet the prettiest lady in town."

Jeff groaned, apparently expecting a real live cowboy to have a better pick-up line than that. "Does that one ever work?" Becky blushed prettily.

His rich baritone laughter filled the diner. "I don't know. I've never tried it before. My name is Scott," he held out his left hand. Being right handed, she took it somewhat awkwardly, his larger hand completely swallowing up her smaller one. He shook it once, giving her ring-less hand an expert once-over, surmising correctly that she was unmarried.

She felt her face reddening again when she realized what had just occurred. "I'm Becky, this is my daughter Jen, and my son Jeff."

"Nice to meet you," both kids said in unison.

He looked doubtful. "Your daughter and son? You don't look old enough to have two kids their age."

She laughed as both kids emphatically nodded their heads. "Oh, I'm definitely old enough."

With a look of disbelief, he asked, "How old are you?"

She gave him a withering look. Jen clapped a hand over Jeff's mouth before he could answer. "Don't you know you're not supposed to ask a woman how old she is?"

Realizing that Jeff was going to be no help, he gave Jen a winning smile in an effort to coax the answer from her. "Come on. How old is she?"

She shook her head and gave him a sweet smile, heeding the warning look her mother shot her. "I'm not telling. I've got to live with her." Again, his rich laughter echoed off the walls.

"You've got some cute kids," he said, still chuckling. "Where did you move to?"

"We're renting a place from a Mr. Pickles," Jeff grinned at the name.

It was Scott's turn to look confused. "Mr. Pickles, huh? Not that old rundown farmhouse?"

Ruefully, Becky shook her head. "Trust me. The picture I received looked much different."

He shrugged his shoulders. "It may not look like much, but it's sturdy. Just needs a little bit of work, that's all. Been around for years," he said thoughtfully. "If you need any help, I'd be glad to give you a hand. Mr. Pickles is a real nice guy. Forgets a lot, but he's pretty good. He should do you right."

Reluctant to accept his offer of help, she took a sip from her Coke. "Thanks."

"There were some raccoons in the closet in the kitchen," Jeff said, anxious to impress his newfound friend.

Duly impressed, Scott arched his eyebrows. "Raccoons? In the house? Be careful. They can be really mean."

He sighed, leaning his head on his palm as he swirled the straw in his glass. "I know. Mom swept them outside."

"No kidding. Your mom sounds pretty cool." He winked at her, making her blush. "Well, I'd better get back, but," he said, turning to Becky, "if you'd like, I could show you around sometime."

She smiled and fingered her paper napkin as a deeper crimson crept up her already flushed face. "Oh. Um, thanks. That's very kind of you. I'll think about it." He gave her a slow, crooked smile and tipped his hat to her before walking back to his friends.

As if on cue, their waitress suddenly appeared, a tray of food balanced expertly on her arm. "That was Scott Boone. He's such a flirt," she said, throwing a look of utter contempt in his general direction. Roughly, she set their plates down. "Enjoy."

Becky watched her retreating back, her heart sinking. "Thanks," she called after her. She hated to admit it, but she had been flattered that a young man as handsome as Scott had shown interest in her. But now, all she felt was stupid. Defiantly, she flipped her hair over her shoulder and ignored the laughing group at the other end of the diner. No self-respecting woman wanted to be just a notch on a man's belt.

"Let's pray," she said, grabbing the kid's hands. They thanked God for all their blessings and began to eat. She managed to disregard Scott, even to the point of turning her head and looking out the window when he and a friend waved at her, keeping a steady stream of conversation up with the kids.

Jeff leaned back against the seat and sipped his soda when he was finished. "What are we going to do now?"

Becky checked her watch. "I suppose we should hustle on out of here and find the nearest furniture store. We need some mattresses." She dug in her purse and pulled out a few bills, handing them to Jeff. "Will you please go pay our bill?"

Gathering her purse and leaving a tip, she was surprised when a muscled brown arm held the door open for her on her way out. She looked up into Scott's twinkling blue eyes. "Well Becky, I hope I'll see you again."

She smiled in spite of herself as she walked past. "Thanks, it was nice meeting you." Pausing next to her truck she asked, "Could you tell me where the nearest furniture store is?"

He pointed down the main street. "Go to the light and turn left. The store is on the right, but you'll find better prices the next town over. It's a bigger place and they've got a lot more to choose from. I can show you how to get there tomorrow if you want."

She pretended not to hear his last comment and climbed in her truck, pulling the door closed behind her. "Thanks. Bye!" She waved as she left him standing on the sidewalk, chuckling.

Jen gave her a disapproving look. "Mom, he's going to think you don't like him."

"Yeah," Jeff chimed in, "he liked you!"

"He did not. Look for the furniture store."

After a moment, Jen pointed to a sign that hung above the large window of an ancient building. "That's it." She unbuckled as she parked. "You probably scared him off and we'll never see him again."

"If he's really interested, that won't scare him away."

"It'd scare me off," Jeff said, trying to be difficult.

Becky waved flippantly at them and walked into the store, smiling brightly at the clerk. "I'm not listening."

Jen clutched her arm, her voice tight with excitement. "Then I guess you wouldn't hear me if I told you that he just parked next to our truck."

"Jen," Becky said, rolling her eyes and not paying her much attention. "Very funny."

The sales associate zoomed up to them. "Can I help you?" Becky wondered fleetingly if it was possible to whiten teeth too much, and if it posed a health risk.

"Do you have a delivery service?"

His smile faltered at the prospect of losing a sale. "No ma'am, but we're having a sale today, and I'm sure you could find someone to help…"

She shook her head, disappointed. "Thanks anyway," she turned to leave and found herself staring straight into Scott's broad chest.

"If you need help hauling something, I can do it," he smiled down at her as Jen stood beside him, grinning triumphantly.

14

She ignored Jen's smug look. "I couldn't ask you to do that," she said, faltering a little.

He had her and he knew it. "It's no trouble at all. Love to help."

She frowned slightly. "Well…"

"Please mom," Jeff whispered loudly. "It's going to be really heavy, and if he hauls it for us, he can help us carry the stuff in."

"Yeah mom," he teased, his eyes twinkling merrily. "I can help you carry the stuff in." Becky looked from one pleading child to the other, finally relenting with a loud sigh.

"I guess we could use your help after all," she said to the sales associate who had been listening to everything with a hopeful gleam in his salesman's eye. "We're looking for mattresses and box springs."

Thirty minutes later, they were heaving some of their purchases into the bed of Scott's truck while the lighter mattresses for the kids were lifted into her older, in-much-need-of-repair truck. They were ready to head home.

Jeff stood next to Scott, his eyes pleading. "Can I ride with him?"

"Jeff!" She scolded, surprised and a little embarrassed at his putting her on the spot like that in front of him.

He winked, his face breaking into his now well-known crooked smile. "I don't mind. It's just down the road and it won't take long. You'll be able to watch me all the way."

She put her hands on her hips and gave her son a stern look before turning her attention back to Scott. "I don't want to put you out."

"You're not putting me out," he answered smoothly opening his door. "I've got to go over there anyway, right?"

"Well I guess if you put it that way. I suppose he could if you don't mind."

"I'll ride with him too, if it's okay?" Jen invited herself quickly before her mother could change her mind as Jeff climbed happily into Scott's big truck.

"Jen!" Becky said, surprised and somewhat horrified at her

plucky children. "You both know better than to behave that way," she said, more than a little irritated at their behavior.

"It's ok," he intervened, settling the cowboy hat back on his head. "They've probably never been around a real cowboy before. I'll go first if that's okay with you," he offered, guessing that she'd be more comfortable if she could keep her kids in view. "I know where it is."

She gave the kids one last glance that told them they were going to be dealt with at home before sighing in resignation. "All right. I'll follow you."

"Jeff, would you please keep the door open for us?" She called, grabbing the end of a mattress after she'd unlatched the tailgate of his truck.

"Sure mom," he called over his shoulder, running up the steps and standing by the door.

Scott smiled and waited for her to get a good grip on the mattress. "Ready?" She nodded as they heaved the mattress out of the bed. They worked well together, only fumbling once as Becky misplaced her foot on the porch step.

They hauled all the mattresses and box springs in and put them into the rooms where they should go, Scott making it much easier than it would have been with just her and the kids.

Amused, they watched as Jen fussed around making her bed, patting corners and pillows so they were just right. Becky glanced at him as he wiped his sweaty brow. "Would you like something to drink?"

He gave her a grateful smile and followed her into the kitchen. "Sure, what do you have?"

"Water," she blushed. "I haven't gone shopping yet."

"Water is exactly what I was hoping for."

Jeff grunted and rolled his eyes. "Yeah right." He ducked a playful punch from Scott.

"As you can tell," Becky said, opening a box looking for a glass. "My son isn't as crazy about water as you are."

His brows furrowed in surprise. "Why not?"

"It doesn't have any taste," he complained, searching for a glass.

Becky turned on the faucet and jumped back as thick brown muck came out. "Yuck!"

She caught just the tail end of Scott's amused grin as he reached over and turned on the other faucet as well. "It probably just needs to be run for a while. If I remember correctly, they had well water and it would do this every once in a while. But when you got to the clear water, it actually tasted pretty good."

"You've been here before?" Waiting a moment longer after the water had cleared, she filled a glass for Scott and one for her.

As if to show them how good it was, he took a big swig and smacked his lips. "I've been here lots of times." Cautiously, Becky sipped hers, waiting for some disgusting taste to fill her mouth. "Not too bad, is it." He said, smiling impudently.

Surprised, she nodded. "Actually it's pretty good." She colored under Scott's scrutiny, not realizing how attractive she actually was.

"What?"

He grinned at her discomfort. "Nothing. Anyway, Mr. Pickles' son and I were pretty good friends there for a while, and we hung around a lot."

"He has a son? I didn't know that."

Looking absently out the window, he fingered his glass. "He joined the army and was killed in the war. After he died, Mr. Pickles just wasn't the same anymore."

She managed to swallow past the lump that formed in her throat. "That's so awful."

He stared at her a moment, a lopsided grin on his handsome face and the mischievous gleam back in his blue eyes. "Well, I better get going." After an awkward pause during which Becky wondered if he were waiting for some sort of invitation to come back, he finally touched the brim of his cowboy hat and headed toward the door. "Thanks for the water. I'll see you around."

Following him out, she leaned on the porch railing as he started the truck. "Thanks Scott, I appreciate all your help. Come by anytime." She wondered at herself as the words tumbled out, seemingly without thought, and was immediately rewarded with a bigger smile.

It was rather nice to have another adult to talk to, but she couldn't deny that at times he made her uncomfortable.

Chapter 3

They spent the next few weeks cleaning and fixing things around the house, taking junk that had been left laying around to the dump, sweeping and polishing floors, painting walls, cabinets, and closets, washing windows, and unpacking boxes. The kids helped, but she gave them plenty of time to explore around the house, preferring to do things her 'own' way.

"Mom," Jeff yelled, running into the house excitedly one day while she was finishing the last box of kitchen stuff.

Her face red from exertion, she stood and arched the kinks out of her back. "What is it, bud?"

Hardly giving her time to straighten back up, he grabbed her hand and almost yanked her out the front door and to the shed. "We can mow our grass now because I found the lawnmower!"

"I didn't know you could be this excited about mowing the grass."

He pointed triumphantly at an old, motorless walk-behind mower with a push handle. "See? Can I try it out?"

"That old thing probably doesn't even work," she said doubtfully, eyeing the rusted blades and hard rubber tires. It didn't look like it had been used in ages. As if reading her mind, Jen grabbed it and pulled it out into the yard behind her, tines singing and leaving a swatch of cut grass to prove her wrong.

Jen gave her a triumphant look, her eyes bright as she continued to push it around the yard. "This is a lot better than that other mower we had before. I couldn't even pull the string to start it, and this one all we have to do is push."

Jeff made a grab at the old handle when she went past. "Here let me try."

"Wait your turn," Becky said, laughing. "I'm sure Jen won't do the whole yard. There's plenty for you both to do. Take turns."

Curious to know what other treasures there might be, she went inside the shed and was amazed at all the antique gadgets stashed everywhere. Finding a pair of old gardening shears, she began to cut away at the overgrown hedges. Before she knew it, she had trimmed her way into the front of the house where Jeff was now trying his hand at mowing, whooping and hollering with excitement as he blazed a haphazard trail around the yard.

Jen came up beside her, her face flushed with the effort of work. "I didn't know mowing could be so fun." She eyed the shears Becky was holding. "Can I try those?"

Becky grinned and handed them over, involuntarily thinking of Tom Sawyer and how he had tricked his friends into doing his work for him. Leaning against the porch, she watched them both for a little while, proud of how willing they were to help and make the best of things.

As usual, when she considered how blessed she was with her kids, her thoughts raced back to the early days of their lives. When Frank had been alive and life had been good. True, she'd learned a lot over the past few years, but things were far from easy. Having to scrimp and save, even to the point of wondering what she was going to do if extra sewing or odd jobs didn't come in. But what scared her the most, was thinking about when Jen and Jeff would leave home.

Who would she have to console her? Who would walk Jen down the aisle on her wedding day? Who would teach Jeff to be a fine, upstanding, hard-working man? Shivers ran down her spine as thoughts of a future without them chilled her heart.

The snipping of shears nearby brought her out of her dark reverie. Shaking her head, she headed into the house to unpack the rest of the boxes in an effort to console herself with work.

Putting the last of the mismatched glasses into the cabinet a little while later, she jumped when Jen appeared beside her seemingly out of nowhere. "Where are we going to church tonight?"

Rolling her eyes, she put her hand over her heart and tried to give her a stern look. "Would you please make some noise next time, and quit sneaking up on me! Sheesh, nearly gave me a heart attack." She grinned and gave her a quick hug. "I forgot it's Wednesday. Good thing you reminded me. I thought we'd try that one down the road this time. What do you think?"

She considered for a moment before slowly nodding her head. "That one we tried Sunday, I didn't really care for it. They didn't even talk about Jesus and I didn't know any of the songs."

"Yes, that one was a definite no," Becky said, shaking her head. "I didn't know it could be so difficult to find a church that taught from the Bible."

"I'm done with the yard," Jeff called, poking his head inside the front screen. "Come see what me and Jen did."

"Jen and I," she corrected automatically, tying her black polka dotted apron around her waist as she followed.

Beaming with pride, she wiped away a stray tear as she surveyed the newly mowed lawn and somewhat misshapen hedges. "Wow! You both did an awesome job, thank you. Now," she said, trying to sound light hearted, "who's going to help me with dinner?"

Not without misgivings, Becky turned off the truck and stared at the small country church they were going to try that evening. Her stomach lurched at the uncertainties of going into a new place and she sighed. Emptiness filled her heart as she longed for the old-fashioned church that they had belonged to before they had moved. She had always loved spending time with the Lord, and it never ceased to amaze her when she heard someone complain that church was boring or dull. Somehow, after Frank had died, Heaven seemed so much sweeter than ever before.

Jen looked quizzically at her, one eyebrow arched. "Mom? Aren't we going in?" Startled back into reality, she realized she had one hand on the door handle. Grinning sheepishly, she led the way into the building as though she were on a death march.

They scooted into an empty pew, trying to be as nonchalant as possible and not create any disturbance around them.

With her face red, Jen immediately picked up a hymnal and started turning pages so she wouldn't have to look a stranger in the eye. Jeff, on the other hand, wasted no time and looked around in search of some boy he could be friends with, while Becky sent a cheery smile to anyone who happened to look their way.

Becky was relieved to find this particular church was different from all the others, as people around them were anxious to greet them and make them feel welcome. She was talking to an elderly woman who was telling them how happy she was they were there, when she heard someone clear their throat behind her.

"Hello Becky."

Surprised, she turned to find an old childhood friend grinning at her. "Jack Anderson! I didn't know you lived here!" Jack held her at arm's length, as if inspecting her, his green eyes twinkling with mirth.

"I've been here for the last seven years. What's it been? Over ten years since we last saw each other?"

"At least," she said eagerly, grasping his hands in her own. "What are you doing out this way?"

He shrugged his broad shoulders and gave her a humble look. "Oh, nothing much."

The woman that had been talking to Becky earlier spoke up before he could give any more details. "Why honey, he's the pastor of this little church."

Shocked, Becky stared at the elderly woman for a moment before turning her attention back to the handsome young man. "The pastor? I didn't know you were a pastor."

He laughed at her look of incredulity. "Didn't think I'd make it, did you?"

A faint blush crept over her damask cheeks. "No, I always thought you'd make a great pastor, but the last time I saw you, you were about to be married and were supposed to go work for her father."

A shadow crossed his face and he gave a quick nod of dismissal. "Yes. I was supposed to get married, but it didn't work out. She left me at the altar I guess you could say," he grinned sheepishly.

Embarrassed, she laid a hand on his arm. "I'm sorry. She must have been a silly woman to let you get away."

"It's okay, really. God knows what He's doing. Speaking of, I guess I'd better start. But don't hurry away," he said over his shoulder as he made his way to the pulpit, "we've got a lot of catching up to do."

"I'll stick around for a couple of minutes, unless the preaching is bad," she teased in return, ignoring a few stares coming from some of the other parishioners.

Unable to bear it any longer, Jen jabbed her in the ribs with her book during the first song. "Mom, who was that?"

"An old friend. Nothing more," she said, shooting her a warning look not to romanticize the situation. Jen and Jeff grinned at each other, not in the least concerned about seeing more than there really was.

Love was so simple to them. Everyone that Becky met loved her immediately. The only problem they saw, was finding the right husband for her.

They had both liked Scott right from the beginning, and it was obvious he liked Becky, but now that Jack was on the scene, it seemed only natural that they would be more suited because they were old friends. They continued to mull over the matter all during the service, not paying much attention to the preaching.

After Jack ended in prayer, she shook hands and talked a little with a few friendly people around her while she waited patiently for him to get a chance to join her again. She had just said goodbye to a white haired widow and was about to sit back down in the pew when a deep voice rumbled behind her, giving her a start.

"Excuse me, ma'am?"

"You startled me!" Becky said, her hand on her chest. Turning around, her smile faltered a little as she stood transfixed by the sad brown eyes of a handsome man standing behind her.

Obviously not a stranger to the outdoors, his thick, dark brown hair waved in all the right places, while his chiseled, perfect nose sat atop a generously full mouth. He had a natural air of confidence that didn't fit with the uncomfortable expression he wore. With surprise, she realized *she* was what was making him uneasy and managed to tear her eyes away and glance toward a small girl that was peeking around his legs, holding a pen out to her.

"I believe you dropped your pen." He gently but firmly pulled the girl forward.

"Why, thank you," Becky took the pen from the shy child and petted her silken blond hair, smiling warmly at her. "What's your name?"

She clutched her father's knees and looked at the floor, her thumb tucked safely her mouth. "Emily."

"Hi Emily," she said, holding out her hand to shake. Solemnly, Emily shook her hand and dropped it almost immediately. "That's such a pretty dress you're wearing."

"Thank you," she replied almost inaudibly, burying her face into his black pants.

Becky beamed up at Emily's father as he protectively patted her back. "I'm Becky Callis, and these are my kids, Jen and Jeff."

"Nice to meet you," he said politely, shuffling his feet. His face red with embarrassment, she shouldn't have been surprised when he suddenly said, "I've got to go. Good-bye." He gave a half-nod, picked Emily up and hurried out the front door, leaving Becky to wonder what she had done to scare him off.

Jen looked miffed. "Wow, it's not like we were going to try to make him go home with us or anything."

"Sheesh," Jeff echoed, wanting to please his sister.

She shrugged her shoulders and pasted on a smile, trying to act as though it hadn't bothered her. "Give the guy a break. Maybe he just didn't want to talk. Not everyone likes to chit chat as much as I do."

Unconvinced, Jen crossed her arms and pursed her lips, her forefinger beating a rhythm against her arm. "He snubbed you, mom."

Embarrassed, she turned to see if anyone were within hearing distance and spied Jack coming toward them. His expression told her he'd seen the whole thing, and she gave him a rueful smile as she whispered out of the corner of her mouth, "Jen, stop. It's not a big deal. Be nice."

Jack stopped next to Becky and gave her what seemed to be a sort of half-grimace and a half-hearted grin. "Well, I see you've met Pearce Morgan and his daughter Emily. He's a nice guy."

"Nice?" Jen fumed. "He just…" she stopped as Becky gripped her arm and smiled a warning at her.

Confused, Jack looked from mother to daughter. "What?"

Safely out of his mother's reach, Jeff decided to spill the whole story before his sister could. "He wouldn't talk to mom. Treated her like she had the plague or something."

"Did he really?" Jack said, amused. "Give him some time, he's had a rough way to go. Divorced, if you wanted to know," he said, grinning slyly at Becky, watching her turn bright red.

He laughed softly and turned his attention away, giving her a moment to compose herself. "You must be Jen," he said shaking her hand. "The last time I saw you, you were just a few weeks old. And I've never met you," he turned to Jeff and waited for him to tell him a little about himself.

He stood as tall as he could, trying to look and act mature as he puffed out his chest and shook the proffered hand. "My name's Jeff. I'm eleven."

"Are you sure? You look older than eleven," he said, giving Jen a quick wink that made her giggle. Suddenly becoming serious again, he turned his attention back to their mother. "Last time I went home, I heard your husband had passed away. What happened?"

"He was killed in a car accident," Jeff said before anyone else could answer.

"He died when Jeff was almost three, so he doesn't even remember him," Jen announced importantly, glad to finally have a chance to say something.

Becky frowned her displeasure at her children. "Thank you. Now if you wouldn't mind, perhaps I could continue the conversation that was meant for me?"

Jeff grabbed his sister's arm before Becky could announce 'go sit in the back pew until I'm done talking,' or worse, 'go wait for me in the truck,' or some sort of horrid punishment like that. "We're going to look around."

Becky watched them go and waited for them to be completely out of hearing range before she deemed it safe enough to continue. She turned her attention back to Jack as they turned the corner.

"I'm sorry, they only do that when they think I'm going to be upset. I don't know what's gotten into them the past couple of days."

"Becky." Jack tenderly took her arm. She glanced at him, a bit surprised but not unpleased at his touch. "It's okay. They didn't bother me. I thought it was cute the way they stuck up for you. Plus, we're too old of friends to be worried about something so simple. You used to be able to talk to me about everything, remember?" He looked kindly at her for a moment, making her heart flutter a little as she stared back. He always had been good looking, but she couldn't help but notice how nicely he'd aged. "I'm sorry I brought up your husband. I shouldn't have mentioned him."

Her shoulders sagged as if a heavy weight were pressing down upon her. "It's okay. It's been nine years, I'm slowly getting used to it. Time heals all wounds, right?" She tried to make light of it, but he could tell just how much it still bothered her.

His green eyes searched hers for a moment, and finding a few stray tears hiding in the corners, he pulled her into a comforting hug. "No. I'm really sorry. I know you two were close. I wish it didn't have to happen that way."

Accepting the hug for what it was and ignoring just how wonderful it felt, she pulled away from him after a moment and tried to speak around the large lump in her throat. "What did you say earlier? God knows what's best? Well," she felt her cheeks burn with the memory of his strong arms wrapped around her and hoped he couldn't read her mind. "I happen to agree with you. It's not an easy road, but I know Jesus is with me."

Unaware that they were being spied upon by a conniving matchmaker and her ever faithful sidekick, they were foolish enough to be completely at ease and enjoy each others' company, taking the opportunity to catch up on lost time.

"Well?" Jeff whispered, peering around the corner with his sister.

She gave him a smug smile and turned her attention back to the unwary couple as Becky laughed at something Jack said. "They are definitely happy to see each other again. They've known each other for a long time so this is going to be easy," she sighed approvingly. "And he's *very* handsome."

It was a very silent drive home that night. Becky kept her eyes glued to the path the headlights cut into the murky blackness and drove a little slower than normal. Throwing their efforts of small talk to the wayside after several attempts to get her to respond, they decided it would be to their credit if they took the initiative and apologized before she could fuss. Trying to act more penitent than they really were, they apologized for their behavior, even going so far as to admit they had been *inexcusable*, (which was one of Becky's favorite words). They weren't, however, expecting her continued silence, and were starting to squirm when she finally spoke up as they were having a snack before bedtime.

"I appreciate your apologies, but just the same," she said, fixing them both with what they called her death stare--they had always assumed that if they so much as twitched during such a stare, they would suddenly be turned to stone or a pile of ash--"you two have been really obnoxious, and I expect it to stop. No more saying whatever pops into your head. Stop and think before you act." She paused for effect, while her next words dashed all their hopes of a complete pardon. "What do you think your punishment should be?"

Jeff, always the clown, ventured an answer. "No TV?"

She glared. "We don't have a TV."

"Sorry."

"Jen, you will wash, dry, and put the dishes away for a week, and you,"--she gave Jeff a stern glare, almost daring him to make his punishment worse by having a smart comment--"sweep and mop the kitchen, sweep and dust the living room, and sweep the porch for a week." Her words fell like the knell of doom, earning a groan and expressive roll of their eyes as she prescribed exactly the chores they hated doing the most. "You have to do a good job, or I'll add a week every time you don't. Understand?"

Glumly, they nodded and stood to their feet in an effort to escape before she could add anything. Giving her a peck on her cheek, they both mumbled a quiet 'goodnight' and left her to her ruminations.

Jen found her still sitting at the table with her head propped up and a far off look in her eyes a few minutes later. "I'm really sorry mom," she said, her bottom lip trembling just a tad as she poured herself a glass of water. "I didn't mean to embarrass you."

Never one to hold grudges, Becky pulled her into a bear-hug and gave her a quick peck on her forehead. "It's okay babe, I forgive you."

Jeff bound into the room and threw his arms around her neck, managing to wiggle past his sister as he planted a wet, noisy kiss on her cheek. "Me too."

Chapter 4

Nursing a steaming cup of coffee, Becky watched the epic battle for control of the skies the next morning. Dark blue grudgingly gave place to light cerulean that finally pushed pink and golden fingers upward as if to announce that all that might have been wrong the day before was suddenly in the past. A new day, the wind whispered gently in her ear. A day with no mistakes in it. A gift just for you, so watch what you do with it, the birds sang as they started to flit through the brightening sky.

She took a deep breath and let it out slowly, her sadness and loneliness nearly overwhelming. She loved sunrises and couldn't deny their singular beauty, was even drawn to them as a moth is to a light, but they always reminded her of what she had lost. A memory of her and Frank sharing a similar morning so very long ago, flirted with her mind.

Shaking her head and setting her mouth in a determined line, she pushed away the sadness that threatened to envelope her and surveyed her surroundings; looking for something to do that would help her out of her morose temperament.

It was time to make the dilapidated farmhouse a real home.

"Here," she said, piling a load of tools in Jeff's awaiting arms later that morning. "Please take these and put them on the top of that bench so I can at least try to organize them." Becky brushed a piece of unruly copper hair out of her eyes. Jeff moaned quietly and she gave him a stern look. "Sorry, bud, but this shed is in dire need of our undivided attention." He glanced over her shoulder and smiled, letting her know that Jen had made a face behind her back.

"Watch out, Jen, or I'll be finding you more work to do when I give Jeff a break," she said without turning her back. She heard a soft groan coming from her daughter's direction and couldn't help smiling a little. Oh how well she knew them both! She grabbed a broom and started swiping at years of cobwebs in the corners of the ceiling, when a large dust cloud down the driveway announced that they were about to have a visitor.

Sensing that an opportunity to get out of work was about to present itself, Jeff haphazardly ditched the armload of tools onto the shelf and went in search of their guest. "It's Scott!" he shouted as he came to a stop next to the shed. Becky smoothed her hair, embarrassed at how she must look.

Scott's boots sent a puff of dust scattering in the wind as he jumped out of his truck and scuffed his way into the shed. Ruffling Jeff's hair as he passed, he smiled at Jen and made her face turn crimson before he turned his attention—and charm—to their mother.

"Howdy. I just thought I'd come over and be neighborly."

"Hi Scott." Jen finally managed to eek out.

"Hey there. I see your mom's got you out here working," he winked, making her red flush take on an even deeper hue. He hooked a thumb over his shoulder toward the house as Jeff snuck out the door, "I think one of your helpers just escaped."

"I know it. Good help is hard to find these days. Why don't you go ahead, Jen? Take a break." Jen left a little more reluctantly, not quite as anxious as her brother to get away from the shed. And consequently, Scott.

Picking up a mass of tangled chains someone had thrown into a dusty corner, Becky began to separate them so she wouldn't have to meet his appreciative stare. "Don't you have a job?"

He grinned, unruffled. "My boss sent me over with some stuff to see if I could help you fix the place up any."

"Your boss?" Unknowingly, she'd stuck her tongue out a little and was biting it as she concentrated on the hopeless mess, which captivated him even further.

"I told him all about you and the kids. Where you were living, how the place looked, stuff like that, and he wanted me to help you with whatever you might need." He watched her work at the links and stifled a chuckle. Almost. "Would you like some help with that?" he asked when it was obvious she was getting it more tangled than ever. She sighed and tossed it to him, ignoring his dancing eyes.

"Where do you work?" Having tired of playing at the pond's edge with Jeff, Jen had come back to listen to their conversation, taking residence next to her mother.

He managed to get a few links to separate, making it look easy. "I'm a ranch hand at the Circle M."

"You work with horses?"

"Yep, I sure do." He gave her a quirky grin that made her cheeks flame.

"I love horses," Jen said, a dreamy look in her eyes.

"That's putting it mildly," Becky grinned fondly at her daughter. "Go play with your brother and let us talk a little." She waited until she was out of earshot before she voiced just a little of her concerns. "I don't understand why your boss wants to help us," she asked a little warily, making sure to stay busy and as far away from him as possible without being rude.

He set one chain on the workbench and continued on the rest. "He's a pretty nice guy. He knows you're staying here and he also knows that Mr. Pickles means well, but," he touched his head expressively, "forgets a lot. By the way," he said, looking around, "the yard looks great. Where'd you get a mower that would go through that mess?"

She hooked a thumb over her right shoulder. "The kids used that."

He gave an incredulous look at the antiquated mower that hid in the shadowy corner, his brown hands momentarily halting their work. "You're joking, right? They didn't use that."

"They certainly did," she laughed at his expression. "And they loved every minute of it too. Although, I don't know how long *that* will last."

He gave a low whistle and glanced out the window just in time to see Jeff thrust a green frog under Jen's nose, making her squeal. "Wow. I am impressed. Those are some hard working kids."

She beamed with the praise. "Yes they are. Sometimes I worry about Jeff though." She gave a slight grimace as the words escaped before she could close her lips over them.

His keen eyes followed her as she fidgeted with some antique tools. "Why? He seems like a great kid."

A hundred uneasy thoughts bombarded her as she struggled to figure out a way to answer his question without seeming as though she were desperate for a man. "He is," she finally said, her embarrassment apparent. "But he needs male influence too. I don't want him to grow up not knowing how to do manly stuff. You know, like how to fix things or make things. How to be a hard worker, that sort of thing."

"Where's his dad?"

She busied herself with organizing the mound of tools on the bench, thankful that an unruly piece of hair somewhat hid her expression. "He died when Jeff was two, and Jen had just turned five."

There was a slight pause before he spoke. "I'm sorry. I wish I could take that back."

"It's okay," she sighed. "It's been a long time. We manage."

"How come you never remarried?"

She gave a short, brittle laugh. "At first, I didn't want to. Then there just didn't seem to be anyone good enough."

Grabbing a pair of hay tongs, he held them above her head in an attempt to lighten the mood. "Good enough for you?"

The sad grin she gave him tore at his heart. "No. Not good enough for them," she nodded toward the kids. "They deserve the best."

He contemplated her answer for a moment, wondering what his childhood would have been like if his own mother had had a tenth of Becky's standards. *Better yet,* he thought to himself as he tugged a large box from her arms and set it on the top shelf, *what would the world in general be like if more parents saw the worth of their own children and put their needs before their own selfish desires?* His admiration for her grew as they worked steadily side by side, joking around and carrying on as if they were old friends. When they were finished, Becky stood back with her hands on her hips and admired their work.

Arching her back to work out the kinks that had settled in while she'd squatted down on the floor to sort various nuts and bolts, she gave him an impish grin. "You did a good job in here. It's just too bad you made me do all the hard stuff."

His eyebrows nearly flew off his forehead as he tried to vindicate himself. "Me? Make you do all the hard stuff? I don't think so." He waggled a finger at her and grinned his maddening half grin. "Looks good, though. You should be proud."

"Thanks for your help. It would have taken a lot longer without you."

He glanced around the ship-shape shed, nodding his approval. "So what are you going to use this place for?"

Leaning on a few crates next to him, she paused for a moment before answering. "I'm going to build a lean-to and put some chickens in here. It shouldn't be too difficult." He snorted, giving her a doubtful look.

"Don't look at me like that," she laughed. "I know exactly how I'm going to do it." Seeing he was unconvinced, she began to explain. "See those trees over there?" She pointed at two tall pine trees, not too far away from the shed. "I'm going to use them as my two fence posts, then I'm going to build a frame to sit on the ground to keep animals out and the chickens in. Then, I'm going to run chicken wire around the pine trees and nail the bottom of the wire to the frame on the ground."

He gave her a self-satisfied smile. "Yeah, but how are you going to keep coons from climbing down the trees and into the coop?"

"Let me finish," she grinned, holding up her hand. "I'm going to nail up a board here," she pointed excitedly to the length on the backside of the shed, "so I can build a frame to go around the top of the pen and staple the chicken wire to the top. Kind of like an arbor." She stopped and smiled exultantly, her eyes shining.

"How are you going to get inside?" He asked, still trying to give her a hard time.

With a haughty glance, she pointed to the door at the back of the shed. "Right here."

"Sounds like you've got it all figured out," he laughed, enjoying their playful banter. "But I still see a problem."

She frowned. "What?"

"Where are you going to get the chickens?" He asked softly, grinning from ear to ear, glad to have found something that she had overlooked.

She glared at him for a moment, perplexed. Brightening, she replied in a deep, mocking voice, "If you build it, they will come!" He burst out laughing, slapping her on the back.

"Well, let's build it before they get here."

The stubborn tilt of her chin as she stood in his way told him she wasn't accustomed to asking others for help. Nor accepting any if it was offered. "I can manage. I was just going to work on it a little here and there."

"Actually, I do have to help you. My boss told me to, and I've got to do what the boss-man says." His eyes twinkled merrily as he considered just how pretty she was with one hand on her thrust-out hip, her eyes flashing defiance.

Her chin lifted even higher. "Oh really?"

"Yep."

"What if I don't want you to?"

His grin was maddening. "Then I'd go back to the ranch and he'd be mad at me, and I might lose my job. You wouldn't want that to happen now, would you?"

Throwing her hands up in frustration, she moved over, making it a little easier for him to maneuver around her. "Why is he doing this? He doesn't know me, I don't know him, so why?"

"I told you. He knows you're here and might need help. He's a pretty nice guy, and he likes to help other people. And," he gave her a sly grin. "He does know you. You met him already."

"I've met him? What's his name?"

"That was the one thing he told me not to tell you, so you'll just have to figure it out." He grabbed a few needed supplies for the chicken pen and went outside, Becky close at his heels.

"You're really not going to tell me?"

"Nope."

"Give me a hint," she wheedled, changing tactics.

"I already did. You met him and he was impressed with you," he smiled, oblivious to her glares.

"Where did we meet? The grocery store? The furniture store? We've met dozens of people!"

"I'm not telling." Irritated that he was enjoying himself so much, she finally stalked into the shed in search of another hammer so she could help.

When she returned, he was laying out the wood for the base of the pen. "What are you doing?" he frowned up at her.

"Helping."

"No you're not."

"Yes I am," she said stubbornly, her lips in a thin, determined line.

"I thought you said earlier that you wanted Jeff to learn how to do things like this?" She could hear his amusement. "How is he going to learn if you're doing it and he's not?" he let the words sink for a second before continuing. "Why don't you let him help me, and you and Jen can go do whatever it is girls do." He grinned, knowing he was about to get a lecture by her defiant stance and furrowed brow.

"You're just afraid I can't do it, or I'll get in your way." Rich baritone laughter filled the air so delightful, that no matter how she struggled against it, she finally had to join in.

"No, I'm more afraid you'd put me to shame."

She caved. "How do you expect me to argue and give you a rough time when you give me a compliment like that? I'll agree on one condition. That you'll stay and have lunch with us, and you'll take something back to your boss from me as a thank you."

"Sounds more like two conditions."

"Nope. One condition, two parts." He laughed and accepted all terms.

Becky watched as Scott and Jeff worked on the chicken coop for a little while before she and Jen went inside to prepare lunch and spend some quality girl time together.

"Well, we're almost done, but I was thinking about baking an apple pie for Scott to take back to his boss. What do you think?"

Jen, who loved baking almost as much as she loved quality alone time with her mother, jumped at the chance. "I love making pies! Can we make one for us too?" Without waiting for Becky's approval, she started piling the baking supplies on the small counter.

"I don't see why not. We'll start right after lunch."

"Wow!" Becky said admiring the work the boys had done later that evening as Scott was preparing to leave. She wouldn't admit it to her kids, but she had really enjoyed having a man around the house again. Her face flushed with her treacherous thoughts. "I didn't expect you guys to get so much done."

"You hear that?" Scott said, poking Jeff in the ribs. "She didn't think we could do it." Jeff grinned, proud of a job well done.

She swatted playfully at him. "That's not what I meant and you know it."

"I'm going to leave before you get more violent." He laughed, backing away toward his truck.

"You can't leave yet," Becky said, going into the house and coming back out carrying a steaming box. He could smell cinnamon and nutmeg as he gingerly took it from her.

"What's that? It smells delicious."

"It's the second part of our one condition." She opened his door for him.

"Apple pie." He gave her an impish grin, his eyes dancing with mischievousness. "Do you want this to actually make it there whole, or can I help myself to a piece before I get there?"

"You have to share it with your boss." Jen giggled.

"Did you make this?" He asked, sliding the box gingerly across the seat.

"I helped."

"Then you're going to make a great wife for some lucky guy."

Becky waved as he closed the door behind him. "I appreciate

all your help today. Tell your boss I said thanks."

The truck danced a little when he put it in reverse as if it were anxious to be going. "I will, but," he tipped his hat at her. "It was really my pleasure. Thanks buddy," he said, waving to Jeff. "I couldn't have done it without you." They watched him make his way down their driveway, waving until he was out of sight.

"Let me show you the parts *I* did," Jeff said, grabbing her hand and tugging her toward the shed without waiting for a reply.

Jeff showed her around the almost finished pen, explaining what they had done and what Scott had taught him, who put what where, and how Scott had promised that he would be back to help when he got the chance.

"Mom," Jeff said, finally winding down as they walked into the house holding hands. "I really had a great time. Thanks."

"Why are you thanking me? You need to be thanking Scott." Baffled, she returned his impulsive hug, a feeling of impending doom gnawing at the pit of her stomach.

"Yeah. I'm glad he likes you." He said over his shoulder, running to his room to get ready for bed.

There it was. She wasn't the only one who had liked having a man around the house. Sitting at the table and nursing a glass of cool water, she wondered what she should do about her dilemma. She liked Scott, as a friend, but she had to be honest and admit that both kids seemed to have a special fondness for him. They even seemed to want him to be *more* than a friend.

Pearce's sad brown eyes and handsome face suddenly popped into her mind. *I could get lost in those eyes*, she mused.

Slapping her hand down on the table and standing so fast she nearly pushed her chair over, she went to talk to Jeff.

Pushing his door open, she knew by the sounds of his breathing it was too late. Covering him in his blanket and turning off his light, she vowed to take care of the situation with both kids--tomorrow.

Chapter 5

"Jack," Becky called as they climbed out of the truck the next morning at church. "Good morning!"

"Good morning. You're here early." He looked genuinely pleased to see them as he warmly grasped Becky's hand in his own. Jen and Jeff exchanged a knowing look.

"I wanted to talk to you about something."

He unlocked the door and stepped aside to let them enter first. "What about?"

"I was wondering if you needed a Sunday school teacher or something?" It had been a long time since she had taught Sunday school. The kids looked at her, surprised.

Jack looked thoughtful. "As a matter of fact, we need a preschool and kindergarten teacher, but," he hesitated, "you have to be a member of the church first."

"That's not a problem," she said, grinning. "I knew this was where God wanted us to be as soon as we walked in. Of course," she grinned and gave him a sly wink, which neither child missed, "it may help just a little that a very good friend of mine just happens to be the Pastor!"

Sensing a matchmaking opportunity, Jen pulled Jeff away to discuss the best way to get them together as they talked about joining the church and what Becky's responsibilities would be.

"I don't want her to like the pastor," Jeff said stubbornly, crossing his arms.

"Why not?" Jen asked, exasperated. "It's perfect. They've known each other for years, neither of them are married, what else do we need?"

"I like Scott."

Her face instantly turned crimson, a fact that usually alerted Jeff to a possible crush and a prime opportunity to pick on his sister. "Scott? Which would mom like better?"

"Scott," he said, sticking to his guns.

"We'll have to wait and see which she seems to like better, and then we can plan how to get them together. Deal?" she asked, sticking out her hand.

He pumped her hand up and down a little more forcefully than was necessary. "Deal."

It turned out that Becky was needed to teach far sooner than either of them had expected. The regular teacher, Mrs. White, had to be rushed to the hospital when her water broke and they were going to be unable to make it.

"Good morning class," Becky began later that morning, closing the door after Jack had left the room. "I'm your new teacher, Miss Becky." She smiled, trying not to be nervous with all the little children staring at her wide eyed. "Mrs. White won't be in today…"

A soft knock interrupted her.

"Pardon me," Pearce Morgan said, opening the door and gently pushing Emily through. "Oh excuse me," he said, surprised to see her there, his face turning dark red.

"Come on in," she smiled kindly, remembering her first uncomfortable meeting with him. Wisely, she directed her attention to Emily and showed her to a seat at a tiny table next to a pretty little girl in the back.

"This is the right class, right?" He said awkwardly, looking at the name on the outside of the door. She hid a smile at his bewildered look.

"Yes it is. The White's are about to have their baby, so I'll be the new teacher for a while." Her eyes twinkled merrily at Emily as she managed to look at the child and not him. Barely.

"Ah," he frowned as he glanced at his daughter. Becky wondered if she was going to pass his exam when he abruptly turned and walked away without another word, leaving Emily behind. Startled and slightly annoyed by his brusque manner, she turned back to her class trying desperately to control her flushed face.

"My name is Miss Becky, and I'm your new teacher." Pausing a moment, she heard a small child crying. Looking around, she found Emily sitting at her table, her head in her arms, sobbing as though her world was about to end. The little girl next to her shrugged her shoulders—just in case Becky thought she had done something to make her cry.

Becky's heart went out to her instantly. "Emily," she put a comforting hand on the child's back. "Could you come here with me?" Tearfully, she looked up at her while Becky knelt on the floor beside her chair. "You see," she began, "I've never taught a class with so many children in it, and I'm scared. Would you come up and sit on my lap to make me feel better?"

The change was remarkable. With only a slight hesitation, Emily took her hand without a word, led her to the big chair at the front of the class and sat in her lap, cuddling next to her as if they had always been the best of friends.

The rest of class went so well, the kids groaned when the bell was rung, signaling the end of Sunday school.

"I'll see you next week," Becky said smiling, as each child wanted to give her a hug before they left the class, which was kind of difficult with Emily still hanging on tightly.

"Emily?" Her father said in surprise, as he walked into the class and saw her sitting snugly on Becky's lap.

"Daddy!" She sang happily, jumping off and running into his legs, wrapping her chubby little arms around him. He looked up at Becky, shocked at the change that had come over his daughter in such a short time.

"How was she?"

"She was terrific," she said simply, gathering all her things and getting ready to go upstairs. "She was scared, but it all went away, didn't it Emily?" Becky said, stroking her head affectionately.

"Daddy, Miss Becky was afraid at first, and she asked me to help her, and I got to sit in her lap the whole class, and she was so brave, she didn't even cry once." She beamed up at him. He smiled tenderly down at her, petting her soft blond hair.

"Thank you," he gave Becky such a warm smile that it made

her heart flutter like it hadn't done in years. As she looked at him, a little of the weariness seemed to disappear, giving her a glimpse of what he could be if circumstances were different. If he were happy.

She could feel the blush creeping up her cheeks. "You're welcome. I'll see you next week Emily, okay?" She bent down and gave Emily a hug.

Clearing her throat, she managed a quick goodbye and left them to go upstairs, afraid of spending too much time with this man and little girl who were wreaking havoc on her emotions and causing unwelcome memories to force themselves upon her.

Small footsteps sounded behind her and a little hand grabbed her own and swung it around. "Miss Becky, can I come see you some day?" Emily danced around happily.

"Of course you can, if your daddy says it's okay," she said, being careful to look at Emily and not Pearce.

"And can I see your little girl and your little boy?"

"Sure you can! They'd love to have you come over." Becky laughed, twirling her on one finger.

Suddenly very serious, she stopped and gave Becky a grave look. "And can my daddy come with me? Cause I don't like to be without my daddy. He needs me." Becky tried to swallow the lump in her throat, longing to hug this child and make her smile and dance again.

"Of course your daddy would always be welcome. And you're right," she said softly, stroking her head lovingly as she fought tears. "Every daddy needs their child, and every child needs their daddy." Quickly, she disentangled herself from Emily, gave her one last pat, and without looking at Pearce, went to find the ladies room so she could cry.

If she could have looked back, she would have seen a sad, gentle man looking back at her. Someone who seemed to understand exactly what she was feeling, and who wished with all his heart he could take away her pain.

"Mom?" Jen called, peering into the ladies room a few minutes later. "Are you in here?"

"Yes," came the muffled reply.

"Are you okay?" Jen asked with concern, hearing the tears in her mother's voice.

"I'll be right out," Becky answered, blowing her nose. She waited a moment longer, hoping Jen would take the hint and go find their seat. Cautiously, she opened her door and looked out, hoping no other women were in there.

She hated to cry in front of people. Her face always turned red and blotchy, and she didn't like having to explain to well-meaning but interfering people what was wrong. How could she explain this one? Tell them that she missed her husband so much she ached inside? Or, that one of the men in the church and his little daughter had wheedled their way unbidden into her heart? She hurried to the sink and turned on the cold water to splash her face.

"Are you crying?" She jumped as Jen walked up behind her.

"It's okay," she mumbled, trying not to cry afresh.

"Did your class go that bad?" Jen asked, astounded. "I thought that was an awful lot of kids in there." Becky burst out laughing.

"No, the class went pretty good actually," she said, feeling refreshed like she always did when she laughed. "Thanks Jen. I needed that." She gave her a bear hug, grateful for her presence.

"What was it that made you cry then?"

"Just a lot of thoughts, that's all." She patted her face dry and fanned herself with a paper towel, trying to hurry her face to its normal complexion. "There. Do I look like I've been crying?"

Jen tried to look optimistic. "It's not that noticeable."

"Well, it'll have to do," Becky replied, still fanning. "Church is about to start." Bravely, she walked out into the auditorium, and was immediately accosted by an older woman who asked her if she'd been crying. Looking sourly at Jen, she just smiled and greeted her as pleasantly as she possibly could, and went to find their seat.

"Have you been crying?" Jeff asked, gaping at her as she sat next to him. Jen smacked him on the arm, giving him a look that told him to hush up.

After his finishing prayer, Jack made a beeline for her. She could tell by the look on his face he was a little concerned. "So how did it go this morning?" She breathed a sigh of relief that he had the goodness not to mention her red-rimmed eyes.

"It went really well. That little Emily is adorable."

She saw a hint of surprise pass across his face before he answered. "Yes she is. But she doesn't usually stay in her class. She cries uncontrollably until the teacher lets her go back to her dad. Did she stay the whole time with you?"

"Yes. She sat on my lap, quiet as could be." For some odd reason, the knowledge that Emily had stayed with her when she refused everyone else, gave her a great deal of satisfaction and delight.

"Well I never would have thought it. You must have touched her, then. She doesn't seem to like people other than her daddy."

"She seems like she's a really sad little girl. They both have a lot of sadness surrounding them. Almost despair." She remarked after another couple walked past them and shook the pastor's hand.

He gave her a rueful smile, his green eyes speaking volumes. "They both have good reasons to be sad."

"Ah. I see." Uncomfortable that he might think she was a gossiping old biddy, she continued before he could say anything else. "Well, I'll let you go. We'll see you tonight."

Knowing her only too well, he couldn't resist a chuckle at her flustered appearance. "Have a good one."

She managed to say a decent goodbye to several people on the way out, trying not to be unsociable. Watching as Jeff and Jen raced to the truck, she breathed in the refreshing air and lifted her face toward the sun, resisting the urge to hold out her arms and spin around like a child.

"Miss Becky!" Turning, she saw Emily running toward her, Pearce not too far behind.

"Emily," she smiled as the tiny child wrapped her arms around her legs, her strange delight resurfacing as she patted her back.

Emily looked at her, her eyes wide with anticipation. "Can I come over and be with you today?"

Completely taken off guard, she stood speechless. Pearce, mistaking her silence as disapproval frowned at his daughter, his tanned face a little red.

"Emily, you don't behave like that! I'm sorry. She's made up her mind that she likes you, and when she likes someone, she loves them." He managed an embarrassed smile, and she was struck by what a difference it made. A little of the weariness and sadness disappeared and his eyes lit up with just a hint of a twinkle, making her wonder what kind of transformation would take place if it had been an unreserved and easy smile.

When she realized she was staring, she gave a delighted smile at the young girl. "You want to come over today? Well, I think that would be fun," she said finally, smiling fondly at her, making the little one's face light up with joy. "In fact," she whispered loudly, "why don't you invite your daddy to come too, and we'll have dinner together."

Emily turned her rapturous face toward Pearce, who was surprised but pleased by the invitation. "Daddy, you're invited to dinner!" She jumped up and down excitedly, tugging at his hand. Suddenly, she stopped and grew very serious. "Do you have enough? He eats a lot." Becky laughed, delighted at his stricken look.

"I have plenty. I hope you like roast chicken."

"Roast chicken? Emily, are you telling me you would trade peanut butter and jelly for roast chicken?" He tweaked her chubby cheek affectionately.

"Oh Daddy," she smiled patiently, "we can have that tomorrow." She stared at Jen and Jeff as if she had just noticed that they were there. "Can I play with your little girl and little boy?"

As if on cue, Jen took one hand while Jeff took the other. "Of course you can." They led her over to see a bug on a leaf Jeff had found, making her squeal with delight when he placed it on her palm.

As soon as they were out of hearing, Pearce asked, "Are you sure this is okay? If it's not, I'll tell her no. She really put you on the spot. She doesn't usually do that."

"It's not a problem. We'd be glad to have you over."

He stared at her, transfixed for a moment, then cleared his throat and started backing away toward his truck. "I'll follow you." Tearing his gaze away from her, he turned his attention to the children. "Come on Emily."

"We'll see you there."

"We're going to have company," sang Jen happily as they drove home. "It's been a long time," she whistled out the window.

"What about Scott?" Jeff asked suddenly. His miffed manner didn't escape his mother's notice. "Isn't he company?"

"Yes," Jen answered sheepishly with a quick glance at Becky. "I forgot about him."

"Speaking of Scott," Becky began, remembering that she needed to address a few issues.

"He's a great guy, isn't he mom?" Jeff asked.

"Yes he is," she hedged. "It's nice to have a friend, isn't it?" He nodded silently, watching out the front window.

"Don't you think he's handsome?" Jen asked mischievously, and to Becky's wise ear, a little wistfully.

"Well," she answered, taken by surprise at her bluntness. "He's all right I suppose, but he's not my type. Can we continue this conversation later?" She parked beside the shed, leaving enough room for Pearce to park next to the house.

Jumping out of the truck before she'd even had time to turn it off, she heard their "Sure," as they ran over to greet Pearce and Emily.

For some reason, she felt their little chat didn't go as well as she had planned.

Taking Emily by the hand, they started toward the pond, leaving her to deal with Pearce. Alone. "You both keep an eye on her. Is that okay?" She asked suddenly, unsure if he would be all right with them watching her or not.

"Sure," he answered, smiling as he watched them. "It's nice of them to be so kind to her. Nice of you too. I still can hardly believe how quickly she took to you. Generally, she's a lot more guarded."

Becky laughed, and he admired the soft blush that crept up her cheeks. "I know how she feels. People make me a little nervous too."

"I don't believe that for a second." He laughed, and nodded toward the cleaned-up farmhouse and shed. "You've done a lot with this place."

"Thanks, but we've had some help," she answered, pleased with his praise.

"Help?"

"A guy named Scott came out to help us a bit. He practically built the chicken coop over there," she pointed. "He said his boss sent him out to help us." She flushed at the memory. "It was weird. He just showed up one day and told us that he was going to help. When I told him that everything was under control and we would be fine, he wouldn't take no for an answer. He wouldn't even tell me who his boss is so I could thank him properly."

Pearce walked over to inspect the new coop. "He put the wire on the top too?"

"No," Jeff answered as they came back toward the house. "Mom did that after he left."

This time, his smile was warm and unguarded. "Looks good."

"Jeff and Scott did most of it," she said honestly, a little annoyed with how her heart sped up with his praises and smiles. "He wouldn't let me help, so Jen and I made some apple pies."

"We had apple pie." Emily said, smacking her lips. "It was yummy."

"You like apple pie?"

Emily nodded her head and rubbed her stomach with such enthusiasm Becky couldn't help but laugh. "Mmm hmm, it's Daddy's favorite!"

"We'll have to see what we can do about that," she winked at him, enjoying his discomfort as his flush grew deeper. "I'm going to check on dinner. Make yourselves at home. I'll be right back." She hurried away, leaving Pearce at the mercy of the kids.

Chapter 6

"That was the best roast chicken I've had in years," Pearce said after dinner, pushing his chair away from the table, grinning as he rubbed his stomach.

"Better than Curly's," Emily piped, putting her dishes in the sink.

"Curly?" Jen laughed at the silly name, sure she was joking.

"Sometimes he cooks for us when daddy's busy."

"Tell Miss Becky thanks for dinner," Pearce said abruptly, getting up to put his dishes in the sink. She was surprised at how comfortable both Pearce and Emily seemed with them, chatting and laughing as if all the earlier barriers were completely gone. She found that she herself was really enjoying their company and a little sad that dinner was over now, thinking the comfortable manner would soon be at an end.

Emily threw her arms around her neck and planted a sloppy kiss on her cheek. "Thank you Miss Becky."

"You're welcome sweetie," Becky smiled, patting her back. "Why don't you guys take Mr. Morgan and Emily and show them the pond," she said, starting to clear off the table.

"Look," he said, giving her a stern look. "Call me Pearce. This *Mr. Morgan* stuff makes me think of my dad, and I'm not that old."

"How old are you?" Jeff asked immediately.

"Jeff!" Jen admonished, frowning. "You're not supposed to ask people how old they are."

"Why?"

"Because that's what mom told Scott when he asked her, remember?"

"That's stupid. I don't see what the big deal is about age," he frowned, rolling his eyes.

"Actually, I think you're just not supposed to ask *women* how old they are," Pearce said, winking at Jeff. "They're afraid of getting older." He grinned slyly at Becky.

"We're not afraid of getting older. We just don't want to announce it to the whole world," was her tart reply. She grinned broadly and started the water to wash the dishes.

"I should stay and help with the clean up," he offered, grabbing a towel off the stove.

"Absolutely not. Do you see how small this kitchen is? You'd just be in my way," She said playfully, taking the towel away and pushing him lightly toward the door. "Go play with the other kids."

He stood holding the screen door open as his eyes challenged her. "Play?!"

"Hey mom," Jeff asked excitedly, ducking his head around Pearce's arm. "Can we go fishing?"

"Fishing? A man Mr. Morgan's age probably doesn't like fishing." Becky teased, soap up to her elbows.

He let the door close and grabbed the sink's spray nozzle. " 'A man Mr. Morgan's age'?"

She shook her head, backing away slightly. "You wouldn't dare." In answer, Pearce grinned and liberally squirted her, drenching the apron she still wore.

"Mr. Morgan!" She shouted, laughing in surprise, purposefully using his proper name. He promptly squirted her again.

"Say it! Say Pearce!" He growled playfully, brandishing the nozzle at her.

"Pearce!" She cried out, water dripping everywhere.

"There. That wasn't so hard, was it," he laughed, handing her a dish towel to dry off with.

"Yes it was," She giggled, taking the towel. He watched her, admiring the brightness of her eyes and easiness of manner.

"What?" She asked, catching his look of approval.

"Nothing."

Jeff, who was still standing with his head poking through the door, broke into their repartee. "Does that mean you want to go fishing?"

Suddenly very grateful for a distraction, Pearce tore his gaze away from her and lay the towel over the stove's door handle. "Of course I want to go fishing. Show me the way."

"Are you coming out when you're done?" He paused at the screen door.

"Absolutely not!" She said hotly. "You're dangerous with water."

"Don't make me come in after you."

She held her hands up in mock surrender. "I'll be out when the kitchen is finished."

"Fifteen minutes or I'm coming back and we're having another water fight," he called over his shoulder, making her laugh.

She finished the kitchen before her fifteen minutes were over, but she decided to press her luck and make some coffee. She had just finished pouring a cup for both of them when Jeff came to the door.

"Pearce wants to know where you're at," he called noisily, walking in.

"Oh he does, does he?" She laughed, her eyes twinkling. "Will you please tell Mr. Morgan that I'm on my way?"

"Do I have to call him that?" Jeff asked, doubtfully. "I really don't want to be thrown into the pond."

"No," she chuckled, ruffling his hair. "I'm coming. Here." She handed him a small basket filled with creamer and sugar and grabbed the two cups of steaming coffee.

"Want some coffee?" She asked, walking carefully up behind Pearce as he sat next to the pond, his fishing pole stuffed into a crook of a large oak tree.

He grinned and took the proffered cup. "Thanks."

"Here's cream and sugar if you want any," she said quickly, pointing to the basket.

"Black is the only way to have coffee." He laughed, taking a sip. "Mmm, this is good. A lot better than I've had in a long time." Sighing with contentment, he leaned back on the tree trunk.

"Thanks," she smiled, leaning against a smaller tree not far away, stretching her legs out in front of her. They sipped the hot liquid in companionable silence as they watched the kids.

"She might need a change of clothes," Becky said thoughtfully a few minutes later as Emily, Jen, and Jeff tried to catch frogs in the mud surrounding the pond.

"What?" Pearce asked as if he had been in a preoccupied daze.

"Emily," she said softly, nodding her head toward the mud spattered child.

The look of utter shock on his face threw her into a fit of soft laughter. "Well, I definitely have to get her new clothes before church."

"It's okay. I've got some old dresses of Jen's that she could use," she offered hopefully, suddenly anxious to keep them there just a little longer. He gave her such an odd look that she wondered what she had said that had irritated him. "Never mind," she said awkwardly.

"No, that's okay," he gave her a guarded smile and shook his head as if trying to get rid of a pesky thought. "In fact, that'd be great."

"I didn't mean to offend you," she blurted, wishing they could get back to their previous friendliness. "I just wanted to help. I know some people don't like the thought of hand-me-downs."

"No really. That doesn't bother me at all. But I was just wondering," he looked at her warily, "if you're always this way."

She stared at him, confused. "What way?"

"Nice. Helpful. Playful. I mean, is this the way you always are, or is this just your best-behavior-because-you-have-company act." He turned away from her, but not before she saw the distrust in his eyes.

Disheartened, she plucked a stem of grass and started to shred it into long, curly strips. "Pearce," she said quietly after a moment. "I don't act any different with you than I do with anyone else. Not everyone is a hypocrite." Throwing the pieces of grass aside, she stood and brushed off her pants and managed a bright smile. "I'll be right back."

In the warm, dusty attic, she sat on a plastic tote and opened a box that held some of Jen's old dresses. With a heavy sigh, she pulled out a beautiful party dress Jen had adored and held the whisper soft material to her face. The floodgates of memories suddenly burst and unheeded tears rushed down her cheeks, her heart yearning for what was lost.

The soft wisp of Pearce's shoes announced his presence at the top of the staircase.

"Becky?" Keeping her face averted, she wiped her eyes and took a tremulous breath to steady her nerves.

"I'm sorry," he knelt next to her, his hand on her shoulder. "I didn't mean to hurt your feelings."

"It's not that," she said with a sigh, embarrassed that he had caught her crying. "It's all right."

Squatting down next to her, he peered into her red face, his eyes dark with remorse. "I'm really sorry. Will you forgive me?"

Wiping at a late tear that suddenly streaked down her cheek, she gave him a small smile. "There's nothing to forgive."

"I guess I'm not very good with people. I'm always saying or doing the wrong thing. I didn't mean anything by it."

His tone melted her heart and she smiled kindly at him to put him at ease. "Is this dress okay for Emily? It should fit her, Jen was always very small," she changed the subject, holding up the dress.

Caressing the fabric gently, he glanced at her tear streaked face. "Are you sure you don't mind her wearing it?"

"I don't mind," she answered softly. "It was Jen and my favorite," she paused, taking a deep breath. "And my husband's. She wore it to his funeral."

"I'm sorry."

"She had just turned five, and Jeff was two. He was on his way home from work one night, and a drunk driver hit him head on. He was killed instantly, and the drunk walked away. He was my best friend." She sighed and struggled against the sudden burst of bitterness that welled up inside.

"How do you handle it?" He asked quietly after a moment.

She shrugged and shook her head. "I don't. I finally had to let it go and give it all to the Lord, because it was making me bitter and eating me up inside. It made me realize how good God is to me, and how much I take him for granted. *And we know that all things work together for good to them that love God, to them who are the called, according to his purpose.*" She quoted sadly, stroking the dress in her lap. "I think that's my life verse. That's the one I quote when things really hurt."

Silence filled the air as he studied her a moment. "I've never met anyone like you."

"Count your blessings," she said with a small laugh, wiping a fresh tear off her cheek.

Emily was adorable in her borrowed dress, prancing around like a princess before everyone at church that night, even going so far as to give a small curtsy to Jack when he complimented her on it.

"Pearce," Jack said after services were over, "Emily has really come out of her shell," he smiled as she floated by.

"Yes she has," he grinned. "Becky loaned her that dress today and she's been that way since she put it on."

"Becky?" Jack asked, somewhat surprised. He looked at her musingly, then brought his gaze back to Pearce, who was also watching her as she talked to some people that stood near.

"She looks nice tonight, doesn't she?" Jack watched him closely for his reaction, trying not to notice a small pang of jealousy.

As if he were talking from a far off place, he answered, "Yes she does. Real nice." On cue, Becky turned, saw them, and waved.

"I've known her almost my whole life. She's a good woman." Another pang of something akin to jealousy stabbed at him.

His words brought him out of his reverie and he shook his head, his face red. "What? I'm sorry. I wasn't paying much attention."

"I said she's a good woman."

Pearce felt a twinge of annoyance. "I guess so," he answered a little defensively, shrugging his shoulders. He hated it when he felt people were trying to fix him up with a woman, but he hated it even more that Jack had caught him staring.

"Hello Becky," Jack called over Pearce's shoulder as she walked toward them.

He grabbed Jack's hand, pumped it once and dropped it, suddenly in a hurry to get away from them. "Well, I better get going. Have a good week, Pastor."

"Hi Jack," she said faintly as she watched him go stand near Emily while she played with the other kids. "What's wrong with him?"

"I think you scared him," he laughed, releasing her hand reluctantly.

She looked bewildered. "Well I didn't mean to. I thought he was getting used to me. I guess I was wrong."

"Give him time. He's a very private person and doesn't handle change too well. He'll come around," he said quietly, laying a hand on her arm.

Shaking off her irritation, she gave him a brilliant smile and changed the subject. "Did you have a good day?" They talked amiably for a little while, oblivious to the fact that they had Pearce's undivided attention.

"Oh, I almost forgot," Jen said on their way home from church. "Pearce asked me to tell you that he'd bring back the dress as soon as he could, thanks again for dinner, and that he had a good time." She looked at Becky doubtfully. "He said he had a good time, but it seemed like he was upset about something after church."

"It did seem like he was upset," Becky agreed, "but I don't know what it could have been about."

"He stared at you a lot," Jeff said importantly. "Maybe he likes you."

"He doesn't like me Jeff," she sighed knowingly, a little tired of their matchmaking schemes.

"How do you know?"

"Because he can hardly stand to talk to me!" She blurted edgily, avoiding his penetrating eyes.

"What about today after church?" He wasn't giving up without a fight.

"I don't know. Maybe because Emily wanted to come over so badly. Please," she sighed tiredly. "Can we stop talking about this? Just believe me that he's not interested." She parked the truck, got out, and went inside without waiting for either of them.

"Whoa," Jeff whistled. "Is it just me, or is she crabby?"

Jen nodded, her eyes wide. "She's definitely crabby. Do you think he doesn't like her?"

He shot her a scornful look. "I think he likes her a lot. Why wouldn't he?"

"I agree. And I think she likes him too. Well, *now* who do we pick for her? Jack, Scott, or Pearce? I didn't know it could be so complicated!" She tossed her coppery hair over her shoulder and started for the house, Jeff fast on her heels.

Chapter 7

They were too busy with school over the next few weeks to give Becky's love life much attention, but they did notice that although he was polite, Pearce tried hard to stay away from her and only talked to her when it was absolutely unavoidable. They also saw that she had given up much hope for any kind of friendship between them and kept her attention focused almost wholly on Emily whenever they were around.

Becky was outside sitting on the porch one afternoon watching Jeff as he worked around the yard when Scott drove up. Giving her his signature crooked smile, he lazily jumped out of his truck and smashed his hat on his head. She watched, grinning as a small puff of dust wafted through the air around his cowboy boots.

"What's up Jeff?" He gave Becky a quizzical look.

Jeff grimaced and refused to look up at his friend. "Hi."

Becky couldn't help but grin at his surprised look caused by Jeff's less than boisterous greeting. "What brings you here? Did your boss send you again?"

"Maybe. Or maybe I was just on my way to get some things from town, so I thought I'd stop by and see how you guys are doing." He pointed to Jeff. "I see he's not doing too well."

"Have a seat," she offered, waving to the rocker next to hers. "Actually he's not doing too well."

He took the proffered seat and dragged it just a little closer to her. "That's one thing I hated when I got into trouble. My mom was always so creative in finding work for me to do. Weeding was the worst. What'd he do?"

"He was misbehaving in school. Not listening. Giving an attitude. Sassing. You name it, he was doing it." She said softly, the discouragement showing on her face.

"Sometimes it's hard to fit into a new school. He was probably just trying to impress the other kids."

"You know, I'd agree with you if he went to a public school, but he's homeschooled." If there was a limit on how many times a person could be shocked in one afternoon, Scott was well on his way to fulfilling his quota.

His drawn out "Oh," told her that was the last thing he'd expected.

"What do you mean 'oh'?" She asked tartly, casting him a sideways glance.

Shaking his head, he muttered a quick, "Nothing."

"You're not getting out of it that easily. Explain yourself." She crossed her arms and pursed her lips, stifling a giggle that wanted to erupt. She enjoyed watching him squirm and try to dig himself out of a hole.

"I was just surprised that you homeschool, that's all."

"Why? Do you think I can't handle it?"

"It's not that," he said, turning red. "I just thought that seeing as how you're a widow that you wouldn't be able to, you know," he cleared his throat, "afford it."

Her sudden laugh made him a little more comfortable. "Well if it makes you feel better, we're okay. Before my husband died, we felt the Lord leading us to homeschool any kids we were lucky enough to have. So, we started putting as much money away as possible so we could handle it financially. We had a pretty good nest egg by the time Jen was born, and even bigger and better by the time Jeff arrived." A large sigh escaped before she continued. "After Frank died, I got the life insurance and invested all I could. So we're living off what the investments make, and taking it one day at a time."

"But what if things go wrong?"

"If and when, you mean. When things go wrong, I sell off some things that I can to make it by, or I take in laundry, or I take cleaning jobs that will allow me to take the kids with me. I haven't had to do that too often, though. God's been good and met every single need we've ever had. Does that make you feel better?" Her playful grin set the butterflies whirling in his stomach and he couldn't help but admire her even more for her determination.

"I guess so. By the way, I brought you something." He said over his shoulder as he jogged back to his truck. Pulling the door open, she watched as he leaned in a little and retrieved the glass pie plate she had sent with him. "The boss said thanks for the apple pie. He said it was the best he's ever had." Thinking he was getting ready to leave, she joined him at the truck so he wouldn't have to walk back.

"I'm glad he liked it," she said with a sly look as he handed it to her. "So. Are you going to tell me who your boss is yet?"

"Nope." He laughed at her playful pout and winked. "He also sent you something else."

"Sent something else? What is it?"

"Come see." When he opened the tailgate of his truck, she heard some scuffling and a very weak cock-a-doodle-do only a moment before she saw a proud, and somewhat disheveled, Rhode Island red rooster and six hens crouching in a cage.

"Oh my goodness, they're wonderful!" She looked like she had a little bit of trouble keeping herself from clapping from excitement. After she had a moment to think about it, her expression became troubled. "Why did he send me chickens?"

"Because he knew you wanted some," he answered simply, taking the cage and carrying it to the chicken pen. Unlatching the door, he set the cage down and opened the gate, dust and feathers flying as they scattered and scrambled to get out.

"Chickens!" Jen yelled excitedly as she and Jeff joined them, "where'd you get them?"

Jeff, who had barreled his way inside the coop, stepped back toward the fence with a look of awe on his face. "Look at that huge rooster! He almost comes up to my knees. I say we name him Bird-zilla."

"Scott's boss sent them," Becky answered after a moment. Jen glanced at her mother, and her heart sank at her grim look.

"Your boss has to be the coolest guy around." Jeff crouched low and tried to coax a hen to come near him.

Scott grabbed a bag of laying mash and marched toward the

shed. "He is pretty cool. I'll tell him you said that. Where do you want me to put the feed?"

Becky chewed her bottom lip, her brow furrowed. "I can't take them."

He didn't look surprised that she was going to argue. "Why not?"

"Because it's not right."

"Why isn't it right to accept a gift?"

"Why does your boss do such nice things for me?"

"Because he thinks you're pretty terrific," he said, looking at her fondly. "And just for the record, I agree with him."

Exasperated with his compliments, she held up her hands. "Stop. I don't want to hear it." She backed away from him, and re-crossed her arms with a stubborn tilt to her chin. "Is he married? I'm not taking anything from him if he is. I'm not that kind of woman."

His deep, throaty laugh resonated through the small shed. "He's not married. Trust me. If he thought you were 'that-kind-of-woman', he'd have nothing to do with you. Me, on the other hand," he scooted out of the playful swat she threw his way and continued with a mischievous twinkle, "Come on and show me where you want this feed."

"I'm paying him back you know."

"He won't take it," he grinned stubbornly.

"Then I'll pay for the feed."

"He won't take that either." He put the bag down in an empty garbage can Becky had bought a few days before and closed the lid tightly.

"We'll see." Turning, she went into the house and came back a few moments later, a disappointed look on her pretty face. "I've only got a twenty. I'll give him the rest later." She held out the bill for him to take.

"He won't take it. Especially if he finds out that's all you've got."

Annoyed, she rolled her eyes. "It's not really all I have. It's just in the budget to wait a week before I get more out of the bank," she replied saucily, her eyes flashing. "Please take it."

Reluctantly, he took the bill and put it into the pocket of his shirt before he climbed into his truck. "What if he won't take it?"

"Let him decide what to do with it then." She argued, stepping back. "And please tell him I said thanks."

"Will do. I've got some things I've got to do in town. Have a good one," putting the truck in reverse, he started to slowly back away. He gave her an impish grin and called, "I wanted to tell you. You look very pretty today."

She stuck her tongue out at him. "Oh go on!"

"I got everything we needed to fix that fence in the south pasture," Scott said later that afternoon, walking into a handsome barn. Running his hand down the soft, velvety muzzle of a gorgeous white mare as he passed by, he came and stood next to his boss.

"Good," the rugged man said, not looking up from the clipboard he was holding. "Did you make it to Becky's place?" An old man that was spreading out fresh hay in a stall gave them a curious glance.

"Yes I did," Scott answered slowly, handing him the twenty. "She said thanks."

Fingering the money, he gave Scott a frown. "What's this for?"

"She wanted to pay for the chickens," he said with a shrug and turned to leave.

"Wait a minute," he said, looking at him crossly. "You should have told her that I wouldn't take it."

Scott grinned. "I did. She wouldn't take no for an answer. In fact, she told me that she wasn't going to accept the chickens at all."

"Why not? I thought she wanted them."

"Oh she wanted them all right. She just thought that you might be married, and she wasn't going to accept any gifts from a married man. She said she wasn't 'that kind of woman'." He leaned against the doorway, smiling at the memory of Becky's determined look. He'd always heard redheads were mean, but after knowing Becky better, he considered her more spicy than mean. *Yes,* he thought to himself with a private grin, *she'd probably keep me interested a little longer than usual.* His boss's chuckle brought him out of his pleasant reverie.

Without thinking, Scott said, "Did you know she homeschools those kids? I guess Jeff was giving her a hard time today, so she had him outside doing work when I got there. She's pretty spunky, if you ask me."

For some reason, the grin on his face didn't set well with Scott, and he suddenly wished he hadn't said anything about her. "Huh. You don't say. Sounds like she's got everything under control. Thanks for going to town for me, Scott."

"Sure." he said over his shoulder as he walked away. Then, turning back before he got all the way outside, he said in an effort to make him feel guilty, "That twenty she gave you is all she had."

"Thanks." Watching him leave, he took the money out of his pocket and looked at it, imagining her stubborn refusal to take help without doing something kind in return.

"She sounds spunky all right," the old man laughed quietly as he came to stand next to him. "What're you going to do with that?"

"Give it back," he said with a twinkle in his eye as he placed the bill back inside his shirt pocket.

"Mom, I got the mail," Jeff shouted a few days later, letting the screen door slam shut behind him.

Becky gritted her teeth and managed to hang onto the stack of plates she'd almost dropped. "Jeffrey Allen, stop shouting!"

Leaning on the counter, he held out an envelope toward her, his smile unabated at being fussed at. "But you got something." Setting the plates carefully in the cupboard, she took it and stared at the bold hand writing, flipping it over after a moment.

"Who's it from?"

"I don't know," she said honestly, sliding her finger through the flap. As she pulled out a plain piece of white paper, a twenty dollar bill fell to the floor. Jeff stooped to pick it up and handed it to her.

"What does it say?" Burning with curiosity, Jeff leaned over her shoulder in an attempt to read it for himself.

Aloud she read:

Dear Becky,

Thank you for paying me for the chickens and their feed, but I can't accept the money as it was a gift from someone who hopes to become a good friend. You have helped me in ways I cannot explain, but I wish to show you my gratitude for all you are, and all you've done. I am indebted to you, and am honored to know you.

Very truly yours,

Scott's Boss

Jen, who had joined them just after she'd opened the letter, was now crowding around her brother. "Who do you think wrote it?"

Becky gave her a puzzled frown and tried to remember having helped someone in the little town out recently. Drawing a blank, she refolded the paper and slipped it into her Bible for perusal later when the kids were in bed. "I have no idea. It's probably a mistake." A thought came to her, unbidden. Could it be Scott's boss like he said, or could Scott just be putting up a front to confuse her?

Becky poked her head into Jen's room where both kids were playing their favorite board game later that afternoon. "I've got to go to the store, anyone want to come with me?"

Jeff didn't bother to look her way and muttered, "Not me."

"Jen?"

"I'll stay here too, or Jeff might cheat." He glared at her in answer.

"Alright, then. I've got to get a few things for dinner, but it shouldn't take too long. Please don't fuss and argue," she said over her shoulder. "I love you. Be back soon."

Driving down the country road, she couldn't help but notice the sky was getting very black and the wind had picked up. She considered turning around and going back home to wait out the storm, but practicality changed her mind. Instead, she began to hurry as much as possible before the storm hit.

It didn't take her very long to acquire the items that they needed and was paying for her purchases when a terrific crack of thunder almost made her drop everything she had onto the black conveyor belt.

"Oh my," said the little old lady at the counter, her hand pressed to her chest. "I just hate them thunderstorms! You should probably wait until it passes, my dear."

Becky took her change and shook her head. "I can't. My kids are at home."

Grabbing her groceries and running through the downpour, she threw the dripping and now torn bags inside the cab. By the time she herself got into the truck, she was completely soaked to the skin.

With her hair in her face and her wipers going as fast as the old truck could muster, she leaned closer to the windshield and tried to make out the road through the thick blanket of rain.

Please keep the kids safe, she prayed over and over again, worried that they might be scared. Breathing a sigh of relief and gratitude when she reached her road, she was beginning to relax a little when a car suddenly pulled out in front of her. Screaming, she yanked the steering wheel to the right to avoid colliding with the small car, and careened off into the deep ditch, slamming into a gigantic oak tree just on the other side, shattering the windshield and knocking her unconscious.

"Jeff," Jen said, trying not to sound worried. "How long has mom been gone?"

"I don't know," he said, looking out the front window for any sign of her. "I'm scared Jen," he whimpered, his eyes red. Jen came over and gave him a hug, patting him on the back.

"What should we do?" Feeling silly, Jeff pulled away from her and went back to staring out the window, his nose pressed onto the glass.

"I guess we should wait a little bit longer." She attempted a smile to soothe herself as well as him, but it was a dismal failure. "She'll be home soon."

Pearce stuffed the change into his back pocket and grabbed the tractor hose off the counter, winking at the blue-haired old woman he'd known since he was a boy. "Thanks Lill, 'preciate it," the old woman blushed and made shooing motions at them. Her inability to speak didn't hinder her in the least to get across what message she wanted to relay, and Pearce's boyish grin grew twice in size as they left the hardware store.

A brilliant crack of thunder shook the store as both men stood under the eave just a little longer, hoping the downpour would slacken a little and allow them to avoid a complete drenching.

Pearce jammed his cowboy hat securely onto his head and turned toward his friend, a drop of rain dancing down the rim when it was obvious the storm wasn't going to let up anytime soon.

"Time to make a run for it, or Emily's going to drive Curly crazy!" Without warning, he took off through the pelting rain and landed safely inside the cab, his breath fogging up the windshield almost instantly as he waited for the younger man to join him a few seconds later.

"You run like an old lady!"

Guiding the large truck expertly through town, he was about to go home by the quickest route when he was struck with a strong desire to drive by Becky's house. Unable to dissuade the niggling thought, he finally gave in and turned down her road.

"What are you doing?" The young man peered at him as the wipers kept up their methodical rhythm in the nasty downpour. "Did you forget where you live?"

"No. I'm going to drive by Becky's house and make sure everything's all right."

"I didn't know you two were that close," he said with a hint of a smile.

His enjoyment was short lived. With a look of horror, Pearce yanked the truck to the edge of the road, slammed it into park and jumped out before he could be teased any further. His headlights rested eerily on an old Chevy pick-up truck, smashed and disfigured by a giant oak tree.

His friend jumped out to help, grinning as he remembered that just a few minutes ago they had both been reluctant to get wet, and how they were sure to be soaked through.

Pearce pulled on the door handle and was finally successful, when, with a sickening groan, he managed to pry it open much against its will. Unable to make anything out, he turned the wipers off, stopping their now purposeless trek across the missing windshield. Shielding his eyes from the spattering rain, he peered into the cab and noticed a figure lying halfway off the bench seat.

"Becky!" Sweeping broken glass off the seat and onto the floorboard, Pearce felt for a pulse and sighed with relief at her moan.

Squinting against the bright white headlights, she frowned at him. "What are you doing here?"

Pearce managed to squelch the sudden rise of bile when he saw the large, ugly gash on her forehead, and helped her free herself from the confines of the stick-shift and the seat. "I think you need to go to the hospital." He swallowed again and looked at his friend, his nostrils flaring as he tried to remain calm.

A fresh rivulet of blood oozed when she shook her head, making him gag anew. He'd always hated the sight of blood, but it was worse when it was on someone he knew. And cared about.

"No. I'm not going to the hospital." She clutched the headrest and swayed slightly, her eyes closed tight against a sudden onslaught of nausea. "I just want to get home. The kids…" she fell forward into Pearce's strong arms in a dead faint.

Scooping her up as though she weighed no more than a small sack of potatoes, he sheltered her from the driving rain and propped her on his friend's willing shoulder and turned the heat on full blast to ward off any chill she might get as he drove her home.

Still stationed at the window like a sentinel, Jeff was relieved and more than a little angry when headlights finally flashed across the room. He scuttled off the couch and ran out the door, flinging a curt, "Jen, she's home," over his shoulder. The reproof he had prepared died on his lips when he saw Pearce cradling Becky protectively against his chest as he brought her up the steps and into the house.

His legs like wooden blocks, Jeff followed him into his mother's room, his face turning white when he caught a glimpse of her bloody face as Pearce laid her on the bed. "Mom?"

Pearce stepped into his line of vision and forced him to look at his broad chest instead of her. "We need some washcloths. Can you get some for me?" Uncomprehending, Jeff stood rooted to the spot, his eyes white with fright.

"Jeff." He gave him a gentle shake and tilted his head upwards to meet his face.

Silently, Jen wafted past them and knelt at her mother's bedside. "I've got them." Tenderly, she picked bits of glass out of her mother's hair and put gentle pressure on the oozing gash. Although the blood flow was slowing down, Pearce was relieved that Jen had taken over and seemed to know what to do.

Pulling off his sopping coat and laying it across a chair, he knelt beside the bed and took the washcloth from Jen and held it in place over the wound. In a conversational tone as though nothing was out of the ordinary, he spoke. "Scott, I'm going to need you to keep them calm."

The mention of the familiar name had the desired effect. Turning toward the tall cowboy standing in the doorway, it finally registered to both children that he was indeed there. They had seen him hold the door open for Pearce as he carried their mother inside but were in such a confused state of mind, that *who* it was hadn't registered until that very moment.

"Right. I'll take care of them and get you some hot water." Scott put a warm hand on their shoulders and pulled them toward the door. "Let's go see what's in the kitchen, all right?"

As soon as they were safely out of the room, Pearce leaned close to her ear and whispered, "Becky, can you hear me? It's time to wake up."

Her eyelids fluttered open at the sound of her name, she turned toward him, inhaling sharply as a stab of pain shot through her head. "Mmm." She lay a hand atop the wet washcloth, another groan escaping before she could bite it back. "What are you doing here?"

"You were in an accident. Lay down." He lay a restraining hand on her shoulder as she tried to sit up. Obediently, she lay back against the soft pillows, wincing as she touched her bruised face.

"Wow." A fresh trickle of blood began oozing down her forehead when Pearce took the washcloth away for a momentary glance at the wound.

"Is anything broken?"

In answer, she wriggled a little here and there to prove she was fine. "Nope, all good." She sat up slowly and clutched the edge of her bed, the room spinning around her.

He gritted his teeth as her nose started to bleed and put his arm around her to steady her, keeping his eyes locked on hers. Embarrassed, she turned and grabbed a tissue off her nightstand and dabbed at the blood. "I'm taking you to the hospital."

"I don't want to go."

"You need stitches, or you'll have a scar."

In an effort to look stubborn, she squinted at him, succeeding only in looking more adorable. She set her jaw and he had the distinct feeling that had her hands not been busy cleaning her bloody nose, she would have put them both on her hips as if ready for a long, drawn out argument. "I'm not going, Pearce."

He bit back a smile and gave her a frown instead. "Are you always so difficult?"

"Try to be."

"Well," he said, leaning in to take a closer look at her bruised face. She tried not to notice how her heartbeat was escalating nor how warm and flushed she felt with him being so close. "You're definitely going to have a nasty black eye." He drew back and gave her his prognosis.

She gave him a rueful grin. "Just gives me something to be proud of." He stared at her as if he were thinking hard about something important when Jen and Jeff peeked around the door, breaking the spell.

"Mom? Are you okay?"

"You can come in," she said after noticing with a slight twinge of pleasure that Pearce's arm was still wrapped around her. With two great bounds and a flying leap into the air, Jeff burst in between them—making Pearce lose his grip—and lay his head in her lap. Jen, on the other hand, took things a little more slowly and sat behind her so she could rub her hair.

Scott poked his head through the doorway, smiling. "I thought it was time to break you two up. You looked way too cozy sitting there like that."

"Scott? Why are you here?" She wondered fleetingly if she should introduce the two men, but gave up cordiality for the moment as thinking hurt her head.

"Uh, I was with him when he found you," he shrugged his shoulders in Pearce's direction, earning a stern scowl for his efforts.

"I didn't know you two knew each other." Becky stood shakily to her feet and grabbed the small night table next to her bed when a sudden whoosh of dizziness assailed her.

With a quick grab at her waist, Pearce was successful in catching her before she tumbled backward onto the bed. "Where are you going?"

Weakly, she tried to pull his hands away. "I'm going to change, make dinner, then I'm going to try to get my truck."

Pearce scowled and refused to drop his hands from her small waist. "Don't worry about the truck, I'll take care of it for you. Will you please just take it easy?"

"I hate to put you out like that," she said reluctantly sitting back down. She had to admit, sitting down and relaxing for a few moments was exactly what she wanted to do.

"It's no trouble."

Just as she was about to argue, Scott came to stand at the end of the bed and she was suddenly grateful that she'd made it a habit to always try to keep a clean house. "I made the kids some sandwiches. I didn't know if you'd want anything or not, but if you do, I'll make you one."

"I'm not hungry, but thank you for fixing for the kids. I'm sure they appreciate it." She sighed and gave him a weary smile. "If you all will excuse me, I need to use my bedroom for a bit. My clothes are soaked, and I'm getting a little chilled."

Pearce was about to close the door after a few seconds of chaos and a final glance into the room, when he paused and said, "If you need anything, just call for Jen. I'm sure she won't be too far away." She waited for the soft snick of the latch and slowly made her way to her closet.

"Hey mom," Jeff smiled happily, looking up momentarily from the game of UNO the three of them were playing when she emerged a little while later, wearing her pink bathrobe and fuzzy slippers. With her hair tied back into a ponytail, she looked like she felt much better, even if Pearce's prediction of a black eye was, without a doubt, going to come true.

"Hi kiddo," she sat down gently at the table, joining them. "Where's Pearce?" Disappointed, she looked over at his friend when it was obvious he wasn't around.

"He went back to your truck to get the groceries out," Scott's warm look and smile made her blush and look away.

"He didn't have to do that."

"I guess he wanted to," he replied, continuing to stare. "You look like you're feeling better."

"I am, thanks. The dizziness has almost stopped, but the headache is still there. It'll go away soon," she said with a weary smile. "Who's winning?"

"*I* am," Jeff grinned and gave a gleeful snort and a nod in Scott's general direction. "I don't think he's ever played UNO before."

"Hey now, keep it up and you're going to make me try harder." He winked at Jen and smiled at her giggle. "Want to play?"

"I think I'll just watch you for a while," Becky yawned and rested her head in her arms. Without realizing it, she almost immediately fell asleep as troubled thoughts about what she was going to do for a vehicle tumbled about her dreams.

"Hey there!" Pearce said loudly, setting the soggy groceries down next to her a few minutes later, making her jump. "How are you feeling?"

"Good," she said with a yawn. Eyeing the battered cans and the soggy, torn bags that now adorned her kitchen table, she was suddenly struck with his kindness and a shy "thanks for getting that stuff for me," and "you didn't have to, but I appreciate it," managed to escape her lips even though she couldn't bring herself to look up into his handsome face.

"No problem," he answered, lifting her head so he could peer at her forehead, unaware that his touch was like fire to her. "That doesn't look so good." With almost a tender look, he gently brushed a lock of hair away from the bandaged cut on her head. "And your eye is already turning black. I wish you'd let me take you to the hospital so you could get that fixed up." They stared at each other for a moment, quite oblivious to the looks the kids were giving each other.

"Well," Scott, who was starting to grow a little uneasy with their camaraderie, slapped his cards down onto the table and cleared his throat. "I suppose we should get going so you can check on Emily," he grinned. Suddenly conscious of the others, Becky dropped her gaze and looked anywhere and everywhere but at Pearce.

"I suppose you're right," Pearce said with a peculiar smile as he noticed her discomfort. "Will you be all right tonight?"

"Oh yeah," she said, her head bobbing up and down a little too quickly. "We'll be just great. Nothing to worry about, right kids?"

A little reluctantly, Pearce followed Scott to the front door. Pausing with the door open, he waited while a brilliant flash of lightening finished its trek across the sky. "You two take good care of her and don't hesitate to call me if she needs anything." He was speaking to the children, but his eyes were fastened on Becky, and with a quick smile and nod, he was gone.

Chapter 8

Her fingers curled around the large mug, Becky inhaled the aromatic coffee and tried to let go of some of the stress that had gathered in her shoulders through the night.

Casting all your care upon him; for he careth for you... she prayed silently as worry and fretting once again took over her morning meditation. Absently, she shook her head and forced herself to thank God for keeping them all safe the previous night, and, unable to resist the temptation, she reminded God for what seemed the hundredth time that morning of their growing list of needs.

Her mug poised at the tip of her lips, a sudden noise of a door being slammed shut in her driveway startled her, making her drip some of the amber liquid onto her shirt. Irritated that she was so jumpy, she dabbed at the spot and went to peer out the door.

"What are you doing here?" She asked as Emily threw her arms around her, almost knocking her off balance in the process.

"Good morning! How are you feeling?" Pearce stood on the lowest step, his hand resting on the railing. A grin spread from ear to ear as he peered at her shiner.

"Fine," she colored under his scrutiny. "Why are you here?"

"You didn't expect me to just ignore you and not even check to see how you're doing, did you?" His eyes twinkled merrily. "Besides, Emily wanted to come by and see your black eye."

"Well, I suppose I did expect you to ignore me. You've been doing such a good job of it lately. In fact," she knelt down next to Emily and loudly whispered in her ear with a glance his way, "I thought your daddy was mad at me."

"Touché." He had the decency to look guilty.

Releasing Emily, she offered him the smile that she could barely contain. "Well, come on in and let me get you a coffee."

Following her into the kitchen, he stopped when he saw Jen and Jeff huddled over papers at the table.

"What are you doing?" He asked, leaning over Jen and studying the math problems she had been working on. "Is that schoolwork?"

"Yes," Becky answered, pulling out a chair beside Jeff and offering it to the tall man. "Okay. You can have a quick break. Please go feed the chickens."

Instantaneously, they jumped to their feet, grabbed Emily's hand, and rushed toward the screen door with a quick, "Thanks mom," thrown over their shoulders as they hustled outside before she could change her mind.

I could almost get lost in eyes like that, she thought to herself as Pearce stared at her over his coffee cup. "I didn't think you'd be doing school today."

"It's very rare that we take a day beside Saturday and Sunday off."

"Don't you think it's a little early to be doing school?" He admired the flush that crept over her cheeks, and the sparkle that lit up her eyes.

"It's 8:30 already. We start school every day at 7:00 sharp."

His surprise was evident, and she had a strong feeling that it pleased him for some unknown reason. "You get up that early?"

"I can't stand to be wasting my day away when there's so much to do. But we do take Saturdays off, and I sleep in until almost 8:00 if that makes you feel better," she sipped her coffee, noticing how the corners of his mouth turned up just a little when he was trying to hold back a smile.

He shook his head in mock dismay. "Lazy bum." She threw an eraser at him.

"Would you like something to eat?"

"No thank you. I'm here on official business."

She studied his expression, finally deciding that he was indeed being serious. "Official business?"

"I wanted to know what you were going to do about a truck now that yours is banged up."

She colored as she remembered her late night pleas with God the previous night to supply their needs because she had no idea what they were going to do. "I don't know. How bad is it?" She asked, squinting nervously as she tried to prepare herself for the worst.

"It's not good," he drummed his fingers on the table. "But I've seen worse. The frame isn't bent, but there's a lot of work that needs to be done."

"Like what?"

"Just to name a few, you need a new windshield, new hood, the engine, radiator, and water pump need to be replaced, bumper…" he explained, counting the things off on his fingers.

"Maybe I should just have it junked," she interrupted miserably, leaning her head in her hand.

He eyed her curiously as though he'd anticipated that answer. "Can I be presumptuous and ask if you've got the money to buy another one, or have that one fixed?"

She pursed her lips, her discomfort obvious. "Not really, why?"

Laying his hands flat on the table, he took in a deep breath and let it out slowly. "Well, I've got a business proposition for you." As if to create suspense, he stood and walked over to the coffee pot, helping himself to another cup. With his back turned to her, he continued, "Suppose you came and worked for me. Cooking, cleaning, taking care of Emily. I'd need you to cook for a couple of my workers as well." Her eyes bore into his back, her mouth agape. He turned and reseated himself, and she couldn't help but observe that tanned faces can grow pretty red.

She stammered and stumbled over her words. "But I don't have a truck to get to your place every day, and I don't have the means to get it fixed right away. You'd have to come out here to get me, and that would be a waste of your time."

He held a hand up in the air to stop anymore of her objections. "Let me worry about the truck. And…" he said slowly, drawing out the word as if it were a mile long, a sheepish smile slowly spreading across his face. "You could stay out at my place."

"I don't think so," she stood up quickly, her face bright red. "I think…"

"Just sit for a minute and listen," he laughed, pointing to her chair. "I don't mean it that way. Emily's taken a liking to you and I think it would be a good thing for her to have you around all the time. She needs a woman's guidance, and Jeff needs a man around, right?" The look on her face told him she wasn't convinced and that he'd have to hurry and explain before she got angry. "I have an empty cabin that you and the kids could live in. It used to be for ranch hands. What do you say?"

"You mean sort of like a housekeeper?"

He gave her a pleased look. "Yeah, I guess you could call it that."

She walked stiffly to the sink, her stomach in knots as she considered the job he offered. It would be difficult to work for him and she was honest enough with herself to know that being in such close proximity with him every day was going to prove a challenge to her emotions, let alone those of her children.

But, she reasoned within herself, *could this be the answer to my prayers?* True, God hadn't always worked things out quite so quickly before, but that didn't mean He wouldn't or couldn't. She sighed wearily and wished things were a lot easier.

Seeing her struggle, he thought some prodding might be in order. "The cabin's been empty for a long time and it's not very nice."

Looking out the window, she watched the three kids play together around the chicken pen, fits of laughter emanating through the thin glass. *It would be nice to have someone around for Jeff,* she thought to herself. And she really enjoyed Emily and how Jen seemed to have taken up with the little girl. But it would be extremely awkward between her and Pearce. Especially now that she realized how easily it would be to fall in love with him.

"I can't," she said finally, wishing her heart didn't have such treacherous feelings. "I signed a year lease on this place."

Not in the least bit perturbed, he answered, "Okay, you can live at the cabin and keep paying your lease here. You've only got a few months left, right?"

"A little less than six," she answered slowly. "What about the chickens?" They both knew she was trying to find excuses, and that he wasn't going to let her get away with it.

"We'll take them with us," he grinned. "Please? Emily would love having you and the kids around, and I could really use the help. Besides," he continued wearing her resistance down. "I don't like the thought of you guys being stuck here without a vehicle."

"We'll be all right," she answered hastily, her heart skipping a beat at the fact that he was worried about them.

"All right." Standing, he walked toward the door and crammed his cowboy hat on his head and turned to look at her, his left hand on the door knob. "Then I'll be over everyday to see if you need anything." He pushed the screen open and walked out to the porch, looking for reinforcements.

"Pearce," exasperated with his stubbornness, she followed him and let the screen door slam behind her. "Why are you being so difficult?"

With her hand on her hips and her lovely eyes flashing, he wondered what it would be like to grab her and hug her. He swallowed and hoped his face didn't show just how attractive he found her. "I could say the same about you. Why won't you let anyone help you?"

Eyes narrowed to slits, she tilted her chin even higher. "I let people help me."

"Yeah right." He grinned annoyingly at her and she resisted the sudden urge to push his hat off onto the floor. They locked gazes for a stare down to see who would give in first.

She frowned and started tapping her foot with her arms crossed as his infuriating smile grew even larger. His self confidence was maddening.

"What's so funny?"

"I was just thinking that you look exactly like Emily when she's pouting. Except for the black eye, of course."

"I'm not pouting."

"You're doing a fine job acting like it."

She had difficulty in maintaining her resolve not to return his smile, especially seeing as how much it added to his handsome demeanor. Luckily, she was rescued that particular embarrassment by the kids gathering at the porch railing.

"What's wrong mom?" Jen asked.

"Yeah," Jeff piped up brightly. "You look like you're pouting."

With a snort of disgust, as well as defeat, Becky flung her hands up in the air. "It's a conspiracy!"

Pearce gave Jeff a jovial slap on the back. "Thank you my good man."

"What's going on?" Jen asked suspiciously, glancing from one to the other while Emily twirled and twisted around her like a ballerina.

"Nothing. Just go play." Nonchalantly, she lay her hand on the door knob just in case she needed to make a fast getaway into the house before the subject could be brought up again.

Pearce was too quick. "I offered your mom a housekeeping job at my place, and she refused."

Jeff's jaw dropped, an incredulous look on his face. "Really?"

"You said no?" Jen asked in amazement. "Why?" Even Emily seemed to know that something big was up as she stopped swinging and dancing and reached for her father's hand.

"That I couldn't tell you. She didn't have any real excuses," Pearce shrugged and tried to look dejected as he looked from one child to the next. "What were they again?" He asked, his eyes wide and innocent as they finally came to rest on her once more. She scowled at him, knowing he was going to shoot every one of her excuses down.

"Because we agreed to a year lease on this place, for one."

"Oh yeah," he snapped his fingers, "the year lease problem. I told her she could keep paying the lease here, and stay in the empty cabin at my place," he whispered loudly to Jeff as he picked up Emily and slung her onto his back. "It was once used for ranch hands."

"Then we'd have to move all our stuff," she hedged, trying not to notice the disappointed looks coming from all three children.

"That's a new one, but we'd have plenty of help, wouldn't

we?" He winked at them as they nodded their heads enthusiastically.

"Please mom?" Jeff whined, unable to bear the thought that he might miss out on being a real cowboy. "I've never seen a ranch cabin before."

Becky could see her excuses failing one by one as it became obvious she was in the minority. Still, she persevered. "What about school? How would I teach you guys, cook, clean two houses, and take care of Emily too?"

"We'd help!" Jeff offered, jumping up and down excitedly.

Jen ticked the items off on her slender fingers as though that was one of the silliest things she'd ever heard. "You could teach Emily while Jeff and I were doing our work, we'd help you clean and work around the houses, Jeff could help Mr. Pearce with whatever he needed help on, and I'd help you cook and take care of Emily."

Pearce smiled at her, satisfied with the way things were working out. Becky looked at Jen and Jeff's hopeful faces, and decided to give a final, last ditch effort of resistance.

"I thought you guys were tired of moving." This, she knew beyond a shadow of a doubt, was her trump card. If anything would dampen their spirits, it was that, and she let herself smile triumphantly at Pearce. Jen and Jeff exchanged looks at this temporary setback.

It was Emily that came to their rescue. Her eyes wide and innocent, she pleaded, "Please come and teach me Miss Becky. I'll be a good girl." Becky's resolve crumbled as her heart went out to the small child.

"All right." Shaking her head, she leaned wearily on the doorjamb as though she'd just emerged from a major battle. "I give up. Is this what you want?"

Without a moment's hesitation, their resounding answer was, "Yes!"

She turned an accusatory glare at Pearce while all three kids were whooping and hollering around them, and acting like a bunch of nuts. "That was mean."

"I don't know what you're talking about," he answered sweetly. His look of total innocence made her laugh as she finally gave in to the feelings of gratitude.

"When are we moving?" Jeff stopped suddenly in front of the porch, interrupting his onslaught of whooping and jumping around.

With her arms crossed, she tilted her chin up a little and answered, "When the lease is up."

"This weekend," Pearce ruffled Jeff's hair and ignored her completely. "Your mom's being difficult, so we'll do it this weekend. Think you can be packed up by then?" Jeff grinned, enjoying the fact that a man was taking control of the whole situation.

In answer, Jeff raced into the house, yelling over his shoulder. "Oh yeah, I'm going to start right now!"

"When do you want me to come help you move some of your stuff?" Pearce asked cheerfully, breaking into her thoughts.

"I guess it doesn't matter. Whenever you get around to it," she answered distractedly, watching as Jen and Emily walked down the hall to Jen's room holding hands. Shuddering, she couldn't help but wonder what would happen if this didn't work out.

Chapter 9

Although it almost took an executive order to get Jen and Jeff to settle down enough to complete their schoolwork during what was left of the week, they had no problem getting the things they would need packed and those that they wouldn't, labeled for storage.

"Good morning," Pearce called through the open door early Saturday morning.

"Good morning," Becky said smiling brightly, coming out of the kitchen with a steaming cup of coffee.

"Morning Miss Becky," Emily, her face wreathed in smiles, ran to give her a hug.

"Why, hello darlin', have you been a good girl?" Becky asked, her eyes twinkling merrily.

"Yep!" She answered cheerily as she skipped down the hall in search of Jen and Jeff. "I've been practicing."

"Good for you," Becky called after her, laughing. Turning to Pearce, she tried not to notice how his short sleeves and faded jeans showed off his muscular, athletic frame. She cleared her throat and endeavored not to be impressed, or at least not to look it. "Want some coffee?"

"Sure," Pearce answered, not masking his own admiration of the petite woman as he followed her into the kitchen. "You've been busy."

"Yes, it didn't take us long to get our things together, but I think the worst thing was trying to do school. It was all I could do to get them to concentrate!" She laughed and poured him a cup of coffee, sitting down next to him at the table. "I think they're thinking that this is some kind of adventure, and they don't think about it being a job."

"I know exactly what you mean," he said, taking a big swig.

"Emily hasn't been able to sleep a whole night through since you said you'd be my housekeeper. She seems to think that you're her best friend, while I feel like chopped liver whenever you're around." He said, not in the least disturbed about being passed over for her.

"That's nice," she laughed, blushing slightly at his wink. "Because all Jeff has been able to talk about is being allowed to work outside with the men," she lowered her voice, trying to sound manly. His deep, throaty laugh echoed off the small kitchen walls.

"Its been a long time since I've laughed like that," he chuckled as he finished his coffee. "It's going to be nice having you around."

Becky returned his smile, a playful twinkle in her eyes. "Oh yeah? Well then, maybe we'll do each other some good, because I dearly love a good laugh."

"I know we'll do each other some good," he answered matter-of-factly as he took his coffee cup to the sink and rinsed it out. "Which boxes do I need to start loading?"

She led him to a smallish group of boxes and odds and ends they had stacked near the door. "These over here."

"This is it?"

"Yep. That's all I thought we might need for now. I figured if I needed anything else, I'd swing by and get it, if it's okay with you," she added hurriedly, her face turning red. She had forgotten for a moment that for awhile, she'd have to depend on Pearce to drive her wherever she needed to go, at least until she could work up enough money to have her truck fixed.

He gave her a reproving look as he stacked a few boxes together. "Of course it's okay with me. Whatever you need, if I don't have it, I'd be happy to bring you back here. But," he said over his shoulder as he walked out the door, "I should have everything you need."

Not to be outdone, Becky swiftly picked up some lighter boxes and carried them out to the truck, pushing them as far into the bed as they would go. They worked companionably together, talking and laughing as if they had known each other all their lives.

"Come on guys," Pearce called to the kids, who were playing

near the chicken pen. "Let's get going."

Excited to be off, Jeff ran over to them, his eyes bright with anticipation. "You're done already?" Jen and Emily followed a little behind him. "I was going to come help you in a minute, but I thought it would take you a lot longer than that. It always takes mom a long time when it's just her and us," he said, looking admiringly at Pearce.

"What about the chickens, mom?" Jen asked, a little troubled by the thought that they would be left behind to starve with no one to take care of them. *She loves those chickens like a boy would love his dog,* Becky thought to herself, smiling.

"We'll come back and get them later on while your mom is unpacking your boxes," Pearce said, handing Emily inside and deftly buckling her into her car seat, as Jen and Jeff quickly got in on the other side, forcing Becky to sit in the front seat with Pearce.

If Pearce was a little worried about what Becky was going to think about his house, he needn't have.

She caught herself holding her breath when he pulled into a long drive with a beautiful brick ranch house situated happily at the end. Surrounded on all sides by a white picket fence and a gate at the front, she marveled at the rose bushes that were clustered and spaced as though a master gardener had planted them, and she couldn't help a surreptitious glance at Pearce.

Gorgeous horses grazing in the fields were the perfect background, and she found herself wondering if she were equal to the task as several large, well-kept barns loomed up beside and a little behind the house.

"Wow." Jeff took the words right out of her mouth.

"Is this where you live?" Jen asked, wide eyed with wonder. She glanced at her mother and wondered if it would be inappropriate to tell her exactly what she was thinking about their newfound luck.

"That's my swing, and my playhouse," Emily pointed out happily as they rounded the curve and came into view of the back of the house. "We can play there anytime you want. Wanna see it?"

Pearce parked the truck next to an old, rustic cabin that sat a little off behind the house, near one of the well-kept barns.

He looked at her a little uneasily and wondered briefly if this had been such a good idea after all. Would she like it? Hate it? He prayed that God would make her want to stay. *For Emily's sake,* he reminded himself.

"I know it isn't much," he apologized as soon as the kids had jumped out of the truck and ran off to investigate Emily's toys. "Whatever you want to do to make it home, go ahead. I didn't really look inside before I offered it to you, and I know there's work that needs to be done, so I'll get to it as soon as I can. But if you see something that can't wait, let me know."

Pearce breathed a sigh of relief at the dazzling smile she gave him, and he wouldn't admit even to himself that he'd been just a little worried that she would want to return home when she saw what he expected her to live in. He had known deep inside that she should be here.

"I think it's just perfect! Can I see inside?" She walked up to the porch and peered inside the smudged window, cupping her hand to cut the glare.

"Sure, but you have to remember that a bunch of men lived here once, and I've kind of let it fall apart," he said regretfully, unlocking the door for her.

She laughed and stepped inside before he could warn her any further. "I don't trust a man that can clean better than me." Stepping lightly about the dusty room, she left tracks in the countless years' worth of dust on the wood floor. Pearce watched her keenly as she ventured around and wished he'd had someone come in and clean up before she had gotten there. Hurriedly, he brushed his hand over the small table that had once served as a dining table, wiping the cobwebs and dust onto his jeans.

Making a thorough search through the small cabin, she smiled as she opened the cabinet doors in the small kitchen, grinned at the bunk beds that lined both walls, knowing the kids were going to love sleeping in them, and looked out all the windows, envisioning new curtains blowing in the breeze.

His curiosity burning, he blurted, "Well?"

"I love it," she pronounced pleasantly.

Sighing with relief, he matched her bright smile. "I thought for sure you'd hate it, or me, or both." Becky had just opened the door to the bathroom when an ear piercing scream froze them both.

"What was that?" Pearce asked, startled.

Becky bit down on her panic and tried to remain calm as they raced out of the cabin to the swings behind the house. "Jen!" Grabbing her daughter by the shoulders, she swung her around to peer at her weeping face. "What's wrong? What happened?"

When it was obvious Jen wasn't able to answer, she pulled her into a hug. "Jeff? What happened?" She looked around the play area, noticing that no one seemed to be hurt.

Jeff looked almost as confused and terrified as his mother. "I don't know. Emily and I were playing here on the swings, then she started screaming for no reason," he answered, pale as a ghost. Emily started to cry, clinging to Pearce as if she'd never let go.

"He's, he's...." Jen choked out between sobs, pointing to a couple of lounge chairs on the back porch, "*dead!*" She sobbed harder than ever, clinging to Becky for support.

Startled, they looked over to a chair where an old man had been sleeping. His face wreathed in wrinkles and his snow white hair, he did indeed look like he could have been a ghost.

"Huh? What?" He jumped up from the chair and blinked in the bright sunlight, confused by all the commotion. "Who's dead?"

"Apparently you are!" said Pearce, almost doubled over with laughter. Wiping his eyes and trying to control his laughter, he introduced them. "Becky, Jen, Jeff, this is Curly, my right hand man. He worked for my dad then stayed on for me when dad left me the ranch."

"Nice to meet you," Becky was the first to shake hands, more than a little embarrassed. With chagrin, she noticed that several men had run out of the barns and hurried over to see what the commotion was all about. "Sorry to have scared you like that. What a way to make an entrance, Jen!" She murmured softly to her shaking daughter.

"No problem ma'am," the old man grinned, pushing his cowboy hat back on his head to scratch his forehead. "I get it all the time." He stuck out his withered hand and she took it, grateful that he had a sense of humor. "You must be the new housekeeper."

"I'm sorry," Jen said with a half hiccup, half giggle as her tears abated and started to give way to a smile. "You were so still, it didn't even look like you were breathing." He gave her a wink and a nod.

"Don't you worry your pretty little head about it. No harm done." Turning his attention toward her brother, he said with a serious look, "You must be Jeff. I hear you want to be a cowboy and see how a ranch runs."

"Yes sir," Jeff answered stoutly, standing up straight and sticking his chest out proudly. "I want to be the best cowboy ever."

"Well, you'll have a hard time being better than that guy right there," he said, nodding his head toward Pearce, who looked skeptical. Jeff looked up at him with new admiration, impressed that he knew the best cowboy around.

"These guys are the rest of the gang," Pearce said, changing the subject as he turned around to see that they were the focus of attention. "This is Billy, Guy, John, Burt, and Mark," he introduced each of them, giving them time to shake Becky's and the kid's hands. "And this last one is the worst of the bunch, but you've already met him," he continued as a tall young man sauntered up, not paying him any attention whatsoever.

"Scott!" Becky exclaimed, surprised to see him there. "You work here?"

"Yes ma'am, sure do," he grinned broadly, shaking her hand enthusiastically, his eyes twinkling. "And I have to tell you how glad I am you came to work here. It's about time we got us some decent food so this old dead coot don't have to cook anymore!" He laughed, sticking his thumb Curly's way, earning a punch to the arm in return.

"If you work here, then that means…." she trailed off, looking at Pearce with narrowed eyes and a fearful scowl. "You're his boss."

He bowed as if he'd received a standing ovation at an opera house. "Caught red-handed. At your service."

Jen gave him a somewhat downcast smile. "Then those chickens belong to you."

"Nope. They're all yours, so enjoy. They were a gift from one friend to another." His eyes searched for and found Becky's, making her heart skip a beat and her face flush.

"Thank you for all those nice things you did for us," Jen said politely, her face brightening up quite a bit with the knowledge that her beloved chickens were indeed hers.

Becky, who was still pretending to be upset, glared at him as he gave her a boyish grin that no sane woman could ignore. "I didn't do anything. Scott's the one who took all that stuff over to you and helped you with the chicken coop."

At the mention of his name, Scott threw up his hands and backed away slightly. "Don't try to get me in trouble, I find enough of it on my own! It was all *your* idea!" Becky continued to frown at Pearce while the workers enjoyed the fact that the boss was in trouble for a change.

His face red, he decided it was time to send his employees back to work and ordered them away. When everyone but Curly was gone, he turned his attention back to Becky and gave her his most winning smile.

"What?"

"Uh huh." Her foot tapped a rhythm on the porch. " 'Daddy likes apple pie, it's his favorite'," she said in a high falsetto voice, mimicking Emily.

He shrugged and tried to maintain his innocent appearance. "Well it *is* my favorite. And I've got to tell you, that was the best pie I've ever had." Grinning profusely, he switched tactics and tried flattery.

Nodding her head, she turned away before he could see her smile. She felt an inexpressible amount of satisfaction that she had pleased him in some way, no matter how small or trivial it was.

"Come on, let me show you around." Resisting the urge to grab her hand, he led her into the back door into the nicest kitchen she'd ever seen.

Awed by the gigantic room, Jeff pulled off his shoes and set them beside the door. "Wow!" he breathed, glancing around at what was sure to become his favorite room in the whole house. Taking his shoes off before walking through the house had been an unwritten rule ever since he could remember, and he didn't see why anything would be different here.

Pearce led them through the gigantic country kitchen into the adjoining dining room, which held the largest cherry Queen Anne table Becky had ever seen, adorned by twelve matching chairs and a large quilt settled on the top. Next to the dining room was a large living room with an open-style fireplace, which promised to be cozy in the winter.

He led them quickly down an expansive hallway, throwing open the door to three unused bedrooms and bathrooms, and finally into Emily's room which was next to his with a bathroom nestled in between.

Becky was surprised that there didn't seem to be anything special or particularly decorative about her room. She had assumed that Emily's room would be the most beautiful room in the house, seeing she was an only child and was pleasantly surprised to be wrong.

Leading the way into his own room through the adjoining bathroom, he seemed to be more than just a little embarrassed by the starkness and emptiness of it as he threw open the door for her to peer inside, leaving the kids to play in Emily's room.

Pushing open a door to the next room, he seemed to relax perceptibly. Becky could tell that this was where he spent most of his time.

"This is the den," he said, standing aside to let her enter. Stepping lightly down the steps, she sensed that he was sharing a very private part of himself with her, and she doubted he let anyone into this room with the exception of Emily.

As she looked around the room, she noticed a desk set in front of a large window with a spectacular view of the mountains off in the distance. Walking to the window to get a better look outside, she noticed a small, very dusty frame with a picture of a pretty brunette smiling mischievously into the camera. Although the frame was obviously silver and not cheap, what intrigued her was how it had been thrown haphazardly on the back of the desk, almost out of view.

At first, she thought it was perhaps his mother, but as she stepped closer to the desk for a better look out of the corner of her eye, she could tell the woman's dress was definitely a newer fashion.

Catching movement beside and to the left of her, she looked out the window in the nick of time when he came to stand next to her, now making it impossible to see anything on his desk without his noticing.

"It's beautiful, isn't it?" He said vaguely, and she had the impression that he wasn't talking to her at all. They stood quietly for a few minutes, him alone with his thoughts, and her fighting to quell the small niggling feeling of jealousy that arose.

He turned and broke the silence, his smile a little sad. "I just want you to know how much I appreciate you coming to work for me. Emily really needs you."

Becky's smile quivered a little and she tried to ignore her fluttering heart and treacherous wishes that one day he would need her as well.

Suddenly feeling a little overwhelmed, as well as a little afraid of her rampant, unreasonable emotions, she turned to go. "I'm going to go see what the kids are up to."

Moving quickly past the desk and its interesting picture, she didn't slow down until she reached the door to Emily's room, and stood out of sight past the doorframe. Sure she was safer here, she listened while they played and remembered when life had seemed so uncomplicated.

When she was reasonably composed, she peered around the corner and said quietly, "Jen, Jeff, will you two please help me unload the truck and put the stuff in the cabin?"

"Sure mom," Jeff jumped to his feet and ran out the door, escaping just before Emily pushed a Barbie doll toward him. Jen got up a little more reluctantly and lay her own doll down into the plastic tote. She hadn't remembered playing dolls was such fun and wouldn't admit for the world that she still enjoyed something she considered herself to be too grown up for.

Becky smiled at her as she walked past, giving her braid an affectionate tug. Jen stopped and gave her a bear hug, and ran outside, not wanting to be outdone by her little brother.

A small hand finding its way into her own brought her attention back to Emily, and she gazed down at her. "You look like you want to cry. My daddy looks like that sometimes."

Stooping down and wrapping her arms around the child, Becky briefly wondered if it was for the girl's comfort, or her own. "I'll be all right," she said, smiling at her as they walked outside to help.

They had unloaded about half the truck when Scott came over, whistling happily and standing in her way on purpose. "Need some help?"

"We've got it," Becky sidestepped him and carried the large box to the cabin, setting it down right inside the door. Turning swiftly, she almost ran into Scott as he followed, carrying another load. He set it down next to the pile by the front door and went out for another.

She frowned and followed him back to the truck. "We can handle this. Go ahead and do whatever it is that you're supposed to be doing." Whistling louder, he ignored her and carried more things inside the cabin, returning just a moment later for another load.

"Scott!" She ordered haughtily with her hands on her hips, irritated at the maddening grin he gave her.

"You know," he said with an appreciative glance, "you sure do look pretty when you're trying to be mad. I like a spicy woman that blushes."

She grimaced and rolled her eyes at his flattery, trying unsuccessfully not to smile. Giving up, she was tugging another box down when Pearce came to stand next to her.

"Why'd you run away so fast?" He asked softly so only she could hear.

"I didn't run away," she kept her face averted. As he stepped closer, his breath brushed across her forehead, sending chills down her spine. "What time do you want dinner?"

"Whenever you get it done," he answered walking beside her as they carried the next to last boxes into the cabin. "And you did run away." He stopped to let her go inside first. Scott came in after them, giving them curious stares.

"I don't know what you have yet, so I'll have to go check," she hurried to follow Scott, hoping Pearce would drop the conversation. "How many do I need to cook for? Will you please put that small box on top of this?" She held out the box in her arms, indicating to Scott which smaller box she wanted him to add. Obligingly, he loaded her up and jumped out, carrying the last bit of the stuff.

Pearce took the boxes from her and put them next to the rest by the door, and leaned on the door frame, crossing his arms stubbornly. Scott set his things down and walked back out, tipping his hat at her as he passed by.

"Thank you," she called after him, wishing Pearce would go away. She busied herself with rearranging, determined to keep busy while he was nearby.

He allowed her to get away with ignoring him for a few minutes before he nonchalantly stepped in her path. "Are you trying to ignore me?"

She did what any self respecting woman would do. She lied. "No. I was just trying to get something done before dinner, that's all."

"Six."

"Six what?"

"Dinner. That's all you'll be cooking for. You and the kids, Curly, Emily, and me. Scott usually goes out on Saturday nights, and the rest go home. So, six."

Pulling up a flap on the box of linens, she didn't bother to look up. "Okay, thanks." He watched her for a little bit, amused by her evident determination to ignore him.

Taking her completely by surprise, he reached down, grabbed her hand, and pulled her to her feet. "Come here. There's something I want you to see." Obediently, she followed, trying to ignore the fact that he was holding her hand. He led her inside one of the big barns where she had seen Curly go in earlier while they were unpacking the truck. Opening her eyes wide, she tried to see in the dim light as he led her to a stall.

Letting go of her hand, he quietly unlatched the door and pushed it open, revealing two of the most beautiful foals she had ever seen, their mother standing protectively over them.

Enthralled, she tiptoed inside and tentatively reached out to give the mare a gentle pat.

"They're beautiful. Isn't it rare for a mare to give birth to twins?" She held her breath as the more adventurous colt nuzzled her hand while his sister stood a little off, unsure of this new stranger.

"Yes it is," he answered, charmed by her childlike reaction. "It's even more rare that they all three lived," he took some oats and fed their mother, running his hand down her soft muzzle.

Leaning his forehead against the mare's head, he spoke softly. "I come here first thing every morning. It helps keep things in perspective." Becky sighed softly, feeling that she had indeed made the right decision to work for him.

She continued petting the colt who was content to stand still and receive as much of her attention as she was willing to give. The filly, more wary of strangers than her brother, crept cautiously nearer until she was standing alongside him and received a good scratch behind her ears as a reward.

"I can see why you like to come here." Reluctantly, she stood and brushed off her jeans to follow Pearce out of the stall. He showed her around the other barns and pastures, explaining things to her as some cattle and horses grazed happily and the kids played near the house with Emily.

"What about that one?" She stopped and pointed to a barn that he had neglected to show her.

"Aren't you tired of looking at barns and animals?" He said off-handedly, quickening his step.

"No," she stood still and waited for him to turn to look at her. When he kept walking, she decided to investigate on her own.

Pulling the door open, she stepped inside and waited for her eyes to adjust to the dimness, a smell of motor oil and gasoline accosted her nose. Burt and John, two of Pearce's workers she had met earlier, poked their heads out from under the hood of her truck and gave her a friendly smile.

"You weren't supposed to come in here," Pearce apologized, taking her elbow and ushering her out of the barn toward the main house.

Worry lines creased her forehead. "How much is it going to cost to fix it?"

"Don't worry about it." He could tell by the look on her face that he was in for an argument.

"I'm not going to let you fix my truck without paying for it."

A grin spread across his face and he congratulated himself on being right. "How about it's a gift from a friend to another friend."

"A friend." She wasn't convinced.

"Yes, friend. A good friend." He stopped in front of her and stood in her way.

"How about you don't pay me for housekeeping and we'll call it even." She knew it wasn't nearly enough to pay for the parts and labor he would have to put into the truck, but the thought of accepting his generosity went against all her principles. Let alone being a burden to him.

He bent slightly to catch her expression and a pleasant scent of lavender tickled his nose. "Why can't you just let me do this for you? Let me help you."

Becky looked away and watched the kids as they played tag in the front yard. After pausing a second, she blurted, "Because I've had to do everything on my own since Frank died, and I don't know how to let people help me."

"Don't you think it's about time you tried?"

"I'm afraid to," she answered so quietly he had to lean closer to hear her. "Please Pearce. Let me pay for it," her eyes begged him to understand.

He frowned as he considered her plea and finally stepped out of her way. "I'll come up with something if you insist."

"Thanks for showing me around," Becky broke the silence that had arisen between them. "I'll start dinner in a few minutes. I just have to do something in the cabin." He nodded and watched her walk away, disappointed by her refusal to let him help her.

Picking up the worn, black leather Bible she had placed on the kitchen table earlier, she fingered its soft cover and flipped through the pages in search of something. Finding what she was looking for, she pulled the folded piece of paper out and sat on one of the bunks, tenderly smoothing out the well-creased folds so she could read it.

"....helped me in ways I cannot explain....I am indebted to you..."

Lord, she prayed silently, head bent over the letter. *I feel that you've brought me here for a reason, help me find it, and know what it is. I surrender to your will and I ask you to use us for your honor and glory, amen.*

Chapter 10

The sunlight streaming into the curtain-less cabin woke Becky the next morning. Stretching contentedly and telling herself she wanted to start the job on a good note, while ignoring the fact that the sooner she got up, the sooner she would see Pearce, she smiled and prepared for her first day.

Rushing through her morning preparations, she was soon inside the large kitchen preparing a large urn of coffee. Trying to convince herself that she was looking for Emily, she walked through the house, and her bright, cheery smile faded somewhat when she realized she was the only one inside.

Sitting at the small white table in the kitchen, her fingers drummed a staccato as she fought the urge to find Pearce. Unable to stand it any longer, she poured a mug of coffee and went to look for him.

Finding him and Curly in the stall with the twins and mare, she held out the mug to Pearce as the twins frolicked around, the mare chewing contentedly on oats. "Here's some coffee." She colored, feeling rather dumb and ashamed that she hadn't thought to bring a cup for the older man. "Would you like some, Curly?"

His grin let her know he saw through the innocent coffee-ruse, and made her face turn even more crimson. "No. Thanks anyway. Used to be able to handle the stuff, but my gut can't take it anymore." He chuckled and patted his overall-clad stomach. "You just keep on bringing some to the boss-man though, he needs it or he'll be crabby!"

"I heard that," Pearce called after him as he walked away, leaving them alone. Suddenly feeling foolish and a little shy, Becky turned to go back to the house. "Where's your coffee?" He asked bluntly, staring at her as he took a cautious sip of the hot liquid.

"I was just going inside to get me one."

"Are you coming back out?" He asked casually.

She halted by the barn door and turned. The morning sunlight pillowing around her made her look almost angelic, and he was thankful she couldn't read his mind. "I just figured I'd have one while breakfast was going."

"All right," he said, turning his attention back to the playful foals as one pushed into his leg. "Go ahead and get one, and come on back. They're frisky this morning."

With an absurd grin on her face, she fairly ran to the kitchen, poured herself a cup--spilling quite a bit onto the counter in the process--and forced herself to walk back so he wouldn't know that she had rushed.

They talked companionably for a while, unaware that Curly kept peeking around the door every so often to spy on them.

She checked her watch when a loud growl from her stomach reminded her of what she was really supposed to be doing. "I better hurry and start breakfast."

"Thanks for the coffee," he called after her, watching her hurry away. He was gazing thoughtfully at the back door of the house where she had gone inside when Curly rejoined him at the stall.

His thumbs hooked inside the straps of his coveralls, he leaned backward on his feet and nodded. "Pretty little woman there."

Pearce grinned, not in the least perturbed that his friend had caught him watching. "Yes she is."

"Makes a darn good apple pie."

His smile grew bigger, his eyes twinkling merrily as he knew what the old man was hinting at. "Best apple pie I've ever had."

He nodded knowingly, his white hair glinting in the sunlight. "Hmm. Sounds like a good woman then," walking away, he hoped he left Pearce with something to think about.

Scott whistled appreciatively at the tantalizing aroma that wafted through the dining room when he came and seated himself next to Pearce a little later. "Something smells great!"

In answer, Becky smiled and placed a steaming bowl of scrambled eggs next to a plate heaping with crisp bacon, pancakes on the other side. Pearce was just about to ask the blessing when he noticed Jen and Jeff were missing.

"Becky, where's the kids?"

She concentrated on pouring coffee into his mug. "In the kitchen."

"Why aren't they in here?"

Her face flushed as she hesitated. "Well, I wasn't sure where we should eat, so I thought it would be best if we ate in the kitchen." She kept pouring coffee into any cup that was available, moving methodically around the table.

Pearce helped himself to some pancakes and passed the plate to Scott, a stern look on his face.

"Because you're hired help, you didn't think it would be proper to eat with us." Not waiting for her to answer, he pushed his chair back and went into the kitchen, coming out a moment later with Jen and Jeff, holding their plates and placed them next to Emily.

Quietly they helped themselves to some food, and without a word, Becky sat down at the furthest place from Pearce. Listening to the talk around her about what had to be done that day, she jumped up to get whatever anyone needed. When the pancakes were almost gone, she was already refilling the plate and placing it back in the middle of the table before anyone could miss any, and went around pouring coffee for any who wanted it.

Pearce, who had been watching her almost as carefully as she had watched the food platters, stopped her when she came to fill his cup. "Aren't you eating?"

She smiled and shrugged her shoulders. "Not yet. I'll eat later."

"We're big boys here. We can serve ourselves," he answered evenly, drumming his fingers on the table, giving her a warning look. "Go eat before it's all gone." Raising her eyebrows, she boldly returned his stare as she mischievously poured some more coffee for Burt.

"This is the best breakfast I've had here yet," Scott broke in around a mouthful of food. "Is there any more bacon?" He asked, looking up at Becky just as she was about to sit down.

"I'll go get it," she gave an impish smile to Pearce as he stared at her through narrowed eyes. They all glared at Scott, who seemed to have been the only oblivious one in the room.

Mystified, he stared around the table. "What I'd do?"

"It's okay Scott," Curly said, shaking his head as Becky brought out the plate and set it in the middle of the table. "Go back to your own world."

"Thank you Becky. Why don't you have a seat and start eating?" Pearce frowned a warning at Scott who had just drained his cup of coffee and was about to request a refill. Taking the hint, he got up and poured it himself.

Becky perched lightly in her chair, and looked around expectantly. "Anyone want anything else?"

"No thanks," Curly said quickly, glancing around the table, his eyes daring anyone to ask for something. They each mumbled an excuse and concentrated on the remaining food on their plate.

Emily, who had been quietly picking at her food during the whole display, pushed her plate away. "Daddy, I'm done. Can I go play?"

"Sure pumpkin. Put your plate in the sink."

Having only had three platefuls, Jeff gulped down the rest of his food so he could follow the men outside as they left. "Mom? Can I be done?"

Becky nibbled on the only occupant of her plate, a small piece of crisp bacon. "Sure. Jen, you may go when you're finished."

"I'm done," she answered, swallowing the rest of her milk and pushing her chair back to follow Emily outside.

Pearce leaned back in his chair and stared at her, a small grin on his handsome face. "Are you going to eat now?" Curly watched them and finished eating.

She looked a little too innocent. "I've been eating."

"A piece of bacon isn't breakfast. And I expect you all to eat with us. No more of this eating in the kitchen stuff. You're always welcome at my table."

"Thank you," she blushed with pleasure at his warm smile and helped herself to some eggs and a pancake. "Curly, would you like something else?" She offered, noticing his plate was empty.

"I've eaten too much as it is. Breakfast was good, thanks," he gathered his dirty dishes and took them to the kitchen, leaving Pearce and Becky alone for a few minutes.

"So what are you planning to do today?"

"Well, I thought I'd clean up from breakfast first, then clean the house, unpack and clean the cabin, fix lunch and dinner, and then do whatever else you needed." She ticked off her mental list one by one on her fingers.

"That's it?" He chuckled, doubting she'd get everything done. Although he wasn't a dirty person and tried to keep the house clean, he was confident the house would take on a whole new persona when a woman took care of it. Especially a woman like Becky.

Pearce noticed the longer he talked, the quieter she became. So he wasn't entirely surprised when she sighed, lay down her fork and, looking everywhere but at him, blurted, "I need to know what exactly it is that you want me to do here."

"Whatever you see that needs to be done."

He watched as she pursed her lips, obviously not satisfied with his general answer. "Is there anything you *don't* want me to do?"

"I don't think so. Do what you would normally do. I trust you," he smiled as he got up, ready to take his stuff to the kitchen.

"Just leave that," she stood to her feet, hating to see him doing her job. "I'll take care of it."

"You really hate it when others help you," he answered, a smile spreading across his face, the dishes still in his hands. "By the way," he paused at the swinging door. "I'd like you to find Emily some things to do to help you, and if you wouldn't mind, I'd like to have Jeff out helping me a little everyday." She followed behind him, carrying the rest of the dishes so he wouldn't be able to take any more. "Is that okay with you?" He turned suddenly at the sink, making her almost run into him.

Her nose mere inches away from his chest, she stuttered, "I think that's great. I'll have lunch ready at twelve. What time do you want dinner?"

Her nearness unnerved him, and another slight scent of lavender wafted up. He knew he would always associate the scent of lavender with her. Shaking his head to clear his mind, he asked, "What?"

"Dinner. What time?" She asked again, noticing how beautiful his eyes were as he stared at her, his features soft and warm, all weariness gone.

"Six." He backed toward the door, resisting the insane desire to reach out and touch her hair to see if it felt as silky as it looked. "I'm glad you're here," he said softly, and he was gone, leaving her to all the agony and pleasure of wondering what he had meant.

She set to washing the dishes, anxious to keep not only her hands busy, but her mind as well. When she was finished in the kitchen and dining room, she called the girls inside, seeing that Jeff was already helping Pearce out in the barn.

"Would you two please help me today?" She asked as they ran in to see what she wanted.

"Sure mom," Jen answered quickly, knowing it was futile to say anything else. Emily wasn't so sure however, not being used to anything other than playing outside on her toys, or following Curly or Pearce around everywhere they went.

"Come on Emily, I'll need your help in your room," Becky led the little girl to her room, which was in dire need of attention. Emily stood in the hall, her arms crossed stubbornly. "Can you show me where you put your toys?" She considered the question for a moment before suddenly deciding there was no harm whatsoever for Becky to know where her toys went.

"My toys go over here," she answered simply, picking them up and putting them away in a large cedar chest at the end of her canopy bed. "And this is where I put my dresses," she continued showing her around, putting her things away as neatly as a five year old could be expected to. Becky followed her around and showed her how to hang dresses, make her bed, and dust, an hour passing by the time Jen came in to join them.

Checking her watch, Becky looked slightly worried that she still hadn't seen anything of Jeff. "Where's your brother? He should have been in here by now. I hope he's not bothering anyone."

Jen shrugged. "The last I saw him, he was with Pearce, helping with some sort of work. He's fine mom. Pearce looked like he enjoyed having him around."

Standing in front of Emily's large window, she searched for her son until she caught sight of Pearce walking out of the largest barn, Jeff trailing closely behind him. *He's so handsome*, her mind whispered before she could stop the unwelcome thought.

Jen came to stand beside her to see what she was looking at. "Mom?"

Suddenly aware that Jen was watching her, she turned away from the window, mortified that her daughter was grinning at her red face.

Perturbed that she had been caught by her match-maker daughter, she briskly ushered both girls out of Emily's room. "Come help me with the rest of the house."

They did accomplish all that Becky had hoped to do in the main house, but still hadn't made it to the cabin by lunchtime, and they quickly put together a delicious lunch for the hungry men, and not a moment too soon. She was just putting the last of the stuff for hamburgers on the large table when Pearce, Jeff, Curly and the rest of the crew tramped in, sitting down at the table as if they hadn't eaten in years.

Scott pounced on a hamburger as soon as Pearce finished the prayer and started slathering it with ketchup, mustard, pickles, tomato, and lettuce before anyone else had a chance to reach for a patty. "Lunch looks great! How come you never treated us so good, Curly?"

Curly gave Becky a wink while he waited for his turn at the meat plate. "Because I didn't think you needed that much to eat. Becky must feel sorry for you, but I'm sure she'll get over it when she gets to know you better."

"I'm hurt," Scott put his hand over his heart as though wounded, making them all laugh.

"House looks great," Pearce smiled warmly at Becky as she seated herself at the other end of the table. "I can't believe you got so much done!"

She flushed with the praise, and the smile she endeavored to conceal was noticed by her daughter. "I've had lots of help. I couldn't have done it without Emily and Jen."

After a little while, when she was sure the others were busy with their own talk, she turned her attention toward her son. "So what did you do today?" She listened attentively as he talked incessantly of cows, horses, grains, prices, and anything and everything that Pearce had said to him that day, amazed at how fast he was becoming attached.

"Can I go now?" Jeff asked when he finally took a breath. "Burt and John said that I could help with our truck if I wanted to."

"Well," she hedged, worried that he might irritate them if he always followed them around. "I suppose it's okay with me if it's all right with them."

"That's fine with us. We thought he'd enjoy himself working on it. He looks like the type that likes to get dirty." Burt laughed as he stood to leave.

"That's the understatement of the year," Becky quipped as she took a load of dishes to the kitchen. Everyone except Pearce was gone when she came back to wipe the table.

"They left fast. Did the girls go out with them?" She kept herself busy and tried not to be distracted by his presence.

"I told them they could have a break," Pearce answered, leaning back in his chair comfortably as he watched her work. "I think they went to the backyard to play. You really did do a great job on the house this morning. I honestly didn't think you'd get it all done."

Her heart fluttered at the praise and she was suddenly grateful neither of her children were in the room to misinterpret something. "It helps when you have two willing hands helping you. See. I let people help me."

"Just not grown-ups."

She rolled her eyes and made quacking motions with her hand. "Yada yada yada."

"Better watch out," he grinned. "I could fire you for being insubordinate."

Becky turned to face him, her hands on her hips. "I'd like to see you try. I don't think those guys out there would *let* you fire me," she tossed her red hair over her shoulder and stared at him defiantly, her grin infectious.

"I just may have a mutiny on my hands."

"You better believe it, buddy!"

"Good," he said, suddenly serious as he stood to his feet. "Then that means you're stuck here."

"I'm not stuck." She snapped her dish cloth at him. "I could leave anytime I want!" His playfulness suddenly vanished and pain and weariness replaced the humor and laughter that was there just a few seconds ago.

After a moment of acute silence, he placed his cowboy hat on his head and gave her a humorless smile. Her heart sank. "I'll be outside." Dismayed, she watched him walk toward the barn, his eyes on his feet as he went.

Never having been one to hurt people, whether intentional or mistaken, Becky followed him. "Pearce? What's wrong? What did I do?" She asked, bewildered by his sudden change of demeanor.

He gave her a calculated look before answering, "Nothing." He touched the brim of his hat and stalked off to the barn where Curly stood waiting in the doorway.

Rejected, she returned to the house and started cleaning the kitchen with a heavy heart and a fervent prayer on her lips. Finally, she made up her mind that she would apologize and try to make him understand that she had been teasing. With a final swipe over the immaculate counters, she flung the dishcloth into the sink and hurried outside in search of Pearce.

"Curly?" She called as she walked into the barn he had disappeared into earlier, "is Pearce around?"

"Well ma'am," he drawled, scratching his snowy white beard. His curious look told her he hadn't been made privy to her and Pearce's misunderstanding, and she felt a little better. "I don't rightly know where he's gone off too."

Her heart sank in dismay. "Rats!" She jammed her hands into the pockets of her jeans and walked toward the door, kicking at the soft dirt floor of the barn.

Curly, who was always quick to understand people, especially those he liked, called out, "Is there something I can help you with?"

Miserably, she shook her head and attempted a half smile. "No. I think I really messed up, and I don't know how to fix it."

"You? How could *you* mess up?" He teased kindly, trying to ease her troubled mind. "What did you do?"

"I was teasing Pearce in the dining room, and he just suddenly left without hardly saying anything. He was mad. How do I make him see that I was just joking?"

His look of surprise didn't escape Becky's notice. "Pearce can take a joke. He likes to kid around more than most people. He probably wasn't mad, you probably just misunderstood him."

Becky shook her head, her hair swinging back and forth. "No. He was definitely mad. Or hurt. I'm not sure which."

"Well what did you say then?"

"We were talking about mutiny, and he said I was stuck here, and then I said that I could leave anytime I wanted to." She looked up helplessly and shrugged her shoulders. "I said the wrong thing, didn't I?"

Curly whistled under his breath, making her feel even more horrid. "Yep. You said the wrong thing." He took off his hat and scratched his balding head.

"What should I do?" Becky asked, dismayed. "I would never do or say anything to hurt Pearce. I wish I could take it all back." She slumped down on the tack box next to the stall door. Curly sat next to her and gave her knee a reassuring pat.

"You know, I don't think you would do anything to hurt him. I think you would do almost anything for his happiness. In fact," he gave her an odd look, "I think you just might like him an awful lot." He grinned as her face instantly turned bright red.

She tried innocence. "I don't know what you're talking about."

He snorted and gave a little laugh. "Are you sure? I think anyone who might be interested in you would be hard put to gain your affection with Pearce around." His eyes twinkling merrily, he went on. "Yep. I'm pretty sure those young bucks out there don't have a chance."

"All right, all right," she shrugged her shoulders. "I care for him."

"Right." He drew out the word, not convinced. "I think it's a mite more than 'care'."

"Esteem, perhaps?" She joked, trying to lighten the mood.

"More like love if you ask me," he laughed, slapping his leg. "But then I guess no one's asking me, are they?" He struggled to stand, holding his right knee as though it pained him a little. "These old knees just don't like the getting up and going down like they used to," he answered her quizzical look as she walked with him a little ways.

"Curly, what can I do to make it up to him?"

White eyebrows shot up his forehead and a hopeful grin lit up his face. "I don't rightly know. But you could maybe try apple pie."

"Apple pie?"

"It's his favorite," he winked. "not to mention it's mine too. Then you might just try apologizing."

"I'll do that," she said, thankful she had someone to talk it over with. "Thanks Curly," she hugged him, grateful to have such a good friend. "By the way," her ears pinked as he started to walk away. "Um, could you, uh, not tell anyone?"

It was his turn to act innocent. "Tell what?"

"You know," she blushed even more.

"Oh, you mean about your 'esteem'? Don't worry. I won't tell him you 'esteem' him."

"Thanks."

"But I can tell him you love him, right?"

Giving him a threatening glare, she put her hands on her hips. "If you tell him or anyone else, there'll be no apple pie for you."

"You can trust me with our secret. But I'm not promising that the other fella's won't figure it out. Especially Scott."

She frowned, confused. "Scott?"

"You'll figure it out," he said off-handedly as he walked away. Shaking her head, she went in search for Pearce.

Finding him in the third place she checked, it seemed everyone could sense he was in an ill mood and there was little to no conversation while he, Burt, and John worked on her truck.

She cleared her throat to get his attention. "Pearce?" He poked his head out from under the hood.

"Yes?"

"I was wondering if I could talk to you for a moment?" She asked, her voice squeaking at the last syllable. Silently, he wiped his hands off on a grease rag and walked outside.

"What is it?"

Feeling it was best to just get it over with, she blurted, "I just wanted to tell you that I'm really sorry I hurt your feelings this afternoon. I was just teasing with you, and I guess I got carried away."

"Becky," he said quietly, his face softened with kindness, eyes dark and warm. "I'm just a little sensitive about certain things. It's not you that should be sorry, it's me." Feeling like a load had been lifted off her, she offered him a timorous smile that grew as he grinned affectionately back.

"I'm really sorry."

"Thanks," he said, watching her walk toward the house. He watched her until she entered the back door, unaware that he was the focus of Curly's attention.

Chapter 11

It was easier than Becky expected to fall into a routine in the following weeks. Almost without any troubles, the biggest hurdle they had to overcome was Emily. Having been used to following after her father or Curly every day, she didn't like being told to stay put. Fortunately for everyone, her love and affection for Jeff and Jen helped her decide she wanted to attempt school like they did. At the kitchen table.

As for Becky's kids, they had even less problems adjusting. Having always been early risers, they settled into a daily routine of cleaning their bunks, getting ready for school without too many complaints, and most importantly, anxious to be finished with school and allowed to help around the ranch.

Becky promptly brought Pearce his cup of coffee at the stables every morning, enjoying the fifteen minutes they spent together, before their real day started. Jen and Jeff would start their school at the kitchen table while Becky fixed breakfast for everyone, taking a break in between subjects to join the others for eating.

After breakfast, Emily would join them at their studies, happily learning to read and write, color, and obey Becky, which was sometimes the hardest thing for her to master. She was willing to listen to her until Pearce came inside for some reason or other, accidentally interrupting school, or when she just woke up on the wrong side of the bed.

One morning, Pearce made the mistake of coming in the kitchen door instead of the back door, consequently interrupting the morning phonics lesson. "Daddy!"

Giving Becky a chagrined look, he shook his head. "I did it again, didn't I. I can't seem to remember that y'all are in here." Disentangling himself from Emily's hug, he stared at Becky, his grin sending chills of pleasure running down her spine. "You look really good this morning."

He didn't miss her look of surprise, nor how it lit up her eyes. "Thank you." She hadn't put on any makeup and had just tied her hair back into a pony tail at the base of her neck, put on her favorite pair of jeans and an old flannel shirt, nothing special. Just plain and comfortable. "I think you're nuts, but I appreciate the compliment," she teased, her face red.

"Maybe I am," he answered, a small smile playing at the corners of his mouth. "But I think you look better without makeup."

"Now I'm convinced," she groaned and gave a shake of her head. "You definitely *are* nuts!"

Lifting Emily back into her chair, he frowned as if he were thinking hard about something. "I forgot what I came in here for. I think I came in to let you know we're going to have a visitor for dinner tonight," he ran a rugged brown hand through his short, wavy hair, making it stand up slightly.

Jen looked up from her lesson, interest written plainly on her face. "A visitor?"

"Who?" Jeff asked before another word could be said. Or another math problem finished.

"Pastor Mathis," Pearce chuckled at Jeff's enthusiasm. "I ran into him at the hardware store when I went out this morning, and I thought it'd be nice to invite him. Is that all right?" He gave Becky an apologetic look.

"Of course. Scott said that he and a buddy were going out, so it'll just be us and Jack. Is there anything special you want for dinner?"

Seeing her look of pleasure, he couldn't help being a little jealous. "No, I don't think so." If he had known about Scott's plans earlier, he wouldn't have asked the Pastor to join them. He always looked forward to spending an evening with just Becky, and he was a little annoyed now, knowing that he was going to have to share her. "I'll let you get back to work," he said suddenly anxious to get back outside.

"Thanks," Becky called after him, still pleased with the compliment that he had given her earlier.

"Mom," Jeff yelled, running into the kitchen later that evening, startling her as she was just adding the pasta to the boiling water. "Mr. Pearce wanted me to tell you that Pastor Mathis just got here," he waited expectantly at the stove for Becky to offer him a spaghetti noodle. "They're in the living room waiting."

"Jeff, don't yell in the house. You nearly scared me to death! Sheesh, give me a heart attack," she sighed, placing her hand over her chest and took a deep breath.

Shifting anxiously on his feet, he asked, "Can I have one, please?"

"I don't know. Can you?"

"I mean, *may* I have one, please?"

"Here," she said, handing him three uncooked strands of pasta. "Give one to the girls too. Now go on, get out of the kitchen."

A few minutes later, Emily and Jen walked into the kitchen, holding hands. "Mom? Do you need any help?"

"It's just about done," Becky answered, checking the cheesy French bread in the oven. "Why don't you two let everyone know it's time to wash up for dinner."

Becky set the steaming mass of spaghetti and meatballs in the center of the table as Pearce and Jack took their seats. "Hi Jack, how are you today? I hope you're hungry." She noticed he had taken her usual seat at the furthest end of the table, leaving the spot closest to Pearce open.

Jack stared at her in surprise, his mouth slightly askew in confusion. "Becky? I didn't know you were going to be here."

Before she could give a tolerable answer and let him know why, Jeff blurted, "We live here," much to Becky's chagrin. Surprised, Jack looked expectantly at her to supply the rest of the story, knowing her too well to suppose her to go against everything she believed in and stood for.

She gave her son a look that stopped anything else he was about to say. "Actually, we live in the ranch house at the back over there," she pointed out the window before she sat down next to

Pearce.

"Oh," Jack answered good-naturedly, chuckling to himself at Becky's discomfort and Jeff's blunder.

"She's my house keeper and Emily's school teacher," Pearce explained, his amusement evident. "How long have you worked here?" He asked Becky with a smile, pleased that she was going to sit next to him instead of Jack.

Filling everyone's plate with spaghetti, she avoided both men's curious stares. "Um, I'm not sure." *Four months and seventeen days,* her mind screamed. She knew exactly how long she had been there, as she counted every day, almost to the minute.

Jack took the plate she handed him. "I didn't know you worked here. I guess I would have figured it out if I just would have gone by your house. I'm sorry I neglected you."

Pearce scowled slightly at the ridiculous notion that he was the one who was supposed to look after her and the kids.

They talked amiably throughout dinner, and Pearce was diligent in being polite and not envious over the easy friendship that existed between Jack and Becky.

When everyone had eaten all they could, Jack pushed back his chair and sighed with contentment. "That was a great dinner. Thanks for the invitation Pearce."

"Any time, any time," Pearce smiled at Becky when she picked up his plate and carried it to the kitchen. "I didn't know you two knew each other so well," he continued when she returned to the dining room, closely followed by Jen who was afraid of missing something.

"We grew up together. I was just five when I moved into the house next to hers."

His curiosity was peaked. As well as Jen's. "Really? So you can tell me all kinds of stories, right?"

Becky cast a warning look at Jack, her expression grave. "No, he can't tell you anything."

"Actually, I've got lots of stories I could share," he said, not paying her any attention.

"Jack, don't." She sat down, purposely getting in their way.

"What are you afraid of?" Pearce teased. "Go ahead Jack. Tell me some stories about Becky." Becky groaned and put her head in her hand, knowing he was going to tell all the things she didn't want him to hear.

"We were best friends up until Frank came along. We did almost everything together. Fishing, hiking, catching frogs, all kinds of stuff. Our parents were good friends too, so we would often go camping or boating together. Whatever it was, we were pretty much together," he continued, a soft smile of remembrance on his handsome face.

"I bet she was a pain in the rear." Pearce laughed and Becky swatted at him playfully.

"Most of the time she was," Jack laughed. "But that's what made her so fun. I remember that it seemed like she had a different boyfriend every month," he said with an expressive shake of his head.

"I did not." Becky turned red with embarrassment. "He's exaggerating, Pearce." Turning a threatening glare toward Jack, she said, "Tell him the truth or he's going to think I'm some sort of floosie!"

"All right, all right. Maybe every other month," He winked and gave a nod to Pearce, who was laughing at her distress.

Becky slapped her forehead in exasperation. "That's not how it was at all! What would happen was, I'd like someone for a long time, then when he liked me, I didn't like him anymore. I don't know what it was, they just bothered me after they liked me."

"I would sit upstairs in my room and watch her dates bring her home, and it was funny how fast she would jump out of their car and run into her house. It was like she was running away from them." Jack continued as if she hadn't interrupted him.

"I was!" Becky harrumphed. "They would always try to kiss me goodnight. It made me want to scream. It was like they thought I owed them something if they bought me dinner and took me somewhere. Actually," she said thoughtfully, after a slight pause. "It made me mad. I couldn't stand it."

"Couldn't stand what?" Pearce was intrigued. He'd never heard of, let alone met, anyone that had disliked being kissed after a date, which is one reason he hadn't dated often. He found it rather refreshing.

"Dating," she answered simply. "The whole thing bothered me."

"You heartbreaker." he grinned, trying not to let her see just how much he admired her.

"No, I wasn't a heartbreaker."

Jack sat straighter in his chair and wagged a long finger her way. "Yes she was, don't let her fool you. In fact, there were a lot of guys that really liked her and she wouldn't give them the time of day. How many asked you to marry them?"

She rolled her eyes and shook her head at her daughter, twirling her finger around her temple to indicate that Jack was crazy. "Oh stop. I don't know what he's talking about."

"*And the truth will set you free*," he quoted, grinning. "Admit it. There were a lot of guys you wouldn't have anything to do with."

"Sure there were some, but that's true with anyone." She answered impatiently, smiling none the less.

He gave her a challenging look. "True. Now, answer the question."

"What question?"

"How many asked you to marry them?"

Becky wriggled in her chair and fiddled with the fringe on the placemat. "A few," she finally admitted.

"That's an understatement," Jack laughed. "Almost every boyfriend she had would ask her to marry him."

Pearce smiled pensively, an interesting, if uncomfortable, thought taking root. "I'm surprised that as close as you two seem to have been that you two didn't go out." Jen's eyes darted quickly to her mother's face with this new information.

"Actually," Jack said, his face turning red. "We did go out a few times." Jen couldn't help her grin at this interesting development.

Becky suddenly stood up with a huge groan. "That's it. I'm leaving."

"You can't leave now," Pearce caught her arm as she passed and held her in place. "We're getting to the good part. What happened?"

He gave a small snort, a rueful smile spread across his handsome features. "I did what ninety percent of the others did. I asked her to marry me. I was one of the unlucky ones."

Pearce turned his attention toward a very red Becky. "Why did you say no?"

"She had just met Frank," Jack answered before she could. "And I think she knew that she would pick him. Actually, I think everyone knew they would get married."

"It was that obvious, huh?"

"You should have seen the two of them," Jack went on, oblivious to her discomfort. "He was the only one she didn't run from. They were pretty much inseparable right from the beginning. Isn't that right, Beck?"

"Yes," she scratched distractedly at an invisible spot on the chair in front of her. "He was my best friend." She smiled, sorrow darkening her eyes. With a shake of her head and a renewed smile that was almost real, she changed the subject. "Anyone ready for dessert?"

Jack groaned and pushed his chair away from the table and slowly stood to his feet. "Not me, I've eaten enough to last an entire week! I need to go. I've got an appointment early tomorrow morning. Thanks again for dinner."

Walking together to the front door, he shook Pearce's hand and gave Becky a bear hug. "I hope I didn't bother you too much tonight," he said softly in her ear.

"You don't bother me Jack. We're too old of friends for that." Becky answered, smiling. "But you always leave right before the dishes need to be done."

"What can I say? I have a gift," he laughed and winked as he walked toward his old car, his keys jangling loudly at his side. "I'll see you at church Sunday."

Chapter 12

"That went well," Becky said, clearing off the table after she had waved a final goodbye to Jack. "What do you think?"

"I think it was a good evening. It's been a long time since I've had a guest over for dinner. I think it went well." Helping her carry the dinner things into the kitchen, he took the opportunity to watch her. When it was apparent her movements were automatic and her smile forced when she put the salad in a cupboard instead of the refrigerator, he asked, "Are you okay?" Following her back into the dining room, he helped her straighten the table and sideboard.

"Why wouldn't I be?"

"I just didn't want you to be upset about Frank," he said softly, stepping closer to her while she put the unused linen napkins away in the drawer.

She swallowed and kept her face turned away. "It doesn't bother me to talk about him. I miss him a lot, but God knows what I need." Putting his hands on her shoulders, he turned her toward him and peered into her face.

"What do *you* need Becky?"

Her mind screamed a thousand jumbled things at once, and she bit back words she would regret.

"Can't you tell me?"

It unnerved her to have him touching her. Being this close to him. Silently, she stared into his beautiful chocolate eyes. *It would be so easy to just reach up and...* the desire to kiss him was almost unbearable, and she shook her head and set her jaw.

"What do you want, Pearce?" she asked almost defiantly, her voice cracking slightly.

"I want you to be happy," he faltered, confused by her passionate response.

She stepped away, forcing his arms to drop by his side. "I'm happy. You've been very good to us and I have no complaints."

"I'm glad," he said quietly. A look of wistfulness passed over his face, and she realized that all the weariness and loneliness seemed to have vanished in the last few months she had been there.

She swallowed and resisted the temptation to reach up and press her mouth against his, and instead asked, "Do you want dessert?"

His eyes danced with mischief and he leaned against the doorframe. "Can I take it to my den?" he asked, knowing she didn't allow the children to take any food out of the dining room or kitchen.

"This is your house."

"My house huh? I could have sworn that you've pretty much made this your house."

"Well if it's my house," she quipped, lifting her chin. "Then you can't take your dessert to your den."

He threw his hands up in defeat, laughing. "I concede. It's my house, and I'll take my dessert wherever I want to."

"I'll go get you a plate." She grinned and slapped the swinging door open, stopping short when it registered that the kids were finishing up the dishes.

"Wow, you guys already cleaned the kitchen? It looks great!" Her heart swelled with pride and she gave Jen a hug, ruffled Jeff's hair and squeezed Emily when she threw her arms around her legs, all at once. "I thought you were being awfully quiet!"

"We wanted to surprise you," Jen answered, pleased with the praise. "We thought that maybe you'd like to have a little extra time to talk to Pastor Mathis," she said, looking at Jeff slyly.

Becky was instantly suspicious. "Yeah mom," Jeff added, with an attempt at innocence. "We just wanted to do something nice for you, but we've got just a little left to do, so you can go back out there and keep talking if you want to."

"Oh really?" Becky crossed her arms and gave them a playful 'mom' look. "Well, Pastor Mathis is already gone, so it's just us. How about I give you three a little bit of dessert and I'll finish up in here."

"Yeah!" Jeff whooped, always excited at the prospect of dessert and completely forgetting their scandalous endeavors to romantically entangle Becky with someone.

Jen frowned at him and said, "Jeff," as though he had committed a crime of some sort.

He gave his sister an irritated look. "What? Why are you fussing at me?"

"Because," she answered, raising her eyebrows and nodding her head toward the dining room.

"I think I'm missing something."

"Oh my word," Jen said, rolling her eyes expressively. "Men!"

"Go on," Becky said laughing, handing Emily and Jeff a piece of lemon meringue pie. "Go have a seat and enjoy. Jen, will you please give this to Pearce?" She handed Jen two plates, one for herself, and one to deliver.

"Sure," Jen answered happily, backing out the doorway. Coming back in after a few seconds, she asked, "Where is he?"

"I think he's in his den," Becky called over her shoulder, expertly wiping the counter off. "Just set it on the table and I'll take it to him when I'm finished."

"Okay," Jen answered, in a hurry to protect her pie before Jeff could sneak a bite.

Becky quickly finished cleaning up the rest of the kitchen and took the plate of luscious pie in search of Pearce. She found him in his den, sitting at his desk with his back to her, giving her ample time to observe him unnoticed.

He was holding the small picture of the pretty brunette woman she had noticed when they had first moved into the cabin. She had been so busy cleaning, cooking, and teaching, that she had completely forgotten about it.

Walking softly so she wouldn't disturb him, she peered over his shoulder to see the picture better.

"I thought you were never going to bring my dessert. I've been waiting for hours." He said suddenly, scaring her. He turned and watched her, the picture still in his hands.

"It hasn't been hours," she set the plate down beside him and turned to leave, embarrassed that he'd caught her snooping.

"Aren't you having any?"

"I was just going to get some."

"Good. Why don't you bring it in here?"

"Because I only eat in the kitchen or the dining room."

He gave her a playful scowl. "I don't think you heard me. Get your pie and bring it in here. And don't take so long," he called after her as she hurried away, thrilled that he wanted her to be with him.

"You can sit here," Pearce said, pointing to the chair he had placed next to his desk. "What are the kids doing?"

"I told them they could play a few games in the living room while we were in here talking," she answered, settling down in the chair he proffered. Busying herself with her pie, she tried not to seem too interested about the woman in the picture.

Evidently, she didn't succeed. He picked up the frame and held it carelessly. Harshly, even. "I'm sure that you've noticed this picture before. As well as you clean, you couldn't miss it."

"I noticed it a few times," she answered evenly.

"How come you've never asked about it?"

"I guess I figured it wasn't any of my business," she answered honestly, looking him square in the face.

"You're right. It *is* my business," he retorted, almost as if he were talking to himself. "But I want to tell you about it. This is one of the biggest mistakes of my life." He continued flatly, holding it out to her. "That," he said, taking a bite of pie, "is my ex-wife. Emily's mother."

Becky studied the photo, disliking the smug, conceited look in the woman's eyes. "You can take it," he added when she didn't take it from him right away.

"She's very pretty." She took it gingerly and stifled her feelings of inadequacy. Looking up to find him staring at her with a grave expression on his face, she couldn't bring herself to say what she really thought. The woman was drop-dead gorgeous.

"Pretty," he said thoughtfully, as if he were tasting the word. "More like beautiful. That picture really doesn't do her justice."

Becky felt a pang as her heart sank. She was definitely a country mouse compared to this beautiful woman.

It seemed as though God had given her everything, a perfect figure, perfect face, perfect hair and teeth. Nothing was lacking and Becky had to admit that she was far superior than herself.

Pearce continued. "I thought she was the most beautiful woman God had ever made. I loved her with my whole heart," he took the frame from her and gazed quietly at the photo.

Before she could clamp her teeth over the words, she blurted, "What happened then?"

"Did you know Satan can transform himself into an angel of light? He can make sin look so beautiful, but you'll always have to pay the consequences for your sins. Consequences that can last a lifetime. Even eternity," he stared at her, trying to read her thoughts. "Do you have any regrets?"

"Of course I have regrets," Becky answered softly with a shrug. "Everyone makes mistakes Pearce."

"No, that's not what I mean." He leaned forward, his eyes bright and probing. "Do you have regrets about Frank?" At her blank look, he went on. "If you knew that he was going to die and leave you with two kids--even though they're pretty terrific--would you still have married him?"

"Definitely," she answered without hesitation. "God intended for us to be married. I loved him with every fiber of my being."

"I can't say the same about me and Eva," he said, leaning back in his chair and finishing off his pie. "I was a Christian when I met Eva, but she didn't have any interest in God. I knew it wasn't right for me to marry her, but, instead of following God's direction and leading, I chose to believe Satan's lie. I thought I could change her and we'd live happily ever after. And now, I'm paying the consequences for my disobedience." He stared at her for a long moment in silence, his eyes deep in memories.

"I don't know what to say."

He grimaced and sat back in his chair. "There's nothing you can say. I goofed up. I thought I knew better than God, and I tried to force God's hand. Well, I guess I had to learn the hard way to listen. I married her against God's leading and even against my parent's wishes. I thought they weren't being fair, or that they were being too protective over me.

"We were married a year when Emily was born, but even before that, I was trying to keep my marriage from falling apart. She was wild and reckless, as well as adulterous, and she'd try to pick fights with me every day. When I wouldn't fight with her, she'd hustle into town and find a new fling." Her sharp intake of breath drew his attention, and he nodded gravely at her. "Oh yes. I found out about all of them.

"She would do whatever it took to get her own way, no matter who was hurt in the process. She used me for what she could get. Before we were married, I had saved about twenty-three thousand dollars so I could buy a ranch of my own, but she went through our savings like it was water. When there wasn't any left, she would pout and threaten until I ended up working three jobs to support her expensive habits. When I got home, she expected me to cook, clean, and do everything she was supposed to be doing while I was gone. It was even worse when Emily was born." He stopped, his eyes distant and cloudy as he remembered the horrors of what he was about to tell her.

"One day when Emily was just five months old, I came home from one of my jobs and found a letter on the table while Emily was sleeping in her crib. She left with her boyfriend and wasn't coming back. She said she'd made a mistake, and couldn't stand it here anymore. She divorced me and took everything I had without even a backward glance at her tiny daughter." A grin devoid of any mirth, lingered on his face.

"Pearce," Becky said, putting her hand on his arm. "I'm so sorry."

"Sorry?" He looked at her ruefully. "I thought it was the worst day of my life when it happened, but now, it was the best thing she could have ever done for me. It was the best day of my life," he laughed humorlessly. "I thought my world was ending, but actually, she was giving me the opportunity to raise my daughter.

"I quit my three jobs and came back to my parents, begging

their forgiveness, which they gave without even a rebuke. Dad helped me get back on my feet financially and gave me this ranch while mom took care of Emily, but that only lasted a little while.

"While Eva was messing up my and Emily's lives, Dad had been diagnosed with cancer. Mom had to take care of him and Emily while I ran the ranch. Dad passed away about six months after I came back here to live, and Mom died of a broken heart about a month later, leaving me to care for Emily and myself, which I had no idea how to do. Praise God for Curly. He worked for my dad and he stayed on when I took over. I don't know what I would have done if it hadn't been for him."

He took a deep breath and took Becky's hand in his, which was still on his arm. Her heart leaped at the tender smile he gave her. "And now, I praise the Lord for you. Now you know my whole, sordid, messed up life. What do you think?"

"I think you're a wonderful person, and I'm grateful that God has allowed me to be a part of your and Emily's lives," she said, her voice thick with emotion. "I think you're doing a great job, and I'm proud of you. Most people would have turned their back on God." She picked up the picture and stared at the heartless woman who hid behind a beautiful face. "But why do you keep Eva's picture?"

"To remind me that sin can look beautiful on the outside, but it's as rotten as a dead horse on the inside," he smiled at her, his eyes dark with pain and remorse. "I look at it every day to remind me to seek God's will and guidance in my life before I make another huge mistake."

"I wish you didn't have to go through that." Becky sat back in her chair and reluctantly pulled her hand out of his grasp. "I wish it didn't have to be that way."

"You know, I often wonder what would have happened if I hadn't married her, but then I think of Emily, and even though I've messed up her life as well, I couldn't give her up. No," he answered, standing to his feet and stretching. "I need that little girl, and now I'm going to do the best I can possibly do for her."

"Good for you," Becky smiled with pleasure over the lump in her throat. "Too often people forget to see the beauty of their children until it's too late. They forget to see that they're gifts from God himself, and they need to be treasured and guided."

"You really love being a mom, don't you. I bet that's why you homeschool," Pearce answered, flashing her his most handsome smile, making her wish even more that he belonged to her.

"That's just one of about a million reasons why I homeschool." She gathered up the empty dishes and hurried away to the kitchen, leaving him to wonder how he had ever cared for such a woman.

Chapter 13

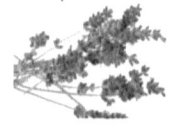

Becky was washing dishes in the kitchen after lunch one afternoon when she turned to find Scott sitting at the small table behind her.

"Scott! You scared me," she pressed a hand to her chest and turned red. "How long have you been sitting there?"

Giving her a teasing look, he said, "Long enough to know that you're thinking pretty hard about something. Or someone."

She grinned sheepishly and sat across from him. "I'm sorry. Next time, say something and I'll know you're there."

"I didn't mind," he chuckled and gave her a wink. "I enjoy watching you work."

"Is there something you need?" She tossed her hair over her shoulder, trying to keep herself from being annoyed. He knew she didn't like his flirting with her, and wondered why he would continue his attentions when it was obvious to everyone that she wasn't interested.

"I love it when you do that," he said, captivated. Something in his eyes warned her that this was no usual visit. He was up to something, and she would have to be on her guard.

"Do what?"

"Everything. I love everything you do," he went on, making her more apprehensive than ever.

"Was there something in particular you needed? I've still got a lot of work to do before dinner tonight." This time, she didn't bother to mask her annoyance.

He drummed his long fingers on the table, restless. "You know that most of us are going out tonight, so I was wondering if you would like to go to dinner with me?"

"Dinner? Tonight?" Her face blanched, and she wished for someone to deliver her from the uncomfortable situation. Normally, the kids would have come in from recess by now, but they had asked if they could give some apples to the mare and twins. The desire to kick herself briefly entered her mind.

"Yeah," he grinned. "The boss would let you off if you asked. He owes you one anyway. You haven't taken a night off since you got here. What do you say?"

"Well…" she hesitated, and wondered if she should just get to the point. Tell him she wasn't interested, wish him the best of luck, and go find someone else as her heart was already taken. "I can't. But thanks," she suddenly blurted, taking the coward's way out.

His smile didn't even falter, and she was faintly impressed. "Why?"

"Scott, you're a great guy…"

"But there's someone else you're interested in," he finished easily, leaning back in his chair. "I thought you'd say that. I can pretty much guess who it is too. Want me to guess?"

She stood to her feet, announcing the conversation was over. "No. You're not my type, that's all."

He quickly stepped in her path before she could walk out of the room. "And who is your type? I bet it's a tall, dark, and handsome rancher. Well, I've got news for you. I'll wait, because after all he's been through, I can almost guarantee that he's not going to get mixed up with anyone else."

Struggling to control her growing anger, she put out her hands, whether to ward him off, or stop him, she didn't know. She gathered her wits and looked up into his dark, flashing blue eyes. Dangerous eyes. "Please Scott. It wouldn't work out, I'm way too old for you," she finished lamely, a little scared. He allowed her to pass by him and watched as she wiped the sinks out.

"I'll give you time if that's what you want. Anyway, I came in here to let you know that your truck is finally done. Sorry it took us so long, but we've had a lot going on."

"It's done?" She breathed again, grateful for the change of subject.

"Yep, it's done. I'll drive it up to the cabin for you. Now you won't have to have the boss drive you to town when you need groceries or something," he watched for a reaction.

"Thanks for working on it for me," she replied evenly, trying her best to ignore his hint. "I really appreciate all you guys have done."

"It was my pleasure," he stood and headed toward the door. "But to tell you the truth, I thought for sure that you really liked going into town with the boss man." She blushed at the hint, knowing he was trying to make her admit her true feelings for Pearce. "There for a minute I thought I was wrong, but I see the truth now," he tipped his hat and walked out the door, letting the screen slam shut behind him.

"I don't think that went well," she announced to the silent room, her heart fluttering in her chest.

Becky was all set to spend some quiet time with Pearce and the kids for dinner that evening, and felt her spirits plummet when Scott came inside.

"I thought you were going out tonight." Everyone usually took off on Friday night, and Pearce was more than a little surprised to see that Scott intended to eat with them.

Scott's eyes were glued on Becky as she placed the food on the table and he purposely sat in the chair next to her usual place. "I changed my mind."

Pearce noticed Becky was quieter than normal, and he wondered if Scott had anything to do with it. He decided to keep a sharp eye on them both.

"I hope you don't mind," Scott said helping himself to mashed potatoes and drowning it with thick, brown gravy.

"I don't mind, I'm sure there's enough for everyone," Pearce answered mildly as Becky went quietly back to the kitchen.

"Pearce," Jeff announced a moment later, coming in from the kitchen and seating himself between Jen and Emily. "Mom sent me to tell you she's not feeling well and won't be eating dinner with us."

He glanced suspiciously at Scott. "Is she all right?"

"I think so," Jeff shrugged his shoulders casually, more

interested in dinner than in his mother at the moment.

"I'll go check on her," Scott said, standing up as if to follow after her.

"No, you sit down," Pearce ordered, sure that Scott's presence was the cause of Becky's sudden malady. "I'll go make sure she's all right. Y'all go on ahead and start without me." He put his napkin down, leaving before Scott could argue. He quickly walked out into the night, heading for the friendly light of Becky's little cabin behind his ranch.

Pearce knocked softly on the cabin door and let himself in when he thought he heard a slightly muffled 'go away' emanate from inside.

"Becky?" Glancing around, he had the uncomfortable feeling that he'd been wrong and she hadn't come back to the cabin, but had instead gone for a walk somewhere. Just as he was about to leave, he spotted a lump nestled under some blankets on the furthest bunk. "Are you all right?" he asked, her head covered by her pillow.

Hearing a sniffle, he suspected she had been crying. "Yes."

"What's wrong?"

"Nothing."

"Is it Scott?" He tried to peel the pillow away from her face. "Is he bothering you?"

"I don't know," she sniffled and allowed him to uncover her head.

"You don't know why you're crying?" He asked, puzzled, looking at her puffy face.

"Pearce," she began, turning slightly to face him, her eyes begging. "May I please have the day off tomorrow?" She looked so pitiful and heartbroken that he was sure he would have given her anything she'd ask.

"Of course, but you do know that it's Saturday, right?"

"Yes," she answered, wiping her tear-stained face. "I just think I need the day off."

"That's fine. You haven't really had a day off since you've gotten here." He moved to the door and opened it, turning toward her just before he left. "But, I just want you to know that if Scott is upsetting you, I'll talk to him."

She frowned. "He isn't bothering me. It's just…" she continued, her face coloring. "Never mind. It's all good. Thanks."

"Anything I can do to help you out," Pearce said, not entirely convinced about Scott.

"Good morning," Pearce called cheerily the next morning to the three children sitting at the kitchen counter. "How's your mom doing?"

"Not too good," Jen answered. Jeff nudged her angrily in the ribs and glared at her.

"What's wrong? Does she feel well?" He helped himself to a large bowl of frosted flakes.

"I guess she's sad," Jeff gushed out before Jen could take over.

"Well?" He prompted gently when it was clear that they weren't going to give him any more information without encouragement.

Jen's spoon paused midway between the bowl and her mouth, the milk shaking a little. "Today is the anniversary of dad's death."

"I'm sorry. I didn't know," he said, putting a comforting hand on her back. She looked at him gratefully, tears threatening to spill over any minute. Jeff sat in stony silence, refusing to acknowledge anyone.

"What does she usually do?"

Jeff gave him a morose look, his lip curled downward. "She mopes around and cries a lot. I don't get it. It's been so long, I just don't understand."

"Understand what?" Jen asked, looking confused.

"Why she still cries. Why she still misses him. Why God allowed him to die before I really got to know him. I don't know. Everything." Jeff answered, pushing around his soggy flakes.

Jen flashed him an angry scowl. "She loved him, that's why."

"All right, all right," Pearce cut in quickly, hoping to head off an argument. "I'm sure she loved him, and I'm sure he was a great guy, but those really aren't very easy questions to answer Jeff.

There are a lot of reasons for each one, I'm sure. But we can be sure that God always does what's best for us. Even when we don't understand it."

"That's what mom keeps telling me, but I still don't understand. She loves God so much, but God took dad away. It's confusing." Jeff shrugged his shoulders half-heartedly, still playing with his cereal.

"Yes, it's confusing, but just trust him. He only wants what's best for all of you," Pearce felt sorry for the two fatherless kids. He wished there was something he could do for them all, but had no idea what.

Jeff stood, grabbed his bowl, and rinsed it out in the sink. "I'm going to be in the barn if anyone needs me." And he was gone, running to find Curly.

"He'll be okay," Jen said quietly, watching him out the window. "He always acts like this when mom's sad."

"What does your mom do about it?"

"I've never told her. I don't want to make her feel worse than she already feels."

"But maybe if you told her, things would be a little different," he said hopefully.

"I don't know," she answered, finishing up and taking her bowl to the sink as well. "I'm going outside, want to come with me Emily?" She held out her hand to the small girl, a sad smile curling her lips. Emily hopped down from the stool, took her hand, and followed her outside, leaving Pearce to ponder over the situation by himself.

Curly nodded as Pearce came into the main barn a few minutes later. "Your coffee hasn't arrived yet this morning, and by the looks of the young visitor that's over yonder with the twins, you ain't gonna get any." He said quietly, jerking his thumb over his shoulder.

"Morning Curly. I gave Becky the day off, so it's every man for himself today." Pearce gave him a curt nod and joined Jeff at the railing. They stood in companionable silence for a little bit, watching the antics of the frisky foals.

"Sorry about all that in the kitchen," Jeff said glumly, resting his chin on his hands. Pearce resisted the urge to chuckle as Jeff's face bobbed up and down when he talked.

"Nothing to be sorry for." They had been silent for a few minutes when Pearce decided to try to bring him out of his dismal mood. "What's your favorite animal?"

"Cats," was Jeff's quick reply. "Jen really likes dogs, and she thinks cats are okay, but I'm like mom. I love cats."

"Really? I didn't know your mom liked cats," Pearce said surprised. He had figured that Jeff would like dogs better, as most boys his age did. He grinned, glad they had something in common. "Did you ever have a cat?"

"We did when I was really little. Dad had given one to her before he died. After the accident, the cat just disappeared. Mom thinks it ran away, but Jen thinks the neighbor took it because it was so pretty. It was black and white with white socks on its feet, and under its chin it had the softest white fur. Jen says that it had an upside-down heart on its nose, but I don't remember. She says mom was really upset that it was gone and cried for days. I remember I used to chase it around and around, trying to pet it or feed it. It always made mom laugh." Jeff smiled at the memory.

Pearce chuckled and went to the door. "Come on. I've got something to show you."

He led him to an empty stall in the back of the barn and Jeff peered through the doorway, his eyes taking a little time adjusting in the dimly lit room. "What? I don't see anything."

Pearce pointed to a lump of sweet smelling hay in the corner. "Look under there."

"Where? Here?" Cautiously, he started lightly spreading the hay around as if he were afraid something was going to bite him. "Hey! What *is* that?" He yelled and jumped back when something scurried further back into the soft mound. Moving in to investigate, he stuck his head closer.

"Kittens!" Joy lit up his face like it was Christmas morning as he tenderly pulled out a fluffy, mewling ball of fur, cuddling it close to him.

"Keep looking, there's about four more somewhere."

"Here they are," he answered as the other four came pattering out to meet the stranger who was holding their brother captive. "I didn't know you had cats." He squatted down so he could pet the rest of them.

"A barn isn't a barn without a cat. If I didn't have at least one, pretty soon the mice would be big enough to carry Curly away. Which one do you think your mom would like?"

His dismal mood was replaced with hope and excitement as he looked at Pearce to make sure he wasn't kidding. "You mean it? Can I really pick one out for her?"

"As long as she doesn't say no when you give it to her."

Jeff examined each one carefully, indecisive as to which one was the best. "They're all so cute, I don't know which one to pick." After looking at each for a long while, he gave a doubtful glance at Pearce. "Can you pick one for her? I love them all."

"Well let's see," Pearce squatted down next to Jeff and reached for a little fur ball. "I think your mom needs a friendly cat," Jeff nodded his head vigorously. "I think she needs a smart cat," he set the first one down and picked up a new one.

"But I also think she needs a beautiful cat," he said, reaching out for another. "What about this one?" He asked, holding the kitten out to Jeff to inspect it. "It seems to be friendly, smart, and cute. Do you think she'll like it?"

Thoughtfully, Jeff took the gray purring kitten out of Pearce's hand, stroked it a few times, looked into its furry face, and smiled his answer. "This is the one. She's perfect." Pearce smiled, gratified in no small way to make Jeff happy on such a discouraging day. "When can I take it to mom?" He asked, carefully cradling the kitten in his arms as if he were afraid to hurt her.

Pearce stood and brushed his knees off, a swirl of dust and hay spiraled into the air. "You can take it to her now, if that's the one you want."

Jeff walked as quickly as his precious cargo would allow, anxious to give Becky the gift. He stopped at the barn door and turned back toward Pearce who had stayed behind.

"Can you come with me? It wouldn't be right to give her the present you picked out for her and act like it was all my idea. Please?"

Pearce hesitated, not sure if it was a good idea for him to give Becky a present. "It's okay if you give it to her. Just let me know what she says."

Jeff gawked at him, his face screwed up in disbelief. "Are you afraid of my mom? You're afraid of a *girl*?"

"No!" Pearce whipped off his hat and laughed, a little embarrassed. "I just don't want the guys to think, well, you know."

"What?" Jeff stared, puzzled. "Oh I get it. You don't want anyone to think you like my mom." Pearce gawped at him, taken aback by his bluntness. "Why? Don't you think she's pretty?" He continued, not one bit perturbed.

Slapping the hat back on his head, he stomped over to the boy and took the kitten out of his hands. "All right, that's it. Let's go give this thing to your mom," he said and walked stiffly out the door, leaving Jeff grinning behind him.

They walked silently to the cabin, one a little embarrassed that he'd been tricked by an eleven year old, the other happily skipping along, proud of himself for his efforts.

"Mom!" Jeff hollered as he unceremoniously threw open the cabin door. "Mom!" He ran through the cabin, not finding Becky anywhere. "I'll go look in your house really quick," he said, running out the door before Pearce could say anything.

Stunned once again by the boy's cleverness, he now found himself in a very uncomfortable position. Pearce wondered what Becky would do if she caught him there alone with a wiggling kitten in his arms.

He looked around, trying to find somewhere to put the cat so he could leave before she came back, when he spied an open book on the table in the tiny kitchen. His curiosity overruling good sense, he walked over and saw that it was an old wedding album, open to a picture of Becky and Frank feeding each other a piece of their wedding cake. Fascinated, he stood over it for a few minutes and flipped through the pages, finding Frank's death certificate pasted carefully on the last page. Splotches where old tears had fallen made some of the type fuzzy and a little difficult to read.

Taking a piece of paper that had been placed between the certificate and the back page, he carefully unfolded it, sure that it was a love letter from Frank to Becky. He was surprised to find it was the letter that he had anonymously sent to her before they had become such good friends.

He sat down abruptly, so deep in thought that he didn't hear the bathroom door open a few moments later.

"Good morning Pearce," Becky said softly behind him, patting her wet hair with a towel. He jumped, almost dropped the kitten, and hastily stood to his feet, cursing his rotten nosiness. "How are you today?"

"Becky!" He stood speechless, his face red with embarrassment and his jaw hanging stupidly open. Trying to look everywhere but at her in her robe, he did the only thing he could think of and thrust the indignant kitten into her arms. "I just, I was, um…here. Jeff said you liked cats." Mortified, he jammed his now empty hands deep in his pockets.

She cuddled the small cat and scratched behind its ears and gave him such a look of devotion and delight, it almost erased the previous ten minutes from his memory. Almost. "She's beautiful! Thank you."

"It was Jeff's idea to give her to you," he said a little more gruffly than he had intended, still embarrassed. She looked down quickly, but not before he had seen the hurt look in her eyes. "Becky, I'm sorry. I didn't mean to sound so rough," he took her elbow. "I'm just embarrassed that you caught me snooping through your stuff. I shouldn't have, and I'm sorry."

"I don't mind if you look through it. If I had anything to hide, I wouldn't leave it out where my two nosy kids could find it," she gave a small laugh, wiping her red eyes with the sleeve of her robe. "It's all the things that I hold dear to my heart," she said simply, shrugging her shoulders. "I have another one for each of the kids with all their baby things and pictures, but this is the one that I keep my most treasured memories in. Mostly a part of me that died," she looked over at the book, absentmindedly rubbing the kitten next to her cheek.

"Except for this," he said jokingly, handing her the letter he had been caught reading, trying to lighten her mood. "This must just be a book mark." He grinned as she took the letter from his hand and looked over it quickly, her face turning pink.

Tenderly, she put it back in the album where he had found it. "No, that's exactly where it's supposed to go. I just haven't gotten a new album for my new memories yet."

Her soft green eyes seemed to beg him to take her away. Make memories that she would cherish for years to come. Be her much needed hero.

And suddenly he knew that was exactly what he wanted to do. "What are you going to do today? Do you have anything planned?"

"I didn't have anything but sit here and mope around the cabin all day, why?"

He smiled down at her and resisted the urge to brush a wisp of wet hair back away from her cherubic face. "I was wondering if you would like to go somewhere."

"Me? I don't know where I would go by myself," she asked, puzzled.

"No, all of us."

"All of us?" She was quiet for a moment. "I don't see how all of us could go. I mean," she glanced up at him, a mischievous gleam in her eye, "where in the world would we put Curly, Scott..."

"You know what I mean. You, me, and the kids. We'll just go spend the whole day together, what do you think?" He caught her arm excitedly, his look challenged her to refuse.

"I don't know," she hesitated, enjoying the warmth and pressure of his hand.

"Come on. You probably need stuff for the cat anyway, right?"

The transformation was instant. The prospect of spending an entire day with him made up her mind. She didn't care if they just went to the grocery store. "All right, I'd love it."

"Get changed, and I'll round up the kids. I'll be back in ten minutes," he said over his shoulder as he walked to the door.

"There's no possible way I can be ready in ten minutes."

"Well then I guess you better hurry," he laughed and closed the door before she could protest further.

He was about to go in search of the kids in the barn, when he saw them standing in a row at the end of the porch, grinning from ear to ear a little too innocently.

"Where were you?" He barked at Jeff whose grin was the broadest. "Your mom caught me looking through her stuff!" He put his hands on his hips and tried to look severe.

Jeff said with a glance at his sister and an innocent shrug, "I couldn't find her." Jen, who had suddenly deemed it a perfect time to hum *Amazing Grace* and look around at the scenery, proved their guilt beyond a shadow of a doubt.

"Oh, I see," he answered flatly when Jen started to hum. "I was set up. You wanted your mom to think I was a sneak."

"Would I do a thing like that?" Jeff asked simply, putting his hand on his chest as if he'd been wounded.

Pearce couldn't resist the urge to laugh. "Uh huh. Well you better get ready to go. We're going to be leaving in about fifteen minutes if your mom hurries," he finished, heading toward the barn to let Curly know he was taking the day off.

He found him in the office reading a newspaper, his feet propped up on the desk in front of him as if it were his barn and he were the boss instead of the other way around.

"Yes, boss?"

"I'm going to be gone all day, so you're in charge." He hung his beat-up cowboy hat on the peg on the wall next to a newer one. Quickly, he looked over his reflection in the small mirror in the tiny bathroom and combed his hair, whistling a tune while Curly watched him shrewdly from the other room.

His eyebrows raised, he repeated, "You'll be gone all day," when Pearce came out.

"Yep," he grinned as he took the new cowboy hat off the wall and placed it on top of his head. "How's that?" He asked, turning to Curly for his opinion.

"Doesn't look like you're going to an auction."

"I'm not."

"Doesn't look like you're going just to the store for groceries either," he said folding up the paper.

"I'm not."

Curly smiled knowingly and gave him a wink. "Looks more like you're going courtin'. And I think I know who you're taking."

Pearce returned his smile and leaned against the door, his arms crossed over his chest. "Who would that be?"

"That pretty little cook you've been mooning over the past couple of months."

He had the goodness to try to look surprised, but his smile grew even larger. "I haven't been mooning over her."

"I say it's about time you took her out. You almost let her get away," Curly picked up the newspaper again and snapped it open.

"Oh really?"

"You're not the only one around here that likes her you know. In fact, I happen to know there's a young man that's going to be a little bit peeved when he finds out she went somewhere with you first."

"Do you think I should leave her alone then?" Pearce looked at him seriously for a moment. "I don't want there to be a problem."

Curly laughed and turned to the page he had previously been reading. "You should have hired an ugly woman to be your housekeeper then! And no. I don't think you should leave her alone. I think you should have taken her out a long time ago."

Dusting off an imaginary fly from his jeans, he asked casually, "Is she interested in this other person?"

"I think you're safe on that account. She lights up like a firecracker whenever you're around. She doesn't even notice anybody else." Pearce flashed a boyish grin at his friend, indescribably pleased.

"How much do you suppose she likes me?" He fingered a stalk of straw.

"I guess that's up to you to find out," Curly grinned craftily, not taking the bait. "I've been sworn to secrecy."

"So you know more than you're telling me. Remember I'm your boss now."

"What are you two talking about?" Becky said behind Pearce, making him jump and hope like crazy she hadn't heard their conversation.

"You look pretty," Curly whistled and tipped his hat at her, changing the subject. "I don't think I've seen that particular dress yet."

"Thank you," Becky answered, turning pink as she smoothed the front of the dress she was wearing. She had decided to wear it on purpose, knowing it made her look very pretty and feminine, showing off her slim figure perfectly. "Are you ready?" She turned her attention to Pearce, who stood mutely gathering in every detail he could.

She frowned after an uncomfortable second of silence grew into five. "What's wrong?"

"I don't think he likes your dress," Curly winked.

"Do you want me to change?" She had so desperately wanted to please him and make him notice her.

"Nope. You look beautiful," Pearce said finally, a faint flush creeping up his throat. "Curly, we'll see you later." He held the door open for her, grinning wildly at his friend behind her back.

Chapter 14

The day passed way too quickly for both of them, and it was late by the time Pearce parked the truck in front of Becky's little cabin that evening.

"I had a great day today," she turned to face him, her eyes shining.

"I did too, and thanks for taking it so easy on me in bowling," he laughed quietly and put his arm on the back of her seat, working up the courage to put it on her shoulders.

"I didn't take it easy on you," she answered, smiling. "I'm a terrible bowler."

Twisting around in her seat to look at the three silent children, she said, "They were so quiet, I figured they must be sleeping." She laughed and turned back, delighted that his arm was now resting on her shoulders. "I can't thank you enough for all you've done for us."

"I haven't done anything for you. I should be thanking you," he said quickly with a shake of his head, his heart beating fast. They were silent for a few moments, enjoying the new level they seemed to have gotten to in their relationship.

Becky edged closer to the door, his arm just barely hanging on. "I should get these two off to bed."

"Yeah, I should get Emily put away too," he grinned. "But I'm really not in a hurry. I was enjoying myself."

"Me too," she answered quietly, biting her lip nervously. It had been so long since she'd been on an actual date that she'd forgotten what to expect or do.

He leaned toward her, and she wondered briefly if he was about to kiss her, when he whispered, "Tell you what, you hurry and put them to bed and I'll meet you out on the back patio and we can watch the stars together." He twisted a silken strand of her hair, sending waves of delight through her as his fingers brushed against her neck.

"I'll meet you in a few minutes."

"I bet I'll be there first," he grinned, enjoying the light scent of lavender.

"Are you rushing me?" She teased, her door open already.

"Maybe."

"Well, I think you should know that I'm American, not Russian," she giggled at the old joke she and Frank used to share together.

"I think you should know that I'll still be first," he picked Emily up in his arms and carried her to the house as Becky ushered a very sleepy Jen and Jeff off to their bunks, wanting to be the first one to the patio.

"I won," Pearce laughed quietly as she joined him a few minutes later. He had pulled a lounge chair next to his, not leaving any room between either of them.

Sitting down in the comfy chair, she grinned. "I bet you just put her into bed with her clothes on!"

"Guilty as charged. Good thing she doesn't mind!"

"I can't believe you'd do that just so you could win. Cheater." Leaning back, she watched the glittering jewels in the dark sky, transfixed by their beauty. She recalled the verse, '*He made the stars also...*' and marveled that it had been a mere trifle for God to make them. A sigh of contentment slipped through her smiling lips.

Pearce, who had been watching her more than the stars, said quietly, "I think you're beautiful."

She froze, wondering if she'd heard him correctly. "Did you say something?"

"I said you're beautiful," he leaned toward her and her heart skipped a beat or two.

For the second time that evening, she thought he was about to kiss her before he suddenly leaned back in his own chair and gazed towards the heavens, his hands folded behind his head.

"I'm so glad that you came to work for me," he said suddenly, his voice husky. "I don't know what I'd do without you now."

"Oh, you'd just find yourself another housekeeper to take my place," she tried to keep the disappointment out of her voice. "I'm sure you wouldn't have any trouble. In fact, you've probably had quite a few in the past." She waited, hoping he would argue with her. He was silent for a little while, surprising her and making her wonder if she'd been right.

"Find someone to replace you? How could I replace you? You're perfect."

With an emphatic shake of her head, she said a little more forcefully than needed, "I'm not perfect Pearce. You'll find out sooner or later."

A companionable silence had settled between them when she was suddenly aware that he was looking at her and not the stars.

Grateful that he couldn't see her blush, she said, "Thanks for taking us out today. I really enjoyed myself."

"Not as much as I did." Without warning, he reached over and took her hand, his thumb caressing the top of her tiny fingers. "I think we should do that more often."

"I agree." Silently, she sent up a prayer of thanks as it seemed her dreams were coming true. They sat companionably a few moments longer content just to be close to one another.

"I think I should be going in," Becky said finally, her voice full of regret. "The day starts pretty early in the morning."

"I guess you're right. Will I see you in the barn as usual?" He walked her to her door, her hand still firmly grasped in his own.

"If you want to."

"Of course I want to see you. It's the best part of my day," he held the door open for her. "Till tomorrow then."

"Tomorrow."

The difference in their relationship in the following weeks was noticed by everyone. Becky no longer sat away from Pearce, but took her seat next to him at the table as well as at church. And while they still had their coffee and chats in the barn every morning, it was mentioned more than once that they seemed to be eating Pearce's favorite meals and desserts. Even small things like going to the store together and leaving the kids with Curly was fodder for the gossiping workers. Scott, the only unhappy one about the whole situation, decided to bring it up to Curly one morning.

"Curly, what do you think about this whole thing?" He flung the pitch fork he had been using into a stack of hay and leaned on the stall door. "They're always together."

Not surprised by the sudden outburst, Curly didn't look up. "I don't see anything wrong with it. Do you?"

"Yes!"

"She's not the only girl out there," he answered quietly, unable to stop himself from grinning.

"I know. But now she won't even give any of the rest of us a chance." He frowned and gave the old man a murderous look.

"Do you mean you?"

"I guess so."

"Don't you think the boss deserves some happiness after all he's been through?" Curly finally graced him with his whole and undivided attention.

"Hmpf."

"Curly!" Pearce interrupted their conversation, his bright cheery whistle seemed out of place next to Scott's glowering disposition. "I'm going into town, do you need anything?"

"Can't say that I do. You Scott?" Curly stared pointedly at the younger man.

"Nope." He stalked out of the barn without a backward glance at either of them.

Pearce frowned his displeasure at the younger man's retreating back, flinching when he slammed the door shut behind him. "What was that all about?"

"I already told you," Curly answered, leaning up against the wall.

"Becky."

Curly nodded, a small grin playing at the corners of his mouth. "You should have hired an ugly one. He thinks Becky's going with you."

"Well he's wrong. She's not going today. School's still going on," Pearce answered, grinning widely as he checked his watch.

"She'd be able to go if you waited a little. She usually gets done about an hour or so from now."

"Yep. That's why I'm going now." Pearce gave him a secretive grin.

His curiosity was now aroused. "What exactly are you going into town for?"

"A little surprise," he answered off-handedly, his smile growing wider.

"How little?"

"You know," he stared meaningfully, raising his eyebrows. "Little."

"Are you going to get her a ring?" Curly asked bluntly, tired of the cat and mouse game.

"Maybe, or maybe not. I guess you'll just have to wait and see!" Pearce chuckled, enjoying himself.

"If it's what I think it is, congratulations then. I don't think you could do better."

Pearce checked his watch. "Well, I better get going before she's finished, or she'll be going with me. See you later."

"Mom, can I please be finished with Science?" Jen asked, tired of learning the names and functions of various digestive organs. Becky glanced up at the kitchen clock, making sure their forty-five minutes were done.

"Three more minutes," she answered, helping Jeff with a difficult math problem.

"Miss Becky?" Emily chirped excitedly, sitting across the table from Jen. "Can I read this to you?" She asked, holding out a small reader she was working on.

"Of course," Becky smiled, glad that Emily seemed to enjoy learning how to read. She remembered how easy it had been for Jen to grasp the concept of reading, and how once she had learned she just took off, reading anything and everything in sight.

Jeff had been a different matter. He had learned the rules of phonics easily enough, but hadn't been as interested, and therefore took a little more prodding than Jen had. His strengths seemed to be science, math, and anything mechanical, while Jen was all English, history, and the arts. She wasn't sure which category Emily would fall into, if either, but she really took pleasure in teaching each one of them.

"Time's up," she said, releasing them out into the wild. Or at least that's the way she thought of it.

Jeff slammed his book shut and jumped out of his seat as though he'd been shot out of a cannon. "Thanks mom!" Jamming his cap onto his head, he ran out the door like a bolt of lightening.

"I always wonder if Curly and the guys are happy when school's out, or if they dread it," she laughed, watching him out the window as he dashed into the barn. Giggling, Jen finished the worksheet she had been working on, and filed her things away in her drawer.

"Is there anything you need me to do to help with dinner?" She asked, helping Emily put away her things.

Becky gave her an affectionate pat on her back. "I can't think of anything yet. Why don't you just go ahead and have a good time."

Jen gave her a peck on her cheek and took Emily's hand and went out into the yard to play.

Becky poured herself a cup of coffee and sat down at the table, relaxing and thanking the good Lord for her wonderful children, including Emily. She had a hard time thinking of little Em as anyone's but hers, and loved and cherished her as much as she did her own.

"Becky!" The screen door slamming shut behind her made her jump a few minutes later.

Ignoring the sudden sinking of her heart when she saw Scott's scowl, she offered him a smile and the seat across from her. "Want a cup of coffee?"

"I'm surprised you're here."

"Why? Where else would I be?"

"I thought you went into town with Pearce."

"I didn't know he was gone," she said, more surprised than

ever. "He didn't even say goodbye," she pouted playfully, throwing her bottom lip out like a little child. Sullenly, Scott stared at her for a moment, not in the mood to joke around. "Is there something wrong?"

He smacked his calloused hand down on the table and leaned toward her, his eyes flashing. "Yes! He'll just hurt you."

"What are you talking about?" She asked, aggravated that he thought he could intimidate her into doing whatever he wanted.

"Pearce can't love you like I can."

"Scott." Laying her hands down on the table, she endeavored to remain calm and discuss the situation like the adults they were. Unless he wouldn't listen to reason. Then she considered the application of a frying pan across his head might make him more reasonable.

"I know you don't want to hear this, but he's just going to hurt you. He doesn't love you, *I* love you."

"You don't love me," she said forcefully, her eyes flashing angrily. "How can you even say you do? You don't know anything about me, or what I like, or what I want to do with my life. You just like the way I look." She pushed her chair back and walked over to the sink, rinsing out her mug. She resisted the urge to get the frying pan.

Scott was behind her in an instant. Angrily, he grabbed her arms and turned her around, pinning her to the sink with his weight. She struggled to get away from his kisses, but her small fists pummeling his broad chest seemed to have no effect.

"Stop it!" Kicking him in the shin and twisting out of his grasp, he yowled in pain as she ran out the door, trying to get as far away from him as possible. Crazed, he rushed after her and grabbed her arm. Yanking her to him, he kissed her repeatedly.

Her blood boiling and rushing in her ears, she continued to resist and faintly heard Jeff yell "Mom!"

As though he were the biggest, brawniest linebacker on an NFL team, Jeff barreled into Scott and knocked him off balance while a few of his punches landed squarely on his jaw.

"Jeff!" Becky tried to pull her furious son away as the two

struggled. Finally successful, Curly, who had followed Jeff out of the barn, punched Scott in the stomach, making him double up in pain, gasping for air.

"You okay?" Curly asked her, standing over Scott in case he tried to get up. "Did he hurt you?"

"I'm all right," she said shakily, spitting blood in the dirt and wiping her mouth, disgusted with the feeling of Scott's lips and tongue pressed against her mouth. She held Jeff to her as he sobbed into her stomach, his arms wrapped protectively around her waist.

"Scott, I think you'd better hightail it on out of here before the boss gets back," Curly said gruffly, jerking his thumb over his shoulder toward the barn. "I don't want to see your face the rest of the day. Now git!" He pushed him as he skulked angrily away, fists jammed deep into his pockets.

"I'm sorry about that," he said kindly, turning to Becky and putting a hand on top of Jeff's head. "You were pretty brave there boy. You did the right thing." Jeff looked at him, grateful that Curly thought he was brave even though he was crying.

Becky now noticed the rest of the workers had come to see what the ruckus was all about, and felt immensely foolish. "Thank you both for helping me."

"I'll let Pearce know what went on so you won't have to. Ma'am," he said, tipping his hat and turning to leave.

"Curly," she called, touching his arm. "What'll happen to him?"

"I wouldn't be surprised if he lost his job," he said, scratching his white head.

"I kind of feel bad for him," she said suddenly, taking him by surprise. "He's just young and stupid. Can't you talk Pearce into giving him a chance? Please?"

He looked queerly at her for a second, thinking about her suggestion. "All right. I'll see what I can do, but don't expect too much." He wagged an old bony finger at her.

Chapter 15

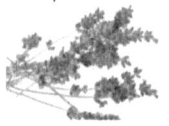

"Something smells great!" Pearce called cheerily, coming into the kitchen where Becky was preparing dinner later that evening. He seated himself at the small kitchen table, taking care that he wouldn't be in her way, but still in a position to watch her every move. "How was your day?"

Suddenly becoming a coward, she decided to skirt the question. "I didn't know you were going into town. I would have had you pick up more potatoes."

Not in the least perturbed, he grinned. "Sorry. Where's the kids?"

"They're in Emily's room." She poured the steaming pot of boiled potatoes into the colander, getting them ready for mashing. Keeping her back to Pearce, she expertly tipped up the roasting pan and spooned drippings into a measuring cup for gravy.

"Did you have a good day?" He repeated, enthralled with her effortless way around the kitchen.

"Mmm…" she shrugged her shoulders, not looking at him.

"That sounds ominous," he said, puzzled by her unwillingness to talk to him. "Did something happen?"

"Boss, I need to talk to you," Curly announced before she could answer, letting himself in the back door.

Now he was intrigued. Watching Becky out of the corner of his eye, he asked, "What is it?"

With a descriptive roll of his eyes toward Becky, who was still avoiding making eye contact with him, Curly shuffled his feet uncomfortably. "Can we go into your den?"

Pearce looked from Curly to Becky, stood to his feet, and after a short pause, followed the old man out of the room.

She tapped on the den door a few minutes later and softly announced, "Dinner's ready," when she was told to enter.

"Thank you," Pearce said curtly, nodding his head and

dismissing her as soon as she poked her head through. "We'll be there in a minute."

Dinner was finished in almost complete silence, the only interruption was Emily asking where Scott was.

His lips pinched and a scowl on his face, he replied, "He isn't eating with us tonight." At the end of the meal, he threw down his napkin, pushed back his chair with alacrity, and gave Becky a grave look.

"May I see you in the den please." Meekly, she followed him and quietly shut the door behind her, feeling as if she were back in school, visiting the principal's office for some crime that she'd committed.

He sat in his favorite seat, pulling a cozy-looking wingback chair over so she could sit across from him.

"Will you please tell me what happened today?" He asked, much more gentle than his manner had indicated. Embarrassed, she cleared her throat and looked anywhere but at him as she told the whole story, word for word. She was especially ashamed to recount the part where Scott had intimated that they had a relationship and were serious about each other. She was still unsure of what Pearce thought of her, as no words had actually been spoken to confirm or disprove his feelings.

"Well," he said finally, rubbing his stubbly chin in his fingers, his expression somber. "I think he should lose his job, but Curly says you don't want him to. I have to admit, that puzzles me." He stared hard at her for a moment. "Is there something going on between you two?"

Instantly irritated, she glared at him. "Of course not! I just don't want to be the cause of any trouble between you and any of your workers. He's just young and stupid. He thinks he has more feelings for me than he actually does. He'll see it soon enough. Can't you please just give him a warning? Please?" She put a hand on his knee only to quickly pull it back after she realized what she had done. He stared at her for a long minute, his face cloudy.

"How can I resist when you put it like that? But I won't let him get away with it. If he tries anything like that again," he spoke through gritted teeth and stood to pace the room like a caged animal, his fists clenched by his sides. "I'll take care of him myself, and he won't get his job back. I don't like it one bit."

He leaned on the back of her chair and reached out to tuck a piece of stray hair behind her ear, sending thrilling chills down her spine. "You know," he added quietly behind her, "you don't have to be afraid to touch me."

Her face turned crimson and she fingered the soft flannel shirt she was wearing. "I'm not afraid. I just wasn't sure if I should or not, that's all."

"I have one question though," he asked, standing in front of her so he could see her face.

"What?"

"Did you like him kissing you?"

Hands clenched into fists, she jumped to her feet and gave him a glare a witch would be proud of. "What in the world are you thinking, asking a question like that? Are you crazy?"

Bursting out in laughter, he clutched the chair to keep from falling. "I'm just picking on you. You would have thought I'd asked you if you liked to kiss an elephant or something!"

"That's not funny." She turned and stomped out of the room, leaving him to enjoy himself alone.

"Well? Did you ask yet?" Curly asked early the next morning when Pearce joined him in the barn.

Pearce stared at him, a confused look on his face. "Ask what? Oh yeah!" he said quickly, snapping his fingers. "Yes I did!" He stopped for a moment when Becky came in, carrying two mugs of steaming coffee. "Didn't I Becky?"

"What?" She asked suspiciously, looking from one to the other, sure that this was some sort of trap.

"I asked you last night, right?" Pearce asked, his eyes twinkling mischievously.

"Asked me what?" She glared at him, knowing what he was talking about, yet daring him to continue.

"If you liked it when Scott kissed you." He smiled charmingly and waited for her to explode. Silently, she turned, placed the hot coffee on a bale of hay that was sitting nearby and stalked out of the barn.

"What did you do that for?" Curly asked, surprised at Pearce's behavior. "I thought you were going to ask her to marry you, not make her feel worse than she already does."

"I'm just teasing, that's all," he answered grinning, kicking the dust with the toe of his boot. "Anyway, I have to be sure that she's not interested in him, don't I?"

"Becky? Interested in Scott?" Curly asked incredulously. "You don't know her very well if that's what you think. Scott's all right," he went on hurriedly. "But Becky has something more. He's not her equal and there's no way she'd waste her time with a guy like that."

"I know. I was just playing," he answered, a tad ashamed of himself. "I guess I should go apologize," he took a sip from the abandoned coffee and made a mental note that it wasn't nearly as good without Becky to share it with. He sighed.

"Sounds like you're too late," Curly said, his head cocked to the side as if he were listening to something.

"What do you mean?"

"I thought I heard a car or truck leaving."

Frowning, Pearce pulled the door open, almost knocking into Curly, who was evidently pretending to be his shadow.

"Oh wait. She's not leaving. You have a visitor."

Chapter 16

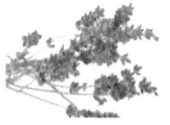

Wiping her hands on a dishtowel, Becky came out to greet the person in the yellow cab. "Can I help you?" She had been busily preparing breakfast when the car arrived, throwing everyone inside the house into fits.

The back window rolled down all the way, and a woman peered over her dark sunglasses at Becky, her gaze snooty. "Is this still Pearce Morgan's place?"

Becky felt her heart plummet to her feet as she returned the look Pearce's ex-wife gave her. "Yes it is."

Without waiting for an invitation, she pushed the door open and stepped out. "And you are…?" she asked smoothly, taking off the sunglasses to get a better look at Becky.

She tried to remain unimpressed, but the more she saw of the woman, the more beautiful she became, and consequently, the worse Becky felt in comparison. "I'm the housekeeper."

At her confession of being the hired help, the woman flashed a brilliant smile, void of any kindness. Gathering her suitcases from the trunk, she placed them on the small verandah, paid the driver and finally turned her attention back to Becky. Her smile fixed in place, she extended her perfectly manicured hand as though she thought Becky should kiss one of the many glittering jewels adorning it.

Without a word, Becky took the proffered hand and dropped it as quickly as she could.

"I don't suppose you know who I am," the woman grinned coldly, a scornful look in her cornflower blue eyes.

She stepped in the woman's way as the pretty brunette tried to step past her into the house. "I know who you are. Is Mr. Morgan expecting you?"

The fake smile slipped a little and her eyes became hard as flint at the temerity of the hired help refusing to let her pass. "Expecting me? Why wouldn't he be expecting to see his wife?"

The barb hit its intended mark and Becky flinched ever so slightly at the term. She quickly replaced it with a look of cool indifference, but not quick enough. "*Ex*-wife," she corrected.

They stood a moment, each eyeing the other as though they were about to spar, when she laughed merrily, completely taking Becky by surprise. "Oh all right, have it your way. I'll wait right here while you run along and let *Mr. Morgan* know I'm here. *He* won't be so rude, wait and see. In fact," she continued as Becky called for Jeff. "He'll be *ecstatic* to see me."

Becky hoped she would be wrong, but she couldn't shake the queasy feeling in her stomach. "Jeff, will you please let Mr. Morgan know he has a visitor."

"Sure," he eyed the woman languishing on the lounge chair.

"How cute," she smiled, not quite succeeding in hiding the disgust she felt for them both as he jogged off in search of Pearce. "Is he your son?"

"Yes." Becky struggled to speak without a quiver. When Pearce had shown her that picture, she had thought that Eva was pretty, but now it was plain to see that Eva was in fact absolutely beautiful. She tried hard to not compare her faded jeans and old flannel shirt to the other woman's high dollar slacks and silk blouse, nor her natural beauty and pulled back hair to Eva's impeccable haircut and perfect make-up.

"Can I get you anything?" Becky asked finally, looking for an opportunity to leave the woman on the porch by herself.

"I'd just *love* a coffee if you wouldn't mind," she answered breezily, inspecting her fingernails as if she were used to giving orders and having everyone jump through hoops to obey them. "Two creams, one sugar." Becky had half a mind to pretend as if she hadn't heard her and continue making breakfast, but Jeff came running back before she could escape.

"He said he'll be right out," Jeff said to his mother while staring at the stranger as if he'd never seen a woman before.

"Jeff," Becky said quietly, holding the door open for him.

Reluctantly, he followed her inside, turning so he could gape at Eva for as long as possible.

"Who was that?" He asked as soon as she had shut the door behind them. Becky had always made sure that none of the kids were in Pearce's den, so they never had the opportunity of seeing the picture on his desk, so she ignored him and stepped inside the kitchen where Jen and Emily were sitting.

Thinking his mother had lost her hearing, he asked louder, hooking a thumb over his shoulder, "Who was that, mom?"

"What?" Jen asked, her curiosity aroused. She had been helping Emily with some of her work and hadn't paid attention as the cab pulled up to the door.

"There's a lady outside sitting on the porch waiting for Mr. Morgan," Jeff informed them breathlessly. "And she's really pretty!" Becky rolled her eyes and continued slicing potatoes and onions into the frying pan.

Jen jumped up from the chair and ran to the kitchen window, pressing her head as close as she could to the glass without actually touching it, trying to get a glimpse of the mystery woman.

"I can only see her shoes!" She whispered, disappointed in not being able to see more. "Do you know who it is?"

Shaking seasonings onto the potatoes as though her life depended on it, Becky answered, "Yes."

Never being one who liked being out of the loop, she pushed the issue. "Who is it?"

"That," Becky turned to face all the children, "is Pearce's business, and you are to let it go unless he tells you about it."

Three miserable faces looked back at her.

"But…" Jeff said.

"No more. I don't want to hear another word about it." She said pointedly, waving a finger in the air for emphasis. They continued in silence, Becky cooking with a vengeance as the children whispered quietly to each other about who it could possibly be.

"Becky," Pearce said a few minutes later as he poked his head through the door, his face pale and tight. "There'll be one more for breakfast." Becky looked at him questioningly, but nodded without comment.

His eyes begging her to try to understand for his sake, he called his daughter to him and took her out of the room after one final glance at Becky.

More curious than ever, Jen and Jeff silently, and without having to be asked, got up and started setting the dining room table for breakfast, being careful to set an extra place for the mysterious guest.

"Who do you think it was?" Jen asked quietly when Jeff came near her to place the forks in their spot.

"I don't know, but she was really pretty," he repeated, obviously impressed with her looks.

"Well what do you think Pearce thinks about her?" She asked nervously, hoping this woman wouldn't come between the romance she had seen growing between him and her mother.

"I think he'd be nuts if he didn't like her."

Always loyal to her mother, she shot him a withering look. "What about mom, then?"

"Mom's pretty, but this woman is definitely prettier."

"That's not very nice!" Jen whispered angrily, setting a coffee cup down onto the table a little harder than necessary.

"I'm not trying to be mean," he defended himself hotly, feeling a little ashamed of liking the looks of the other woman and being disloyal.

Becky poked her head through the door, interrupting them. "Jeff, will you please tell Pearce and Emily breakfast is ready?"

Eager to get away from his irate sister, he answered, "Sure," and sped off down the hallway.

"Curly," cooed Jen, sidling up beside the friendly old man when he came in to take his seat. "Do you know what's going on?"

"Trouble with a capital 'T'!" He answered gruffly.

"Scott won't be here this morning," Burt called to Jen before she went into the kitchen to help Becky. "You set an extra place."

"It's just fine," Curly answered shortly. His smile didn't quite erase the troubled look in his eyes. "Go on and help your momma, girl."

"Gentlemen," Pearce announced, half-dragging Emily into the dining room, "we're going to have a guest for breakfast," he paused and took a deep breath when Becky came out of the kitchen. The kids sat in their usual places and Becky busied herself at the buffet table, reluctant to share breakfast with the beautiful Eva.

"Is it someone that's going to take Scott's place?" Burt snickered and nudged John, while Curly sat stonefaced and impenetrable.

Pearce ignored them and introduced the brunette who was standing behind him. "This is Eva." Obviously loving the fact that everyone was looking at her, Eva stepped around him and gave them all a gorgeous smile.

"Hello," her tinkling laugh seemed to bounce off the wall and bore into Becky's head. With a spiteful glance at Becky, she took the seat next to Pearce, leaving Becky to sit at the other end of the table. "I'm Eva *Morgan*." She made eye contact with each of the men, expertly sizing them up, and Becky squelched the image of a mountain lion sizing up innocent prey.

Her eyes narrowed slightly and lost some of their twinkle when they came to rest on Curly. "Hello Curly," she said with a disdainful curve that was supposed to be a smile. Becky held her breath and wondered if he was going to ignore her completely, or would at least try to be civil in front of Pearce.

"Ma'am."

"I can't believe you're still alive!" Eva snickered while Burt and Mark laughed out loud. "I mean, you're practically prehistoric."

"Well, someone had to stay and help the boss run this place and take care of little Emily," his look of utter contempt spoke volumes of his intense dislike of the woman. Eva's smile froze in place and her eyes once again glinted like steel.

"Curly!" Pearce barked, surprised and embarrassed at his friend's comment.

With a large sigh, Curly slowly stood to his feet. "Excuse me. I'm not very hungry. Boss," he tipped his hat in Pearce's direction as he held Eva's glare for a moment longer before leaving.

The rest of breakfast was strained, the only sound was Eva talking about herself and commenting on how odd it was that a rich man like Pearce would invite hired help to eat meals with him.

Surprisingly, Jeff was the first to push his plate away. "May I be excused?"

"Me too?" Jen chimed in.

"How cute!" Eva mocked, throwing a dazzling smile Pearce's way.

"Yes," Becky answered stiffly, getting up as well and taking the almost empty serving bowls and plates with her to the kitchen.

Immediately, she set to work fixing a plate to take to Curly, whom she knew must be starving as he usually ate like a horse. She slipped out the back door, quietly closing the screen so it wouldn't slam, and made her way to the barn where she knew she would find him.

"Curly?" She asked timidly, poking her head just inside the door, her eyes trying to adjust to the dim light.

"Back here," she heard a muffled reply from the colt's stall.

Following his voice, she pushed the half-door open a little ways, balancing the plate on one hand. "I thought I'd find you here. This is your favorite place, isn't it. The filly's going to get jealous."

He gave a soft snort and shook his head. "Not really. I think she gets irritated when I take up too much room."

She handed him the warm plate, a small smile playing at the corner of her lips. "I thought you might be hungry."

Closing his eyes, he inhaled deeply and gave her a large grin. "Smells good." Soon, the aroma of fried potatoes and onions, bacon, and eggs had taken over the barn. "I think it smells even better out here."

For a moment, Becky watched the colt playing while Curly ate his breakfast, then stood to her feet. "I guess I'll let you go. Not that I really want to go back inside though."

"Well then sit out here with me for a while," he patted the seat next to him. "Horse won't mind. Anyway," he continued as she sat back down. "I think there's quite a bit on your mind right now."

"I guess you could say that."

"Why don't you tell me what you think?" He prompted, taking a swig of orange juice.

"I think she's here for a reason," she finally blurted, sure that honesty was always the best way.

"What do you think the reason is?"

"Pearce." She admitted flatly. Picking up a bit of hay, she twisted it into oblivion.

"You don't think she's here to get to know her daughter?" he looked sideways at her, a little surprised at her candor.

Her eyes clouded with dismay, she looked him square in the eye. "No I don't. I think if she were interested in getting to know Emily she would have shown up a long time ago. I think it would have haunted her and bothered her to no end. Besides," she sighed and threw the mutilated piece of hay down on the ground at her feet. "Didn't you notice that she didn't even look poor Emily's way this morning at breakfast?"

"I wasn't there," he answered, reminding her of his departure.

"Well," she continued, blushing at her blunder. "She completely ignored her as if she weren't even her child. She acted as if Emily were a nasty little bug that she didn't want anything to do with."

"Doesn't surprise me. Anything else?"

"I think she's absolutely gorgeous." Her voice flat and expressionless, tears threatened to spill over and her heart sank to a new low with the honest confession.

"And...?"

"What?" She asked, looking up at him in frustration. "Do you want me to tell you that I think they're going to get back together and that I'm okay with it? Well I'm *not*! I'm discouraged and depressed, and irritated that he could even think of letting her be here after the way she treated him." She stood with her hands on her hips and swatted away any tears that were treacherous enough to fall. "And if you sit there and tell me that you think she's pretty or that they're going to get back together or that you like her, so help me I'm going to knock you off that hay bale!"

He surprised her by bursting out laughing, and pulled her back down next to him. "Wait a minute. Let's get some things straight. I can't stand that woman, I've never thought she was even remotely pretty--in fact, I think that there horses rear-end is better lookin' than she is--and I don't agree that they're going to get back together. If they do, Pearce is a fool. And I think you're one hundred percent correct that she's here for something other than getting to know Emily. I have my suspicions that maybe she's run out of money and thought she could fanagle some from Pearce. She's a sly one she is, so you be careful around her." He took a deep breath after his tirade and patted Becky's hand. "I do think, however, that we really need to pray for Pearce and especially for lil Em. There's going to be some rough times ahead for them."

"What's rough?" Pearce's voice made them jump, and they both briefly wondered just how long he'd been standing there.

Becky started to fan her red face and looked away, not wanting him to know that she'd been crying.

He looked from one guilty party to the other, his eyes narrowed in suspicion. Finally resting on Becky's tear-stained face, he said, "I need to talk to you for a moment. I've been looking for you everywhere, and then I thought I'd check in here before I called the police and filed a missing person's report."

"She brought me breakfast," Curly said, finishing off his orange juice for emphasis.

He was unconvinced. "Uh huh."

"Thanks Beck," Curly said finally as she stooped over to pick up the plate and cup. "I'll be here if you need to talk," he winked as she turned to leave, keeping her face turned away from Pearce.

"Actually," Pearce said, purposely standing in her way so she couldn't leave. "I need to talk to both of you." Curly stared at Pearce, his face expressionless as Becky sat back down next to him.

He looked apprehensive and shuffled his feet in the dirt, sending puffs of dust into the air. "This isn't going to be easy. Obviously you know that Eva's back, and I can only guess that you were both talking about her and me." He looked up at them, daring them to deny it. Neither of them said anything, Curly still expressionless while Becky turned a slight pink under his sharp

152

scrutiny. "That's what I thought. Anyway," he sighed, plunging ahead. "She needs a place to stay for a week, so I'm allowing her to stay here with us. She says that she wants to get to know Emily, and I don't think that's an unreasonable request."

Curly almost succeeded in stifling his disgusted snort. "So what are you saying, Boss?"

"I guess I'm asking you both to put up with her for a week and be nice," he held the older man's gaze for a moment.

"I'll be as nice to her as she is to me," he answered curtly, spitting onto the floor next to him for emphasis. Becky looked down, the tension thick between them. "But I do have one question. If she had wanted to know Emily, why didn't she come see her earlier?"

Irritated, he threw his hands up in the air, a frown etched deep into his forehead. "I don't know, maybe she was busy! Don't you think that as a Christian I should forgive someone when they ask me to?"

"Of course," Curly stood up to leave the little stall. "But I think that woman is the devil in disguise, and I ain't ever heard of the devil asking for forgiveness. Becky," he turned toward her before he left, "you can come talk to me anytime, hear?"

"Thanks." She watched him leave, suddenly nervous and agitated that he'd left her alone with Pearce.

"He's always disliked her," Pearce said, more than a little aggravated.

"Hasn't he had good reason not to like her?" She couldn't help pointing out. Moodily, Pearce turned to look at her. "Remember, he was the one who stayed here to help you when she walked out." She looked at him boldly, her face flushed.

"Look," he said testily, folding his arms across his chest. "I don't like this just as much as you two, in fact, I wish I'd never seen her again. But now that she's here and wants to get to know her daughter, I think we'll just have to deal with this as best as we can. Anyway," he soothed, drawing her into his arms. "Nothing's going to change. She'll be gone before we know it, and then we can get back to the way we were, you'll see. Trust me."

It was a good thing neither of them knew how wrong he really was.

Chapter 17

Becky was of the opinion that a woman who had walked out on her husband and tiny daughter would be embarrassed and try to make amends for her mistreatment of them, yet, quite the opposite was true.

As the days went by, Eva acclimated herself to her new surroundings remarkably well, and showed no signs of the maladies Becky thought should accost her. Or of leaving. What was supposed to have been only a week's stay, lengthened to two, and when the end of the second week came along, it was apparent -- if only to Becky -- she intended to stay another. As a permanent fixture.

Before Eva's arrival, there was much talk and laughter during the dinner hour, but during the weeks Eva was there, everyone listened as she talked incessantly about herself and her acting career.

With each passing week, Jen and Emily ate less and less, and pushed their food around their plates more and more. Jeff and the ranch hands didn't seem to mind her presence, and clung to every word she said, flirting and joking, completely forgetting the fact that it was Pearce's ex-wife and that it might be causing him some kind of grief to hear all the playful banter.

Becky was also becoming disturbed by the attention Pearce was paying her. On more than one occasion, Becky would catch him staring fixedly at Eva, and however she struggled to not see anything out of the ordinary in it, she couldn't stop her stomach from sinking with trepidation.

It was at one such time when, unable to take it anymore, she left the dining room and wandered into the kitchen, with the intention of washing the dishes. But the ladder-back chair looked inviting and enticed her to sit down instead.

Her eyes blank and her thoughts far away, she was startled when a voice behind her asked, "Are you okay?"

Turning to find Jen behind her with her plate in her hands, she gave her a bright smile. Too bright. "Of course." She attempted to divert Jen by picking up her fork and taking a bite of food as if she were ravenous while her ever loyal daughter sat next to her. "I'm all right," she repeated, her voice hollow.

They were silent for a little while, when Jen said quietly, "Thank you for dinner. It's really good."

"You're welcome," Becky answered, aware that Jen was the only one who had thanked her for the evening meal, something that Pearce and the others had made a point to do right from the start. "But it doesn't look like you like it very much."

"I guess I'm just not hungry." She lay her fork down and leaned her head on her palm, worry furrowed her brow.

"What's bothering you?"

Tears sprang up almost instantly and a little pout appeared when she blurted, "I don't like Eva very much."

"Why? Everyone else does." She blushed at her own bitter tone and took a bite of tasteless food to stop herself from saying anything else she might regret.

"That's part of the reason," Jen answered honestly. "Remember when we first came here, they were all so nice to us? They joked around and laughed with us? Now it's like we're not even alive."

"Maybe it's just because she's new here and they're trying to make her feel welcome."

"Maybe," she said doubtfully. "But I also don't like the way she treats Emily. This afternoon, Emily tried to sit in her lap while she was on the couch, and she pushed her so hard that Emily fell off and hit her head on the coffee table. When Emily started to cry and Pearce came in to see what was going on, she lied to him. She told him that we were playing and I knocked into Emily on purpose!" She looked up at her mother, mortified that she had been blamed.

Eyes flashing, she sat straighter in her chair, her fork midway to her mouth. "What did Pearce say?" She had always taught her children that honesty was the only way, and that lying would always bring punishment in some way or fashion.

"He picked Emily up and told me I need to be careful."

"Why didn't you tell him what really happened?"

Jen started a little, surprised at her mother's anger. "I was afraid to," she answered sheepishly. "Eva was looking at me so meanly, that I was afraid of what she would do."

"Always tell the truth." Becky leaned over and pulled a strand of hair out of her eyes. "No matter what."

"But what bothers me just as much, is that Emily didn't even try to tell him what really happened. She let him think that I would do something like that to her."

"She's only five. Maybe she was afraid, too. She probably wants her mom to love her, and wants to please her anyway she can. Or maybe she didn't want her mom to get into trouble."

Jen hesitated a moment, then said finally, "I just feel ashamed I guess."

"You have nothing to be ashamed of, dear. Nothing." Becky put her arm around her shoulders and gave her a side hug, determined that Pearce was going to hear what had really happened.

The next opportunity Becky had to talk to Pearce without Eva around was the next morning. Pouring herself and Pearce a cup of coffee and walking to the barn, she left the kids to start on their spelling word lists as usual.

They were in the middle of writing their third column of words when Eva walked into the room, still in her pajamas. Giving the room a cursory glance and finding Becky was nowhere to be found, she glared at the children and snapped, "What are you guys doing?"

"Our schoolwork," Jeff answered, somewhat proud that he got to answer before his sister.

She sneered. "Why aren't you doing that at school?" She looked around again, aggravated no one was around to answer her beck and call. "Where's that housekeeper at?"

"She went to the barn," Jeff blurted just as Jen's well-placed kick made contact with his shin. "Ow! What did you do that for?" he glared at her.

Eva's curiosity was aroused, and she gave Jen a shrewd look. "What did she go to the barn for?"

Ever studious, Jen resumed her work and muttered, "Nothing," under her breath.

In a somewhat coddling tone, she turned to Jeff and asked, "What did she go to the barn for little boy?"

"She brings Pearce's coffee out to him every morning." He pushed his chair far back out of Jen's reach so she couldn't kick him again.

"Oh really. Well, what do you think of that?" She threw a triumphant smirk at Jen. "I'll just go see if there's anything I can do to help out. We can't have them hanging around together without a chaperone, now can we?" She turned to leave, and was almost out of the room before she turned her attention back to them. "You know, you're really a cutie, little boy. It's just too bad that your mom wants you to be stupid."

Her face bright red, Jen jumped angrily to her feet with her fists clenched at her sides. "She does *not* want us to be stupid!"

Her malicious grin told Jen she'd gotten the reaction she had wanted. "Everyone knows that *all* homeschooled kids are dumb. That's why the parents keep them at home. Because they know their kids are never going to make anything of themselves." Her merry, tinkling laugh echoed on the walls while she walked away.

"I can't believe she said that!" Jen's nails bit into the tender skin of her palms. Her face an angry purple, she turned toward her brother and waited for the quick comeback she knew he would have ready. Surprised, she watched while he sat and contemplated the venom and hatred Eva had spewed.

With a look more forlorn than any Jen had yet seen on his face, he laid his pencil down and stood to his feet. "Maybe she's right." He put his shoes on and walked out the back door toward the barn without another word.

"She's *not* right!" She called after him vehemently. Looking to the little girl for support, she said quietly, "Right Em?"

With a rebellious look at her friend, Emily threw her pencil across the room and crossed her arms. "I don't want to do my work.

I want my mommy!"

"Curly?" Jeff stood on the lowest rung of the fence and watched the old man feed some horses. He had made sure to stay away from Pearce's office just in case his mother saw him.

"What are you doing out here? Aren't you supposed to be in school?" Curly asked, surprised to see him so early.

Without answering, he blurted, "Do you think homeschooled kids are dumb?" He grabbed a handful of oats out of the feed bucket and let it run through his fingers.

Completely taken by surprise, Curly scratched under his hat and studied the young boy who had become the grandson he'd never had. "What in the world brought that on?"

"I just want to know." Jeff refused to look up.

With a snort of disgust, he said, "Absolutely not. I think your momma has done a great job of teaching you kids, and I'd have a problem if I heard anyone say anything to the contrary. In fact, I think you and your sister are about the smartest kids I've ever met." He tousled Jeff's hair, and gave him a peculiar look. "What's going on?"

He shook his head at the appalling story Jeff told him. "I'm going to tell you, just like I told your momma. That woman is the devil, and this proves it!" He spat for emphasis.

"But how can she be the devil?"

"It's just a figure of speech son. I'm just saying she's pure evil."

"How can someone that pretty be so awful?"

"Meanness has many faces. Just because someone's pretty on the outside, doesn't mean they're pretty on the inside. She's one of the nastiest people I've ever met, and that makes her ugly." Jeff thought about this for a few minutes, making up his mind if he believed Curly or not.

"Truth be told," Curly continued after a short pause, "I think your *momma* is the most beautiful woman I've ever met."

It was Jeff's turn to snort and make a face. "Mom? I always thought she was pretty as a mom, but not like a *girl.*"

Curly laughed and slapped his thigh. "How many other women have you ever seen or heard of that put everyone before herself? That's what your mom does. She makes sure that you and your sister are getting an education, not to mention taking in a little motherless girl that's not hers and treating her as if she were one of her own, keeping her own house clean plus someone else's, cooking for a bunch of men she's not related to, and just basically putting everyone else first and herself last."

Jeff was beginning to see what Curly was driving at. "When's the last time you saw your mother do something that was just for her?" Jeff thought for a moment and shook his head. "That's what I thought. That's *real* beauty Jeff, and don't forget it. And I wouldn't let anyone talk about you or your sister that way and make you think you're dumb. You're only dumb if you allow it."

Chapter 18

Becky waited as patiently as she could for Pearce to get off the phone, wondering just how long horse business could take. She began to wonder if he was really even talking to someone or was just trying to get out of talking to her, when he hung up.

"Morning Beck." He said, taking his coffee cup and filling his mouth with the much cooled off liquid. "Great coffee."

From her vantage point in the chair across from him, she had had ample time to study his face and somewhat assess how he might take the conversation she was about to bring up. Usually, she loved to look at him, especially when he was busy doing something, but this particular morning, she was more uncomfortable than usual and it showed.

"So how are you?" He leaned back and put his feet up on his desk, the picture of ease and comfort.

"Fine."

His eyebrows raised slightly at her flat tone. "Something specific is on your mind I see."

"I don't really know how to start this conversation, I guess." She sighed and looked away. "So I'll just plunge right in. Jen and I were talking last night at dinner about an incident that I think you should know about."

"I already know."

"You do?"

"It's all right. They were just playing and things like that happen when kids play."

"Well that's not exactly what happened," she said, her heart pumping. How she hated rocking the boat and making a fuss. "Jen told me what really went on, and…"

At that precise moment, Eva swung the door open and walked in, looking like she'd just come out of a modeling magazine. Becky's words died on her lips, and her throat closed for good.

"Good morning, I was wondering where little Miss Susie Homemaker was." She flashed her a reproachful glance. "And look. Here she is," she laughed merrily and took the chair closest to Pearce. "I'd like a coffee if you don't mind. Two creams, one sugar."

Pearce looked down at his desk, his eyes shut against them both. "Her name is Becky, and she's not your personal attendant. You can help yourself to some coffee in the kitchen. We were in the middle of a chat."

"What a meanie," she pouted prettily. Becky half expected her to leave, but instead, was forced to watch in horror while she drew her chair closer to his. "You know, you can be a lot nicer to me than that. I know you're happy that I'm here. You always did have a hard time whenever I went away somewhere." She waited for him to say something. Disappointed when he didn't, she unleashed a little of her hostility Becky's way.

"Anyway, little Miss Susie doesn't mind me teasing with her, and I'm sure she'd *love* to bring me a coffee out here. That's what you pay her for, right? Then you and I could have that talk we were supposed to have. You know," she looked at him meaningfully, leaving Becky to guess what the talk was about.

"What?" Pearce asked with a bewildered look.

"Don't play innocent with me. Oh," she nodded her head, her eyes widening in mock surprise. "You didn't want anyone else to know. I'm sorry."

His face red and his eyes begging Becky not to believe her, he managed to sputter, "I don't…"

Eva cut him off. "Do you mind? We'd like to be …*alone*… If you know what I mean." She winked at Becky and possessively put her hand on his knee. Pearce jumped up from his seat, and walked to the door, knocking her hand off.

Opening it, he said with an apologetic glance at Becky, "Maybe it would be best." Slowly, Becky walked past, searching his face for some kind of explanation. He shrugged his shoulders and shook his head, letting her know that it wouldn't be coming anytime soon.

162

Becky walked back to the house in a daze, her mind going in twenty different directions at once. What were they talking about? Why was Pearce afraid for her to be there? Did he still love Eva? Is that why he allowed her to act the way she did?

Still lost in thought, she ran into Jen and almost knocked her down when she walked through the kitchen door.

"I was just coming out to look for you," she said breathlessly, kicking her shoes off. "Eva's looking for Pearce."

"I know," Becky said glumly, slumping down in the kitchen chair. "She already found him. Where's Jeff and Emily?"

"They ran off." Jen answered unhappily, seating herself in the chair next to her mother.

Surprised and alarmed, Becky sat up as though she were about to run out the door herself. "Ran off? Where?"

Jen told her the whole sordid story of Eva's nastiness to them, and Becky listened attentively, her anger and dislike rising and almost getting the better of her.

Speaking calmer than she would have thought possible, she asked, "Where are they now?"

"Last I saw Jeff, he was running toward the barn where Curly usually is, and Emily's in her room I think. Do you want me to go get them?"

"No, I'll let Jeff alone for a little bit. I think I'd better see to Emily." Becky sighed as she left the kitchen in search of the little girl.

"Emily?" She found her in her room, lying with her face in her pillows. Becky shook her gently. No reply. "Emily? What's wrong darling?" Emily kept her face hidden in her pillow, refusing to budge.

"Don't you want to come on out and have a hot chocolate with me and Jen? I'll put some marshmallows in it, just the way you like it." Still no reply.

"You know," she said sitting next to her on the bed, rubbing the small girl's back gently, "you can tell me anything you want. I won't get angry with you. I'll still love you. You don't have to be afraid anymore."

She sat for a couple minutes longer, hoping she would break through her tough shell. Swallowing her anger and frustration, she left and wondered how a mother could treat her child so callously.

"Jen," she said her lips in a thin line. "Would you please stay in the house while I go to talk to Pearce?"

"Do you have to?" Jen begged. She hated to cause trouble and knew by the look on her mother's face it wasn't going to be a good conversation.

"I think he should know what that woman is doing to his daughter," she answered grimly. "I'll be right back. Keep Jeff in here if he comes back." Hastily, she walked back into the barn where Pearce and Eva were still talking with the door closed. Taking a deep breath, she knocked with force, more angry than nervous.

Poking her head through the door when he invited her in, she ignored Eva and got right to the point. "Pearce, do you have a moment?"

"Sure," he stood to his feet and with just a few strides was at the door, throwing, "I'll be right back," over his shoulder.

"Oh, how sweet," Eva said glaring at Becky behind Pearce's back. "A lover's chat."

Without a word, he closed the door firmly behind him and led her outside the barn. "What's up?" He leaned on the door, his arms crossed.

He looks tired, she thought with a dash of sympathy. Thinking perhaps it might be better to let it go and deal with it on her own, she was about to turn away, but the image of little Emily crying in her room and not talking to anyone, pushed her to tell him everything Eva had managed to do that morning.

"Do you think maybe it was all blown out of proportion? Maybe the kids didn't understand her?" He asked when Becky finally stopped for air.

"No I don't." She gaped at him, appalled that he was so willing to see everyone else at fault rather than see the problem.

"Maybe Eva was joking," he said stubbornly. "She's got a weird sense of humor sometimes."

"Calling children dumb is not funny or a joke!" She said hotly, crossing her arms across her chest. "And what you think is humor is just mean-spiritedness."

"Now hold on a minute," irritated, he pulled away from the barn and retorted, "you don't know Eva, so maybe you shouldn't be pointing your finger. Just because Curly can't stand her…"

Not waiting for him to finish his sentence, she threw her arms in the air and yelled loud enough for the entire household to hear, "I didn't get my information from Curly! *You* were the one that told me the situation, remember?"

In complete exasperation, he said through gritted teeth, "What do you think I should do? Not forgive her? Not let her see and get to know her daughter? Just what exactly do you want me to do? Throw her out with nowhere to go?" They stood staring at one another for what seemed like hours.

Was it her imagination, or did the door behind him move ever so slightly? Becky swallowed her anger and gave him a curious look.

"Pearce," she said quietly, sure that Eva was listening on the other side. "Can't we talk about this somewhere else?"

"No." He answered flatly with a frown. "Why can't we talk about it here?"

"Because everyone is probably listening." Speaking in a much softer tone, just in case Eva was indeed eavesdropping, she rolled her eyes at him. The last thing she wanted was Eva to think she was pulling them apart. *It might be true,* she thought dismally, *but I don't want to make her happy about it.*

Her fingers curled into the cuff of his sleeve and she tried to pry him away, but he shrugged her off. "Let them. I don't really care who hears. What do you want from me?"

She flinched at his almost hostile look, and all the fight left her, leaving her hollow inside. Her shoulders drooping, she managed to mutter, "I don't know, I guess I want you to explain to Emily that she's not dumb, and maybe while you're at it, you could explain it to Jen and Jeff."

"Fine. Is that it?" Not able to reconcile himself to the hurt he saw so plainly in her eyes, he looked everywhere but at her. Deep inside, he knew she was telling him the truth, but somehow the situation had gotten so out of his control, he had no idea how to fix anything.

Becky sniffled, and he resisted the urge to reach out and pull her into his arms. "Now you can tell me what you think I should do about school, seeing as how I've lost two-thirds of my class."

"Give them a break," he answered simply, a little more calm. "Don't teach Emily anything while Eva's here. Will that work?"

"Why can't you just tell Eva that it was *your* idea to have her homeschooled and that you thought it was a *good* idea?"

"I'll talk to her," he said, shrugging his shoulders lamely and she wondered what had happened to the man she had fallen in love with.

Feeling abandoned, tears of frustration and hurt welled up in her lovely green eyes, but she refused to let any slip. "What happened to you Pearce?"

"Nothing," he answered evenly, hating himself all the more for being unable to admit his cowardice. "Is that all you needed?"

"Yes," she said softly, turning to go back to the house. She wanted him to call her back so they could fix the problem, but he didn't.

Numbly, she walked into the kitchen to find Jeff and Jen sitting at the table doing their work as if nothing had happened, and she started preparing breakfast. No one said a word, which, when she thought about it later, was a good thing, because if she had been required to say anything, it would have come out as sobs.

Breakfast finished, and having no desire to be around anyone, she said quietly, "Jeff, will you please ring the bell for everyone?" He nodded and slipped out of his chair to do as he was asked, giving her a sideways glance when he walked by.

"Jen, will you please set the plates and silverware out on the buffet?" She asked absorbed with finding anything to do that would keep her busy.

"Do you want me to get Emily?" Jen asked after she was finished and everyone was coming inside. Becky shook her head, keeping her gaze averted from Pearce and Eva as they walked in together.

She stood silently apart from the rest of them while Pearce said the blessing, leaving to go back to the kitchen as soon as he was finished without preparing herself anything to eat.

Glumly, she sat at the table and nursed her wounds. The only thing that seemed to be an option was to keep her mouth shut and deal with Eva as little as possible.

The only one that can fix the situation is Pearce, and he refuses to do anything about it, she fumed to herself. Immediately convicted that she'd forgotten to even attempt to pray about the whole ordeal, she leaned her head down in her arms, and prayed, waiting for peace to envelope her.

A few minutes later, Curly joined her in the kitchen, setting his plate down on the table and scooting the chair over in a more comfortable position. "Why isn't the cook going to eat? Did you poison it?" He gave her a suspicious smile and winked.

"I wouldn't do something like that," she smiled weakly. "You and the kids are eating too, and I wouldn't want anything to happen to you four."

Settling himself in, he picked up his fork and paused, giving her a meaningful look, "Are you going to eat with me, or do I have to feel like a pig?"

"I can't." Her stomach flip-flopped at the thought of having to go back out there for food in front of Pearce and Eva.

"It'll only get worse if you let her think she won," he answered gently, knowing exactly what she was thinking. "The best thing to do? Go out there and act like nothing's happened. Don't even look her way. Trust me. It irritates her to no end."

"It's not just her anymore, she's brainwashed Pearce too."

He nodded his head, and she imagined his ruddy face grew even ruddier. "I know. I heard it all."

"You did?"

"I was watching Eva eavesdropping at the door. You can't trust that one, I tell you." He was quiet for a while, thinking over what he'd heard. "But really. You can't let her win. I'm serious. You have to act like she doesn't bother you, or things will get worse. Get something to eat. Maybe Pearce will come out of it when he sees that you're not out there eating with him. Maybe he'll realize what's going on then."

"I don't think it's going to matter," she said softly, shaking her head. "He's completely under her spell. He'll blame everyone else for whatever she does. If she came back for him, she's already won. But," she stood up, straightening her flannel shirt, feeling like the ugly stepsister next to Eva's beauty. "I'll try. For you." With a tilt to her chin, she squared her shoulders and walking resolutely to the dining room to prepare herself a plate.

"Aren't you going to eat in here with us?" Pearce asked quietly when she was about to return to the kitchen, her plate in hand. Becky glanced at him, and couldn't miss the glare Eva sent her way. "There's plenty of room." He pointed to a couple of the empty chairs at the other end of the table.

Steeling herself not to fall under the spell of the soft, repentant look he gave her, she looked over his head and answered, "I thought I'd just eat in the kitchen, thanks."

Eva was delighted and clapped her hands, her tinkling laughter sending shivers of loathing down her spine. "That's a good idea. You're way too nice to let the *housekeeper* eat with you." She smiled around the table, giving a wink to any who looked up at her. "I wouldn't let *my* housekeeper eat with me. I mean," she wiped her mouth daintily with a napkin. "She's being paid, right? That should be enough for her." She laughed as if it were the funniest thing in the world to have the hired help eat with the boss.

Becky held her peace until the vile woman was finished speaking. Giving her a large, bright smile, she said, "If you had a housekeeper, I'm sure she'd be a lot different than me and would actually *poison* your food. So," she smiled ever-so-sweetly at Pearce, making him shift uncomfortably, "you just enjoy your breakfast without *this* hired help at your table."

She sauntered into the kitchen as if she didn't have a care in the world, doing a valiant job of hiding the fact that she was shaking with anger and really wanted to slap the 'guest' across her prettily made-up face.

Curly was grinning from ear to ear when she sat down and she almost couldn't hear his praises over her madly thumping heart. "Now *that's* what I'm talking about! You did a good job, you should be proud of yourself."

"I feel kind of terrible though," she said when he quieted down.

"Why?"

She stifled a giggle. "Because I know what I was *really* going to say."

Chapter 19

After that, Becky stayed as far away from Eva as possible and kept herself in the kitchen mostly with Jen and Jeff, that is, whenever Eva didn't want her to do something.

Eva had mistaken Becky as her own personal slave and ordered her about every chance she got, being especially aggravating and demanding whenever Pearce wasn't around. She had stopped taking him coffee in the morning --as Eva was always with him-- particularly when she thought there was a chance that Becky was going to see him.

She didn't need to worry. He only occasionally looked Becky's way anymore, and she got the hint. He wasn't interested. And she wasn't going to chase.

During Eva's stay, Scott had come back to work and was even more smitten with Eva than the rest of the men seemed to be. He completely ignored Becky as if she'd never existed, and she supposed she should be glad for his attentions being placed elsewhere, but she couldn't help feeling as though he could do better.

She was especially worried about Emily. She had reverted to her prior behavior and refused to talk to anyone except for Pearce, following him about as if she were his shadow. Not being in the position to argue, she had followed Pearce's advice on giving Emily a school break while her mother was around. But, in regard to her own children, she was unwilling to stop teaching them, and looked forward to their companionship each day.

One day when Eva was being particularly nasty, Becky couldn't stand it any longer and escaped to the barn without her noticing. "Good morning Curly."

"Well morning to you, Becky. What brings you out so early?" He smiled kindly at her, not stopping his work of cleaning out horse stalls. "I haven't seen you out here in a while."

"I just needed to get out of the house."

Standing the shovel against the wall, he gave her his full, undivided attention. "That bad huh?"

"I guess it's not that bad. It could be worse, I suppose."

He gave her a doubtful look. "How?"

"She could stay forever," she whispered confidentially with a grim smile that held no humor.

"I know what you mean," he tipped his hat back and scratched his head absent-mindedly. "I feel sorry for you, though. Me, I get to stay out here as much as I possibly can get away with. But you. You have to stay inside with her."

She shrugged her shoulders and sat on a bale of hay. Pulling her cat onto her lap, she rubbed between her ears and made her purr. She kept her head lowered so Curly wouldn't see her dismay.

"So what's bothering you?" He settled down beside her and chewed on a piece of hay.

"Her," she blurted, all the tension and stress that had built up from the past few weeks made it impossible to keep quiet any longer. "She's so nasty and he can't seem to see it."

"I know that he seems to be spending a lot of time with her," Curly began quietly, "but I'm pretty sure it's all her and none of him. I mean it," he shook his head at her disbelieving look. "I know that he's not talking to you, but believe me when I say that I really think he's just enduring until the end. Or that he's trying to protect you.

"He notices that you're not bringing him his coffee in the morning anymore and I'm pretty sure it bothers him. *He* won't tell you that, but I will," he gave her knee a reassuring pat. "Did you know that he doesn't even talk to us workers anymore? The only things he ever talks about are the things that need to be done. None of the friendly stuff we had before she came. Just cut and dry. Then he goes off into his office, or the big barn, or somewhere else and pretty much hides from everybody."

"Everybody except Eva," Becky pointed out bitterly.

"I can't really argue with that," he smiled ruefully. "But it's my guess that she's the one following him around. In fact, I think she's doing it for your benefit."

"Why my benefit?"

"She got wind that something was up between you and Pearce, and she wants to tear it up. She's one of those people that can't be happy for anyone else. She's only happy if she's causing trouble."

"Well she's causing lots of trouble up at the house." Becky pet the cat with a vengeance and a scowl.

"What's she doing?"

She screwed up the side of her face in a half frown. "It's hard to explain. She likes to play head games. Like," she glanced sideways at him, embarrassed, "she tries to be really sugary and sweet when Pearce is within hearing distance, but as soon as she thinks he can't hear, look out. She drops all pretence and is as nasty as can be.

"The other day," she lowered her voice and gave a cursory glance around the barn to make sure no one was listening. "She had me do her laundry, which really isn't a big deal, but then she told me how she wanted me to do them, how to iron them, where to hang them, what hangers to use, which ones needed starching, and how to fold the rest. Then she gave me 'permission' to clean up her room, which was a complete disaster and took me two hours just to clean one room.

"Next, you should see her menus. She's kept me so busy, I can't keep up. I've worked from six in the morning until midnight, only to find out the next day that I did something that she didn't like and I have to redo it all."

Curly gave her a disapproving look, a frown etched into his face. "Does Pearce know she's making you do all this?"

"I've given up trying to talk to Pearce. He won't listen to me, and anyway, Eva's always with him. It's like she's afraid I'm going to tell him something she doesn't want me to."

"Of course she's afraid of you. She knows that he won't put up with her garbage." Becky gave him a look that told him she didn't believe that for a minute, but let the comment pass.

"But what really bothers me is Emily," she said softly, shaking her head. "She's supposed to be here getting to know her daughter, but there's been a couple of times that I've caught her pushing Emily away when Pearce wasn't looking, or giving her ugly looks. There was one time she didn't know I was nearby that I heard her tell Emily that if it wasn't for her, they would still be together."

"You're kidding me!" Curly blurted angrily, his fists clenched.

"Haven't you noticed that Emily is acting the way she did before I came out here? Maybe even worse." She shook her head sadly and briefly wondered why Pearce was so blind to the havoc Eva had created, and shuddered to think what it was going to take to fix it when she left.

"I just thought she was being shy with Eva around."

"She won't eat, she won't speak to me, she won't even be in the same room with me if she can help it,"

"Eva? I thought that would be a blessing." Curly interrupted her.

"I'm talking about Emily," she answered quietly. He stared at her for a moment, considering. "Why can't Pearce see all this?" She stopped and swallowed the lump that formed. When she felt her emotions were sufficiently in check, she went on. "That's why I think he still loves her. Because he can't seem to see what she's doing. He puts the blame all on someone else."

"Maybe I should talk to him," he said finally, scratching under his hat distractedly.

"I don't think it'll matter. He won't listen."

"Becky?" An unwelcome voice said behind her, startling them both.

"Good morning Scott." This was the first time he had talked to her since his return to work and his smirk told her she would probably wish he hadn't.

"What are you doing out here? I thought you would be with Pearce. Or is Curly your new man?" He laughed and slapped Curly on the back.

He glared. "Knock it off Scott."

"I'm just kidding with you. I know she's loyal to Pearce, but he doesn't seem to be so loyal back, does he? Now that his gorgeous ex-wife is here and all." He turned to leave before either of them could recover themselves enough to respond. "By the way," he turned at the doorway, "I owe you an apology Becky. It seems that we weren't meant for each other after all. There *are* other fish in the sea. Much prettier ones."

When he was gone, Curly turned toward her, offering her comfort. "He's still mad. Don't listen to him."

"Sure didn't take him long, did it?"

"Long for what?"

"To fall under her spell," she smiled unhappily.

"I thought you didn't want him to like you."

"I don't, but it still hurts." She kicked the dirt in front of her. "I'll see you for breakfast, right?"

"Sure thing," he called to her retreating back.

"Good morning Susie Homemaker," Eva sneered at her as she set the table for breakfast later on.

"Eva, stop," Pearce repeated for the third time that morning. Eva seemed to be in a particularly hateful mood toward Becky and anything that remotely had to do with her.

"Why do you always stick up for her?" Turning toward him with her hands on her hips, her eyes challenging, she asked, "Do you like her or something?"

"*She* likes *him*, is more like it," Scott laughed, glad to cause any type of pain to Becky, regardless of who may be watching.

Her face crimson she turned on him and almost knocked the stack of plates that were on the buffet over. "Of course I like him. Don't you? He's a good boss, and gave you your job back." The room fell silent, all eyes turned toward her and Scott as they paired off to spar. Pearce watched her gravely.

"Yes," he drawled slowly, the eyes she had once thought pretty, now narrow and hate filled. "But I think you like him a little more than I do," he glanced at Eva. "In fact, I'd say you like him *a lot* more than I do." Eva grinned triumphantly at her, daring her to deny the rumors she had heard.

Becky, refusing to answer to a woman who had held such a

low opinion of her husband and daughter and had treated them so terribly, gave her undivided attention to Scott instead.

"I don't know what your problem is," she said slowly, her lips in a thin line. "But it's time you grew up." She stalked away and took extra care not to give the door a furious swing behind her, even though she really wanted to.

"I think I hit a sore spot," Scott said casually with a forced laugh, trying to act as if he didn't care.

Once again pretending to be the victim, she turned innocent eyes toward Pearce. "She's a little touchy today, isn't she?" Pearce didn't reply, but slowly rose up and went into the kitchen without looking Eva's way.

Curly and Becky were sitting at the table together, talking quietly, oblivious to the fact that Pearce had come in.

"I can't understand for the life of me why he would be interested in her." He overheard Becky say as she stabbed her fork into her scrambled eggs. Curly looked up at the boss man and cleared his throat nervously for her to stop talking. She didn't notice.

"The more I get to know her, the more anxious I am to hear that she'll be leaving soon. She can't possibly stay much longer, or I'm going to go *crazy*!" She screwed up her face as she mimicked Eva in a shrill voice. "Little Miss Susie-Homemaker. Do this! Do that! Be at my beck and call! Two creams, one sugar. Or, you didn't fold this right. Or, you hung this *designer silk* blouse on the wrong hanger, or...." she trailed off, staring at Curly who was making slit marks at his throat. "What in the world is wrong with you?"

"Becky," Pearce said behind her, succeeding in almost scaring her to death. "When you're finished with breakfast, I'd like to see you in the den. *If* you don't mind," he stared at her evenly, his face expressionless.

"Yes sir," she answered quietly, feeling as if she had been punched in the stomach.

Without a word, he turned and left the room, leaving a very embarrassed Becky and Curly behind him.

"I wish I could just crawl into a hole and never come out," she said miserably after he'd left. "Do you think he's mad?"

He whistled through the gaps in his ivory teeth. "I don't have a clue, but I bet you're going to find out."

She pushed her plate away, feeling eggs were her worst enemy and if she were forced to eat any more of them, they'd kill her. "What did he hear me say?"

"Just about the whole conversation." He looked at her apologetically. A slow grin spread across his face as the humor of the situation began to sink in. "I tried to warn you."

"Just kick me next time!" She took her full plate to the counter, and set it down, staring out the window.

"Aren't you going to eat?"

"If I ate, I'd probably throw it all up anyway," she said unhappily, trudging toward the door.

"Where are you going?"

"To face the music. I want to get this over with as soon as possible. Then," she turned wearily toward him, "if it's still light outside, maybe I'll be able to find a new job." She left the room at the sound of Curly singing the funeral march, and felt as though her life couldn't get any worse.

Becky slipped through the door and out of the dining room as quietly as possible, not wanting to draw attention to herself. Silently, she stood outside the door of his den and listened for movement within. Cautiously, she pushed the door open and stepped quietly inside, barely making a noise as she closed the door behind her. Pearce was at his desk with his back toward her, looking at something he held in his hands.

"Pearce?" She said softly, standing just a few feet behind his chair.

Obviously not wanting her to see whatever it was he'd been looking at, he snapped his fingers shut and shoved his fist into his pocket, but not before she'd gotten a glimpse of what it was.

She sat down dejectedly and tears welled up and over. Now she knew exactly what he thought of Eva, and it tore her up inside. It didn't matter anymore that he hadn't listened to her or hadn't taken her side. At that moment, she could have forgiven almost anything he'd allowed to happen, if only she could erase the memory of what she'd just seen in his hands.

"Becky," he cleared his throat. "There's something that I want to talk to you about."

"I'm so sorry," she said quickly, interrupting him so she wouldn't have to hear that he was in love with Eva. "I didn't know you were behind me, and…" he put up his hand to silence her.

"I know you didn't know I was there, but I'm glad I overheard you." His look of kindness, affection even, made her feel worse. "I didn't know she was treating you like that, or I would have stopped her." Her surprised thoughts tumbled about restlessly as he continued. "I've wanted to ask you for the past couple of days why you've been avoiding me?"

She stared at him, uncomprehending. "Avoiding you? I didn't know I was."

"You haven't talked to me, you haven't brought me a coffee in the morning in a long time, and you act like I have the plague."

"I thought you and Eva would want to be alone." As if on cue, Eva popped her head through the door, and gave them a bright, cheery smile.

"There you are!" Pearce quickly pulled away from Becky and sat back in his chair, a look of consternation on his handsome face. "I've been looking everywhere for you Pearce."

She made her way over to stand behind him and leaned her arms on the back of his chair. Becky watched as she plunged her long fingers into his hair and began running them up and down his scalp.

With a look of horror, he stood up and quickly moved across the room, trying to get as far away from her as possible.

"Eva, we were in the middle of a conversation," he said, his back toward her as he stood looking out the large picture window. Eva grinned nastily at Becky, winking at her as if she had intended to interrupt them.

"I'm sorry," she pouted playfully. "Do you want me to leave?"

"If you don't mind," he answered coolly, finally turning to face her.

"All right, all right. Sorry to bother you." She walked toward the door, her hips sashaying provocatively. "But I was just wondering if you told her yet?" She turned and stared at Becky with a malicious smile.

Becky knew she didn't want to hear whatever she was talking about, and was surprised to hear herself ask, "What?"

"Just that you could have the rest of the day and evening off. Pearce and I are going out on a date, and you won't be needed," Eva answered quickly, not giving Pearce a chance to say anything.

"A date?" The room suddenly seemed too close for comfort. The room was too tight and the light too bright. She needed to get out, but wondered how she was going to do that with the floor suddenly so wavy and unstable. She shut her eyes against the dizziness and took a few gulps of air.

"Of course a date, what else would it be?" Eva grinned cruelly at her despair.

"Emily's going with us." Pearce gave Becky a helpless look and hoped like mad she would understand the predicament he was in. He honestly had no clue how he should handle the situation, and knew if he stood up for Becky, Eva would make her life even more miserable. If it was possible. He looked away, but not before he saw her lip tremble slightly and how white her face had gone.

Cursing the day Eva showed up, he wondered what was he supposed to do. Wasn't it wrong to keep Eva away from their daughter? Wasn't it right to forgive her, or at least try? He cleared his throat and kept quiet, expecting Becky would see through her and see what she really was.

Chapter 20

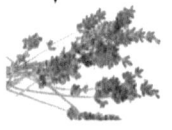

"So," Curly began when Becky joined him later that afternoon in the barn. "Is everything all right between you and Pearce?"

Becky shrugged her shoulders, still reeling from that morning's conference. She hadn't been able to get Eva's smug look out of her mind when she had informed her that 'they' were going out on a date. How could Pearce even like her after what she had done to his family? How could he even think of re-marrying her? She was so preoccupied with her thoughts, that she didn't hear Curly repeat his question.

"Are you all right?" He asked, concerned when she wouldn't answer.

"I'm fine," she said, smiling a little too brightly to be convincing. "Why?"

"It just looks like you're upset," he drawled, continuing his work. Silently, Becky followed him around, just needing someone to be around while the kids were busy with their school work.

"I'm not upset," she answered quietly, just as Scott joined them.

Overhearing her last comment, he stared at her and his spiteful eyes fairly gleamed with malice. "Why are you upset? You look like you just found out that Pearce was getting married again." Curly looked at him, surprised.

"What are you talking about?" She asked, sighing as she sat down.

"You just look like there's something wrong."

"Nope. Nothing's wrong," she answered flatly, looking away, but not before they both saw the tears threatening to fall.

"Kind of hurts when someone you love doesn't love you in return, doesn't it?" She shrank from his venomous words. "I should know pretty well."

Curly had heard enough. With a warning look, he stepped between them to block his view. "Leave her alone."

"Fine. I'll leave you two alone," he shrugged as he walked away. "Maybe you two could get together now that Pearce is out of the way." He laughed raucously on the way out, closing the door behind him.

Curly waited a moment to make sure they were really alone and to give Becky a little time to recover from Scott's verbal attack. "You ready to talk about it?"

She threw him a morose look. "They're going out on a date."

"Who?"

"Pearce and Eva." She said quietly, as if it had cost her quite dearly to utter their names out loud together.

He stared at her, incredulous. "Who told you that?"

"Eva."

"I don't believe it for a minute. It's just a bunch of hog-wash." He spat contemptuously on the ground.

Something about the way she held herself told him it wasn't one of Eva's vicious lies, and he flinched when she said, "Pearce was right there and didn't say otherwise."

"Maybe he didn't hear her." Even he didn't look convinced.

"Or maybe they're really going out on a date. Curly," she said when he was about to argue. "Pearce gave me the rest of the day off. I don't have to cook lunch or dinner. In fact," she turned to look out a small window. "I think they're gone already. His truck isn't here."

"Maybe it's just..."

"And when I walked into the den, I caught him looking at a wedding ring."

He turned to her, his eyes narrowed, and she thought that perhaps this was a piece of news that hadn't quite caught him off guard. "Are you sure it was a wedding ring?"

"It was a complete set in a really nice ring box. I think he's going to ask her to marry him again tonight," she looked away and refused to meet his gaze.

"You're wrong." He hung a coil of rope he had been winding

up on a hook on the opposite wall. "I think you need to get yourself out of this depression you're in. Why don't you go out for dinner tonight? Call a friend, go out and have a good time."

"I'm not depressed."

Rolling his eyes, he gave a rather disgusted snort. "All right then, prove it. Go out and have yourself a good time for once. Leave the kids with me."

With a vehement shake of her head, she answered, "I couldn't do that."

"Yes you can, and you are."

"What am I going to do, go grocery shopping?" She said with a bitter laugh.

"If that's what you call a good time, you've got a lot to learn," he shook his head and grinned at her. "Go to dinner, maybe catch a movie. Go for a drive, you'll find something. I'm not taking no for an answer," he said when she opened her mouth to argue.

Like a martyr, she sighed heavily and stood to her feet. "All right, if it'll make you feel better."

"One more thing," he said before she was completely out the door. "You're not even allowed to *think* of Pearce and Eva."

"Yes doctor." *As if that's even possible,* she thought, opening the door and leaving him alone.

"What in the world am I doing?" Becky said miserably to herself as she drove to town later that evening. "I have no idea what to do or where to go. This is just stupid." She almost turned around, but Curly's warning to not come home early nagged at her to at least try to find something. It wasn't very often she was able to go somewhere by herself, let alone have an entire night to herself, and all she could think about were her kids.

She had cleaned up Pearce's house and her own cabin before setting off, still trying to get out of going. But, Curly had enlisted the help of Jen and Jeff, making it difficult to take a long time. He had offered them some sort of a treat if they helped her, and obviously it had been a good one, because they had the chores done in record time. Jen hadn't even seemed reluctant to see her go this time, which was unusual. Jen had always been one to follow her around like a shadow, and she had grown used to always having one or the other, or both, around at all times.

Driving around the small town twice, the only thing she could think to do was to pick up a few things they needed from the grocery store and put a little gas in her truck. After that, she was completely lost.

Deciding it was better than driving through town for the third time, she pulled into the parking lot and turned off the engine. Suddenly, an ugly thought struck, and she looked around to make sure Pearce's truck wasn't there. When she was reassured of their absence, she got out and walked woodenly to the door.

"Becky?" Someone called behind her as she was getting herself a cart. "How are you doing?"

"Jack, hi," she answered with as much enthusiasm she could muster when he joined her. "What are you doing here?" Wishing she could take the idiotic question back even before it was fully out of her mouth, she gave him an apologetic grin, her face flushing prettily. "Sorry about that, just had a dumb moment."

Not one to let an opportunity slip by, he flashed her a bright smile and answered with a mischievous glint in his eyes, "Well, let me see. I usually come here to buy transmission fluid, spark plugs, and gas. You know. The normal stuff people go to the grocery store for. Where are the kids?"

"They're with Curly tonight." They walked around the aisles together, picking out the things that they each needed, as well as some things they didn't. "Wait. You forgot these." She put a package of Oreo's in his cart when he tried to walk past them.

"I don't really need those," he chuckled, not bothering to take them back out. "I can't believe you remember I like those."

"Like them? Ha! I don't think I ever saw you without one when we were growing up." The memory of him as a chubby boy always carrying around a cookie in each hand flashed through her mind, and she couldn't help grinning. *Perhaps this might turn out better than I had first thought,* she reasoned, thankful to be in good company.

"I've grown out of that. Almost." He patted his much flatter stomach as reassurance. She had to admit that he had indeed grown into quite a handsome man and she admired his muscular frame. He grinned when he caught her staring, and she hastily looked away.

"You've done a fabulous job." Quietly, she threw a bag of chips into his cart when he wasn't looking, glad he could take a joke.

"Oh really?" He sucked in his breath and stuck out his chest in an effort to impress her, causing a few people to turn and stare as they passed by. "You never thought I'd grow up and have such a fine physique, did you?" She laughed, refusing to give him an answer and encourage his ego.

"I think that's all I needed." They came to the very last aisle, and she glanced in her cart, suddenly wondering what she was going to do with herself after she checked out.

"That's it? Why did you come all the way into town for just that?" He gave a skeptical look at her nearly empty cart.

Shaking her head more to keep from thinking of the reason why than in answer to him, she answered, "Pearce gave me the evening off."

"Well that was nice." Her forlorn look hadn't escaped his quick notice, but he decided not to press the issue. "What were you going to do after shopping?"

"I really have no idea, to tell the truth. Curly told me to go out to eat, or maybe catch a movie, or something, but I've had kids so long, I just don't know what to do by myself."

Pouncing on the opportunity, he asked, "Do you want to have dinner with me, tonight? We could just go over to the café, they're pretty good. I'm a frequent visitor, so I should know."

"I'd like that," she said with a shy nod.

Chapter 21

They rode together in Jack's car to the café down the street, joking and carrying on much as they had done as kids.

Becky pushed open her door before he could get it for her, and whistled, her hand pressed to her chest. "Praise the LORD!"

He gave her a suspicious look. "What?"

"I didn't think we were going to make it!" Gulping in deep breaths of air for emphasis, she went on, "You still drive the same."

"Look who's got jokes," he said, pulling the café door open for her. "I drive better than you any day."

"Dream on buddy!" She said with an appreciative glance around them.

There was just something cozy and inviting about the interior of the quaint café. The gingham checked curtains at the windows were clean and curling around the frames in just the right places. Cast iron tables were placed strategically in the middle of the diningroom, their matching chairs made comfortable with fluffy cushions. For those who desired a little more privacy, the booths that lined the walls were inviting with romantic candles and tablecloths that matched the curtains.

Jack, to Becky's immense relief, chose a booth in a corner furthest away from the other customers.

"Well," Jack said, breaking the silence after the waitress had taken their order and left. "What's new with you?"

With a wary look, she plucked at the table cloth and leaned her head against her hand. "Nothing much."

He watched her curiously for a moment and decided to try to draw her out of her melancholic state. "You've been acting a little strained at church the past week. Did something happen between you and Pearce? I've noticed that you haven't been sitting with him and Emily as usual."

Her face pink, she said a little rougher than she intended, "Don't be so nosy."

"I'm not being nosy. I'm just being a friend that wants to make you feel better. Besides," he sat back and crossed his arms, giving her a lopsided grin, "I think you owe me after sneaking the Metamucil into my cart!"

"I bet Patty never looks at her preacher the same again," she finally conceded with a laugh at the memory of the organist's shocked expression when Jack had pulled the laxative container out of his cart.

Not feeling it was right to just set it aside at the counter and make someone else put it away, he'd added it to his items with a baleful glare at a laughing Becky. He shook his head and laughed with her, repeating his earlier question a moment later.

"I just feel stupid," she blurted after a small hesitation.

Usually, she was calm and collected, and her flustered manner intrigued him. He leaned forward. "What do you feel stupid about?"

Sighing and giving it up for lost, she told him the whole story, not hiding any details or feelings for Pearce. More than a little ashamed at how she felt at being so rejected, and concluding with how Scott was acting toward her now.

He whistled and managed to look impressed when she had finally finished. "You've had quite the past few weeks. Are you sure he cares for her after what she's done to both of them? It seemed to me that he was interested in someone else, last I knew."

Twisting her spaghetti around and around with her fork, he briefly wondered if it was possible to put a hole in the plate when she answered, "I thought maybe he liked me a little, but all that changed when she showed up. He hardly speaks to me or has anything to do with me anymore."

Seeing a hint of tears in her gorgeous eyes, he changed gears. "So, what's she like?"

She gave him the disgusted snort he was so fond of from years ago. "Perfect." His smile of disbelief annoyed her. "No, I'm really being serious. She's beautiful and she knows it. She's small and thin, dresses like a million bucks, and has no end of male admiration. You name it, she's got it."

"You know what I think?" He asked, leaning back in his seat. "I think you're jealous and she's really not all that pretty."

"Ha!" She nearly choked on her soda. "I bet you'd like her too if you saw her."

"Well, here's my chance," he said quietly, nodding toward the door. She turned to see Pearce carrying Emily with Eva following close behind wearing a clingy dress that showed off her curves.

Becky groaned and hastily turned around, hoping like crazy they hadn't noticed her.

"Susie Homemaker!" Eva shrilled. Oozing charm as she came to stand at their table, making sure her low-cut dress would give Becky's companion plenty to stare at if he were so inclined. "How are you? And *who* is your *delicious* date?"

"Hello," Becky mumbled as Pearce and Emily joined them. She could feel her face turn three shades of red, each darker than the rest as the other patrons turned to stare at them.

"Evening Becky. Jack," Pearce said in a much quieter tone, his embarrassment at Eva's antics evident.

Grabbing his arm as though it were her very own life preserver, she cooed, "Pearce, you are so *good* to let little Susie here have time off so she could meet her boyfriend. I have *the best* idea. Why don't you two go out with us tonight? Wouldn't that be so fun Susie?" She beamed at her, anxious to inflict pain.

"Sounds so fun!" Becky answered a little too sweetly through a fake smile as she looked at Pearce, trying desperately to give him the hint that she didn't want to go.

He didn't take it. "That's a good idea."

Becky looked helplessly at Jack for support, somehow managing to bite back her frustrated scream.

"Actually," Jack said smoothly, staring at Pearce and completely ignoring Eva. "I had planned to take Becky somewhere else after dinner, but it's really up to her," he looked at her with a small shrug of his shoulders.

"Then it's settled," Eva began, unwilling to let Becky off the hook so easily. "You're coming with us. We'll have *so much* fun, won't we Susie?"

Suddenly able to breathe again, Becky returned Eva's nasty smile with a cheery one of her own and an appreciative glance at Jack. "I already told Jack that I'd go with him tonight, and I wouldn't feel right doing that to him. Sorry."

"Pearce," Eva whined, tugging at his arm as she pretended to pout. "Make them go with us."

Pearce held Becky's gaze a moment, and she wondered if the hurt she saw was because she was out with Jack, or that Eva seemed to want Jack's attention so badly. "They're allowed to have an evening to themselves. Come on, let them finish their meal in peace. Enjoy."

"That's okay little Susie," Eva said sweetly with a glare after Pearce had left to find a table for the three of them. "I'd rather have Pearce all to myself anyway. Unless," she winked at Jack, "you're available."

Jack calmly wiped his mouth with a napkin and returned her gaze. "Sorry, I'm already taken."

Patting his hand and leaning over him just in case he wanted to see some of the charms he was going to miss out on, she said, "Isn't that so *sweet?* But, I'm already taken as well. Bye!" She stalked away, her hips drawing the attention of more than one man in the dining room.

When she was out of earshot, Becky growled, "If you say she's pretty, I'm going to make a scene."

"Actually, that wasn't going to be my first observation," he smiled kindly taking her hand in his own, oblivious to Pearce's stares. "I was going to tell you that you have her all wrong." Becky's mouth fell open, and she was about to argue when he held up a hand to silence her. "Wait. Hear me out. You said she was perfect. She's not that nice, nor is she so pretty."

She gave him a grateful look that told him he was her hero and squeezed his hand affectionately. "Have you gone legally blind and haven't told me? That *would* explain your driving!"

Jack tried his best to keep Becky talking and laughing for the remainder of their meal so she might find it easier to ignore Pearce and Eva, and was almost successful. If every *other* thought instead of *every* thought could be considered success.

"Aren't you finished yet?" Jack asked sometime later when Becky was still playing with her food and he had been done for quite a while.

She gave him an apologetic look and pushed her plate away, turning her head toward the wall and away from Pearce's many glances. "I'm really not that hungry."

Taking her hand again, he asked, "Are you all right?"

"I'm fine," she smiled thinly, squeezing his hand in return. "I'm just not very hungry this past week." She looked up at him and shrugged her shoulders dismissively. "It'll all work out in the end."

"Did you have anything specific you wanted to do after dinner?"

When she gave a gentle tug, he reluctantly let her pull her hand back. "I thought I might drive by the old house and make sure it's still standing. Just in case," she whispered with a solemn wink at him.

He stood and pulled his billfold out of his back pocket. "I'll drive. Just let me pay first."

"Wait," she called after him, noticing that the waitress had left only one bill.

"What?" He turned back to her, standing close to Eva and Pearce's table.

"Come here," she waved him back, embarrassed. "My dinner is on there as well. Here," she held out a twenty dollar bill when he was close enough to take it.

He gave her a ferocious frown and stepped back. "You know me better than that. Be right back."

Becky watched him pay for their meals and gathered her things, ready to meet him at the door when he was finished. How she hated the thought of walking past Pearce's table! Hoping that they wouldn't notice her, she walked quickly by and kept her eyes on a smiling Jack.

"Becky," Pearce called when she was almost past. With a sinking heart, she turned and trudged back, a plastic smile pasted on her face.

"Did you call me?" She ignored Eva's hateful looks, and watched Emily who had pulled her chair as close as she could to Pearce and as far away from Eva as possible.

"Yes," he said quietly, gazing at her. "I was just wondering if I could talk to you later on tonight?"

"I don't know what time I'll be home," she answered coolly, irritated that he thought she would just come running. *Like I usually do*, she thought with a pang.

Eva giggled and winked at Jack, who ignored her while still waiting patiently for Becky. "So your boyfriend has a hot night planned."

"He's not her boyfriend," Pearce answered for her, hating the fact that they were even out together on a date. "He's the preacher."

"Well," Eva looked at him saucily, "looked to me like they're boyfriend and girlfriend. They *were* holding hands just a little while ago, and he *did* pay for her dinner, didn't he?"

"Is there something particular you need?" Becky asked, purposefully not telling either of them if Jack was her boyfriend or not as he gave up his post at the door and came to join them in case Becky needed support.

"Actually," Pearce cleared his throat. "I do need to talk to you. Later on tonight if that's possible."

"Emily, are you all right?" She asked with a frown, surprised that neither of the parents seemed to notice that Emily was holding her stomach as if she were sick.

Pearce turned toward his daughter, and gave her a small nudge. "Emily?"

"Daddy, I need to go to the bathroom," she said quietly, her face turning a little green. Pearce looked expectantly at Eva.

With a disgusted scowl and a wrinkle of her dainty nose, she said, "I'm not taking her. Ask Susie here. She gets paid for it."

Becky shrugged off Jack's protective hand from her elbow and took Emily's sweaty hand. "Come on Em. We'll be right back," she said with an apologetic look at Jack.

When her nemesis was gone, Eva turned a bright smile Jack's

way and patted the seat next to her. "So, can you answer a little question for us? Susie homemaker wouldn't tell us."

"Eva," Pearce took a sip of his soda, "stop." He set the glass down and glared at her.

"It'll be all right," she argued, dismissing him entirely. "He won't mind, will you?" A hard gleam in her eye dared him to refuse.

Refusing her offer of the chair next to her, he answered, "Well, I guess it depends on the question."

"It's an easy one," she smiled. "Anyway, *are* you and Becky dating? I mean, are you two an item?" She fluttered her eyes at him hoping she was irritating Pearce.

"Well," Jack began, clearing his throat uneasily. Instinctively, he knew she wanted to hurt either Becky or Pearce and he wanted no part of it, but he was an honest man and couldn't lay aside his feelings for Becky and act like he didn't care for her. On the flip side, he also knew that Becky had cared for Pearce and didn't want to make her lose any chance of happiness with him. "I don't know exactly what you mean."

She looked irritated. "How many different ways are there to take that question?"

When Becky still hadn't made an appearance, he sat down in Emily's chair next to Pearce. "Let me ask you a question before I answer yours."

"Sure. I don't have anything to hide," she patted her hair and grinned like a wolf that has just seen a fat pig it wanted to eat for its dinner.

"How long are you staying?"

"I thought it was only for a week, but now I'm not so sure," she smiled, patting Pearce's hand affectionately. Quickly, he pulled it away as if he'd been scorched, his face red. "Is that the question?"

"Actually, it's a series of questions," Jack leaned back and took the two in, assessing their actions and demeanors. Years of being a preacher had taught him many things, including how to read body language. "Why are you back?"

"That's two questions and I only asked one. *My* turn. *Do* you like Becky?" Pearce leaned back in his seat and tried not to look interested in Jack's answer.

"Of course I like Becky, don't you? And I bet that's the first time you've used her real name since you've been here." *She's not so pretty when she frowns,* Jack thought to himself, amused.

"Why wouldn't I like Susie homemaker? She's plain and does all the work around the house. What woman *wouldn't* like her? Plus, she's been keeping my handsome hubby company until I was able to come back and settle down," she answered loud enough for Becky to hear as she led Emily back to the table. Jack stood up and gave Emily her seat, and the young child immediately leaned her head on Pearce's arm.

"But now that I'm back for good," she went on as Becky stared at her, her face white. "*I'll* be the one who's keeping him company, so he won't need her anymore."

"Eva!" Pearce slapped his hand down on the table, his face almost purple with rage. Not a few customers turned to stare, suddenly interested in their table.

Unperturbed, Eva looked at him. "What? Wasn't that what you were going to tell her tonight when you wanted to talk to her so badly?"

Pearce gave Becky an apologetic look. "Becky, I..."

She interrupted him before he could answer, her expression carefully blank. "I think she's got a fever. She was sick in the restroom but she did say she was feeling a little better. We'll see you later." Jack ushered her to the door, his hand on the small of her back.

"What do you think you're doing?" He fumed when they were gone.

Her eyes wide with innocence, she wiped her mouth with her napkin. "What are you talking about? I was only playing around. Don't be so sensitive."

"You're *not* back for good, and you have no right to talk to her that way!"

With a cruel smile, she replied, "Wow, you seem to be pretty attached to your little housekeeper, Pearce."

"Let's go." He signaled the waitress to bring him the check.

She knew him well enough to know she'd hit her mark, and she continued, "Watch out, Pearce. Looks to me like you may have some competition with that preacher boy. He's pretty handsome, don't you think ? I'd be interested in someone like him."

At one point in their relationship, it would have deeply hurt him to have her so interested in another man. Now, he found it irritated him much more to have her, whom he considered to be closely related to the devil, speak about Becky with another man.

Standing to go, he picked Emily up and cradled her against him, her fever burning through his shirt. "He wouldn't have anything to do with you, Eva." His lips in a grim line, he laid a tip on the table.

Patting her hair and sauntering through the café, she said loudly, "What makes you think he wouldn't be interested in me?"

Her disgusting selfishness and the disdain for the feelings of others pushed him too far and he blurted, "Obviously he's got taste. Look who he's with," he glared at her, glad beyond words to see that he had succeeded in irritating her. "You couldn't hold a candle to someone like Becky." He turned and stalked out of the restaurant, leaving her staring after him with eyes full of hate.

Chapter 22

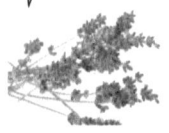

"Becky, I'm sorry about all that," Jack began as they drove toward the old house she was renting.

She gazed sightlessly out her window, her head leaning on her hand. "I just don't understand."

"Understand what?"

Shaking her head in bewilderment, she answered, "Why he would take her back after all the garbage she's put him through," she paused before continuing quietly, "and you really didn't think she was pretty?"

"Absolutely not," he grimaced, a frown furrowing his brows. "She reminded me of that verse in the Bible about jewels in a swine's snout. She'd be the snout, by the way." His efforts of cheering her had the small effect of a return smile, as well as a return to silence for the rest of the ride.

"Here we are." He pulled into the driveway and turned off the engine.

She suddenly had the awkward feeling that they were parking and he was about to kiss her. In an effort to keep him at bay, she fumbled with her door handle to let herself out, the dome light bright and cheery.

"Looks like I need to cut the grass again," she said, trying to be funny as she scooted out of the car. Glancing over her shoulder and seeing him leaning toward where she had been sitting, she again had the feeling that he had leaned over to kiss her.

"I'll wait here for you, don't hurry," he said with a wry smile.

"Thanks Jack." Quietly she shut the door, and walked up to the porch. Taking her house key out of her purse, she let herself in. She walked around a little, remembering all the things she and the kids had done in certain places, smiling to herself.

She hadn't realized how much was at stake back then. She had thought that she could handle just being Pearce's housekeeper and nothing more, but now she realized that she had been wrong. Seriously wrong. She had wanted to be so much more to him, and now that Eva was back, it seemed her hopes and dreams had vanished into thin air. She walked into the kitchen, letting her hand slide over the chair back that Pearce had last sat in, lost in her thoughts.

Dear Lord, she began to pray, sitting down dejectedly at the table. *I've gone and made a mess of things again. There were so many things I was hoping for, that I forgot to ask your will to be done. Please forgive me, and lead me in a plain path. I beg for your peace and comfort in this whole situation. Let me know what you would have me do. In Jesus' name, amen.* She sat still for a few minutes, letting the peace that passes all understanding take hold of her and reassure her.

Jack found her a few minutes later, still sitting at the kitchen table with her head in her hands. "Becky? Are you all right?" He put a comforting hand on her bent head and stroked her silky hair with a racing heart.

"Yes," she answered softly, taking his hand in hers and giving it a squeeze before letting it go. "I'll be all right."

"Is there anywhere else you want to go?"

A tear slipped down her cheek, and he wished with all his heart he could do something to erase her pain and sorrow. "I thought about going to see Mr. Pickles if you don't think it's too late."

Cupping her chin with his hand, he wiped the tear away with his thumb. "I'll take you wherever you want to go. You can always count on me."

"I know." She gave him a halfhearted smile. "I'm so glad God brought us back together."

"Becky," he walked with her to the front door and waited patiently while she locked up behind them. "Have you wondered why God brought us back together again? I mean," seeing her rather confused look, he hurried to finish. "Do you wonder if he had a certain purpose for it, or do you think it was all chance?"

"God doesn't do anything by chance," she answered, allowing

him to open the car door for her. "Why?"

With a shrug, he started the car and drove down the dusty road before taking the coward's way out of the conversation. "I don't know."

She glared at him through narrowed eyes. "Yes you do. What were you thinking?"

"I was just thinking out loud, that's all. Don't worry about it," he said evasively, turning into the overgrown road that was more like a tractor rut than a driveway.

"I'm not worried about it, but I know you too well to just dismiss it," she looked at him seriously. "I'm not letting you off the hook. We'll talk about it more when I come back." Opening her door, she went to talk to Mr. Pickles. She was only gone a few minutes before she returned, a sad smile curving the corners of her pink mouth.

"Well," she said, when they were back on their way toward town, and consequently, the end of their date. "I don't know if that was the right thing to do or not, but at least it's taken care of."

"What's taken care of?"

"The kids and I for a while," she said distractedly. "At least until I can find somewhere else to go," she whispered almost inaudibly.

He didn't like the sound of that. "Where would you go?"

"I don't know," she shrugged. "Wherever God sends me I guess."

He parked next to her truck in the empty parking lot and turned toward her, his arm resting on the back of the seat. "What if he wants you to stay here?"

"I don't know where he wants me. I thought he wanted me to stay here with Pearce, but now that Eva's back, I'm lost."

Jack plucked at the piping on the head rest and looked everywhere but at her. "What if he meant you for someone else?"

"Like who? Scott?" She scoffed, rolling her eyes. "He isn't interested in me anymore, especially after meeting Eva."

"Maybe there's someone else you've never given a chance," he smiled stiffly, finally looking over at her.

"Or maybe," she said slowly, his meaning suddenly becoming very clear. "He doesn't want me to get remarried at all." Uneasy, she hoped he wouldn't pursue the conversation and would take her subtle hint.

He didn't. Turning to her, his eyes spoke volumes that she wasn't ready to hear. "I was meaning that maybe he brought you here to be with me."

"Jack," she said softly, putting her hand on his arm. "You've always been good to me and I've always loved your company. But more as a friend than a husband."

"Isn't that a good start for a marriage?" He took her hand in his and looked longingly into her eyes. "Couldn't you try?"

"Try to love you? I already do, but not in a wife's way." She hated to cause him pain, but knew there was no possible way she could love him. Not with Pearce around. She couldn't imagine trying to be the kind of wife he deserved when her heart yearned so completely for another. She changed tactics in an effort to lighten the mood. "You don't love me, you just like having me around."

"Don't love you? I've measured every woman I've ever met with you, and you don't think I love you? I know we'd make a great team and I'd be a good husband to you. I wouldn't be demanding." Still holding her hand, his eyes implored her to give him the answer he desired.

"Jack," she answered quietly, tearing her hand out of his grasp. "I can't. Please try to understand."

"I understand," he smiled ruefully, "rejected twice by the same woman."

"The first one doesn't count," she tried to laugh through the tears that insisted on gathering in the corners of her eyes. *He deserves so much. I just wish he could find someone that would treat him right,* she thought miserably. "You were eighteen, so you didn't really know what you were doing."

"Was I really only eighteen?" They laughed a little, some of the tension easing between them. With a little grin, he turned toward her, and she wondered if he were about to try to argue with her some more. "Will you promise me something?"

196

"I don't know if I can promise," she hesitated.

"If Pearce and Eva get back together and you stop loving him, will you finally give me a chance?" He pleaded, a small smile playing at the corner of his mouth.

"I'll give you the chance," she said softly, cradling his face in her hand, "my dear, dear friend. You will always be cherished." She fervently prayed God would send him a wonderful woman to take her place in his heart, even if it meant being alone without anyone for the rest of her life. "Thank you for being with me today, I needed a friend."

"I'll always be your friend," he answered quietly. "But I'll be wishing for more."

Becky let herself in the cabin later that night to find Jen and Jeff playing a board game on the tiny table in the kitchen. With a bright smile, if somewhat forced, she asked, "Did you guys have a good time tonight?"

"Yes we did," Jeff answered excitedly, trying to be the first one to tell her what they had been able to do. "First, we helped Curly finish up what he needed to do…"

"…then," broke in Jen, not letting her little brother be the one with all the glory, "he took us bowling with him. You should see him…"

"He's almost as good as a pro-bowler person!" Jeff interjected, bouncing up and down on his seat. "He taught me how to be a better bowler. You should see me now," he stood and pretended to toss a perfect ball down an imaginary aisle, and she figured he must have gotten a strike by all his jumping up and down in glee.

"He taught me a few things too," Jen continued quickly as Jeff was acting out his bowling expertise. "You'll have to go with us someday, because now it's not going to be so easy to beat us," she said, giving Becky a quick hug.

"I didn't think it was very easy before," she smiled tiredly, putting her purse down and starting the kettle for some tea. She sat down at the table to listen to their story.

"Then after bowling," Jeff continued, "he took us to an

awesome restaurant where they had all kinds of video games and toys that we could play with..."

"...and Jeff and I played skee-ball. You know, where you roll the ball up a ramp for points? And I beat the pants off him." Jen laughed and poked him in the side, earning a stuck out tongue for her effort.

"That's only because *my* lane was messed up."

"Well, you really shouldn't beat the pants off Jeff – that's just gross," Becky couldn't help teasing.

Jen rolled her eyes. "Anyway, when we were done eating, Curly took us out for ice cream..."

"...and he let me get whatever I wanted." Jeff couldn't help interrupting, rubbing his stomach for emphasis. "I got a triple-decker double-fudge cone with a cherry on top." He smacked his lips for emphasis.

"Wow, were you able to eat all that?" Becky grinned.

"Of course." He looked at her as though she were silly to ask such a question. "But Curly had to help Jen with hers because she couldn't handle it."

"It was a lot of ice cream," she answered, defending herself. "They were definitely *not* afraid to give someone ice cream."

"Then what did you do?" Becky asked, getting up to make her tea when the kettle started to sing.

"That's it," they said in unison, giggling. "I think we really tired Curly out. He was yawning so much we thought he was going to go right to sleep as soon as we got home."

"I'm really going to owe him a big one, aren't I," Becky murmured, cautiously taking a sip and sitting back down at the table. "Why don't you two get ready for bed?"

"I get the bathroom first!" Jeff yelled, running for the door and grabbing his pajamas on the way. He always accused Jen of taking too long, so he was always careful to be the first one in.

"That's all right with me," Jen answered loudly, looking over her shoulder, "that just means I get more time with mom." She grinned mischievously, knowing it would irritate him. "So what did you do?"

"Nothing much."

"Well, where did you go? What did you do? Did you go with a friend?" Her arms crossed, she gave her mother a stern look.

"I went to the grocery store."

"The grocery store?" Jen frowned, not at all impressed with her night out. "That's it?"

"No, that's not it," she said with a little smile. "I met Jack there and we went out to dinner at that little diner in town."

"Jack?" Jen asked. Becky saw the disappointment on her daughter's face, and was glad she didn't have to tell her about his marriage proposal. "I was hoping that maybe you and Pearce would somehow hook up and get together."

"No, Pearce went out with Eva, remember?"

"Yeah, but I was hoping that he'd ditch her or something," she grinned guiltily, "I don't know, maybe even push her out of the car."

"I don't think he's going to do anything like that." Becky looked down at her fingernails so Jen wouldn't see the gleam in her eyes and see that her mother agreed with her tactics.

"Maybe not, but she can't stay much longer. It's already been almost a month," she answered boldly, her look daring her mother to argue.

"Honey," she gave her a rueful grin and patted her hand, "I don't think things are going to work out here after all."

"What do you mean?" She looked panicked.

Becky swallowed and tried to keep the waver out of her voice. "I think we may have to be moving soon."

"But I don't want to move," she blurted, tears forming. "I love it here."

"I do too baby, but I don't think Eva is leaving."

Her fists clenched in indignation, she stood abruptly to her feet. "But they can't get back together. Pearce loves *you*, not *her*!"

"Please Jen," Becky put a finger to her lips in an effort to quieten her down. "I really don't want Jeff to find out this way, so please hush." Jen sat back down, her expression miserable. "I love it here too, and I definitely don't want to leave, but I don't think we'll have much choice, sweetie. Eva's made it pretty clear tonight what she expects. In fact," she said softly, "I don't think it would be a bad idea if we were to start packing our things."

"Why should we pack our stuff?" Jeff asked, coming in on the tail-end of their conversation.

"Because we're probably going to have to move out of here!" Jen snapped. Without another word, she stalked to the bathroom and slammed the door, letting her mother know exactly how she felt about leaving.

Jeff, who was always a little clueless to women's mood swings, frowned. "What's bugging her?"

"Sit for a little bit, honey," Becky repeated a little of what she had told Jen and got almost the same reaction, but was grateful when no doors had been slammed this time around.

"Mom," Jeff asked after he had cooled down and thought about it, "why would God allow all this stuff to happen to us? I mean, don't you think we've had enough to deal with already? Why does this have to happen too?"

"I know you're not going to like to hear this honey." She tucked the quilt in around him as Jen climbed into her own bunk. "But whether we like it or not, we have to trust that God *always* knows what's best for us. Even when we don't agree or understand." She kissed him tenderly on his forehead and gave him a quick hug.

"Jen." She softly rubbed her back. "Aren't you going to say good-night?"

"Good-night," she mumbled, turning to face her. Becky noticed that her eyes were red and puffy from crying.

"Please don't be angry," she pleaded, hating herself for putting them through this emotional situation. "I was hoping things would turn out differently."

"We're not angry with you." Jen hated hurting her mother's feelings more than they were. "We're just really disappointed."

"Me too. But there is one thing I have to ask both of you to do," she said, getting into her own bunk across the room. "I don't want either of you to say a word to anyone about us leaving, understand?"

"Yes," they answered together quietly. "We promise."

Chapter 23

For very different reasons, Becky and the kids tried to stay away from almost everyone the next day. Jen and Jeff didn't want to get any more attached than they already were. Becky, who was already painfully attached, was reluctant to face anyone for fear of blurting out her plans to leave.

"Becky?" Pearce asked later that morning, poking his head into the kitchen where she was teaching school. "Can I see you for a minute? It won't be long." Becky stood up and looked warily at the kids before following him to the den.

Unable to shake the ominous feeling of trouble, as well as being terrified of what he was about to say, she stood apart and waited for him to speak first.

"I'm sorry about what went on last night."

She plucked at the piping on the back of the wing-back chair and changed the subject. "How's Emily this morning?"

"Emily?" His wearied looked pained her and tugged at her heart strings. It was now painfully obvious that he hadn't been sleeping well, and she tried to ignore his bloodshot eyes. "I think she'll be all right. She's sleeping right now, but I think she might have a stomach virus or something."

"I'm sorry. Let me know if there's anything you need me to do." She figured that would be the best place to avoid Eva, not to mention it would allow her some quality time with the little girl she had grown to love before she had to leave.

"Thanks." He gave her a grateful smile. "I can always count on you, can't I."

"I'd like to think so." Guilt gnawed at her, and she looked away. *Things would be so much easier if Eva would go. You could count on me for anything and everything*, she thought with a pang. "But to be honest, I don't know what's in the future."

"If you're meaning Eva," he said with a sigh, holding his head in his hands, "you just have to realize that she's got a strange sense of humor sometimes."

"I was always raised to believe that humor was when you were joking with someone," she said instantly annoyed that he was trying to make excuses for her again.

"Maybe she *was* joking with you." It was his turn to get irritated.

"Pearce," she chose her words carefully, knowing that a full blown argument could erupt with just one wrong observation. "Joking is what happens between two people who are friends and they both laugh. If only one is laughing, maybe it wasn't a joke or they aren't friends. I think in this case, it was both."

"Becky, I don't want to fight."

She gritted her teeth against the angry tirade that wanted to spew forth and said calmly, "Neither do I. But I don't want you and Emily to get hurt again either." She looked at him, pity striking deep into her heart.

He gave a scornful laugh. "What would make you think that I'd get hurt again?"

"There's so many reasons, I wouldn't know where to start, but I don't think you're happy."

"Why?"

"You don't smile or laugh anymore and you're always tired. Your face has the dark shadows it had when I first met you, you're always sad, and..."

He interrupted with a wave of his hand. "That's enough, I think I know what you're saying. Anything else that you'd like to tell me?"

"Well," she answered slowly, eyebrows raised. It was everything or nothing. His daughter's well-being was at stake, and she was darned if she was going to stand around and let her get hurt without trying to do something about it. "There is one other thing. Have you noticed that Emily is back to the way she used to be? In fact, I think she's worse. She won't play with Jen or Jeff, she..."

"I thought she just wasn't playing with Jen because she keeps knocking her down," he said angrily, wanting to point to something else as the cause of Emily's behavior.

"Don't you think it's weird that they got along great until your ex-wife showed up? And now all of a sudden 'someone' keeps knocking her down?" She responded hotly, her eyes flashing.

"Do you think Emily would lie to me?" He said through gritted teeth, his face red.

Becky wasn't about to let her daughter take the blame for something that despicable woman was responsible for. She planted her feet and crossed her arms, her voice rising in anger. "She's not telling you the truth. Maybe Eva's putting her up to it, but I can certainly tell you that there is no way Jen would knock her down on purpose. Get your head out of the sand and wake up. Eva's the problem and you're blind. You refuse to see her for what she really is and you keep making excuses for her or point to something else as the cause. Why are you being so stubborn?"

"I don't want to talk about it anymore!" He yelled with a slap to his desk, scattering several papers in the process.

"Fine! Neither do I!" She shrieked and yanked open the door so fast, Eva didn't have time to stand back and act like she hadn't been eavesdropping. Becky stopped short and turned a searing gaze on Pearce. "Surprise surprise! I would have never guessed that *you* would be listening in on our conversation. Guess I must be hallucinating, right Pearce? Or is this one of those weird sense of humor things again? Excuse me." She pushed her way past the smiling woman. "Some of us have to work for a living."

Eva giggled and called after her, "Good morning, Susie."

Becky ripped open the door, not caring that it banged on the wall. Both kids looked up from their schoolwork, their eyes wide in shock at seeing their mother in such a tantrum. "School's out. Get your stuff and come with me."

"Mom?" Jeff asked when he and Jen finally caught up with her at the front door of the cabin. "Are you ok?"

"I'm fine," she answered through gritted teeth. "Why?"

"Well," Jen hemmed and hawed nervously, "you seem a little

upset."

They watched in horror as Becky threw suitcases on their bunks, and their hearts sank when they realized what was happening. "Upset? Me? Why in the world would *I* be upset? Start putting your stuff into your suitcase. It won't take us long."

Sudden tears streamed down Jen's face. "We're leaving?"

"Yes." Becky paused for a fraction of a second before continuing shoving more clothes inside.

"When?" Jeff asked the question they both wanted to know the answer to.

"Tonight, when everyone's in bed." Stopping her furious packing frenzy, she sat at the small table, and buried her face in her hands. Both were mortified when uncontrollable sobs erupted.

"Can we tell anyone?" Jeff asked a few minutes later when the crying had stopped.

"No," she wiped angrily at her smeared face. "I don't even want you two to be with any of the workers either. Just stay in the cabin and pack. That's what we're going to do today. Pack!"

Jen whimpered. "Not even Curly?"

Becky hesitated and swiped angrily at her wet face. "Leave Curly to me." She said finally, knowing that she couldn't leave without some sort of explanation for her good friend. He'd always been there for her.

"But I want to say good-bye to him too," Jeff answered setting his jaw stubbornly.

"We'll see," she stood to leave, a crick in her back from bending over so long. "I'm going to go clean up and act like nothing's wrong. If you need me, I'll be in the house."

She forced herself to go back into the main house and was jumpy the rest of the day. At every creak or groan, she held her breath and knew it was either Eva or Pearce coming to talk to her, only breathing again when it wasn't either.

Keeping her secret from any of the workers, with the exception of Curly, would be easy, but Pearce was another matter. There had been times that he just instinctively knew what she was thinking or contemplating, and she figured it would be hard to convince him that nothing was wrong.

Fortunately for her, Pearce was tending to Emily who was still in bed sick, and Eva was nowhere to be found. She sailed through her day and worked furiously, trying to keep her mind and hands busy so she wouldn't have time to dwell on things. She wanted to leave the ranch house in better order than when she had first arrived.

She was scrubbing the bathtub with a vengeance later on that afternoon when she met Pearce for the first time after she had resolved on leaving that night.

With a distracted glance around the room, he asked, "Do you know where Eva is?"

"Nope."

"Ok then," he said lamely when she refused to look his way. He wondered for what seemed the millionth time what he could do to fix the whole situation. "I guess I'll just go back and sit with Emily. If you happen to see Eva, would you please let her know where I am?" He asked softly, turning to go.

That was too much, and she broke her resolution to not speak to him. "Sorry, but no. I will not." She leaned up to give her back a break. "If I happen to see her," she looked at him coldly, "I'm walking the other way. I figure anything else I try to do, is going to come out nasty!" Surprised, he stared and she glared at him in return. With an indifferent shrug and a scowl on his face, he went back to Emily's room, leaving Becky angrier than before.

Fuming to herself, she threw herself into her work like a mad woman and stewed. Scrubbing had never felt quite so good, and she found herself finished quicker than usual. With grim determination not to be the one to apologize first, she started preparing dinner.

Chapter 24

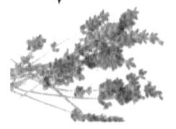

Her stubbornness didn't have the effect she wanted. Instead of Pearce finding her and begging her forgiveness, she grew more discouraged and unhappy when it was clear he wasn't going to seek her out.

Becky was a smart woman, and however upset she was, she tried not to speak out in anger. She wasn't always successful, but she had found that talking to herself, whilst waving her hands around sometimes took the edge off whatever it was bothering her. This was no different. Her oversized oven mitts were flashing around and accusing an imaginary opponent when Jen found her a few seconds after she'd put the casserole in the oven.

"Mom?"

Her oven mitts paused in mid-air, and Becky turned to face her daughter with an innocent expression on her face. "Yes?"

"We're done packing," she tried not to notice her mother's red-rimmed eyes. "Is there anything else we can do?"

"I can't think of anything," Becky answered irritably. "I'm sorry," she said quickly, knowing that she'd hurt Jen's feelings for no reason. "I'm just really unhappy right now." With a grimace, she flipped off the oven mitts and sat down at the table. Jen took a seat next to her.

"We're all unhappy right now. I wish it didn't have to be this way," she said quietly, leaning her head on Becky's shoulder. Becky leaned her head down on Jen's and sighed, remembering so many precious things that had happened in that very room. Leaving was the last thing she wanted to do, but this was her only option.

"I know baby. I know," she kissed her daughter lightly and stood to get her shoes on. "I suppose I need to go talk to Curly. Do you and Jeff want to come with me?" She asked hoping she wouldn't have to do it on her own.

With a nod, Jen stood. "I'll go get him."

They trudged silently to the barn and found Curly in the back, measuring out sweet feed for the horses. They filed silently into the room and closed the door behind them.

Whether Curly instinctively knew what was about to be said, or he had heard whispers of rumors, he wasn't surprised when Becky blurted, "I just wanted to tell you that this will be our last dinner here."

Curly sat down on the stool, his lips pushed out in concentration. Or perhaps he was keeping his words in check. Becky continued.

"We're going back to our house in town."

"Are you sure this is what you want to do?" He asked, casually dusting off his overalls as though things like this were ordinary.

"No." With an emphatic shake of her head, she said, "this is the only thing I *can* do. I don't have any other options."

"Have you told Pearce yet?"

"No. I can't talk to him about anything. I tried talking to him this morning, and he won't listen to anything I say. In fact," she went on reluctantly, "when he knew I was still angry about our argument this morning, he wouldn't even bring it up and try to fix it. Nothing. Zilch. This is my last option, Curly." Her eyes begged him to understand. "Eva's won. That much is obvious, and I *will not* stay here and watch her hurt him and Emily all over again."

"I guess I understand then, when you put it that way," he smiled resolutely. "What are you going to do in town?" He scratched under his hat, a nervous habit he had when he was thinking hard about something.

Distractedly, she rubbed Jeff's head. "I don't know. I guess I'll try to find a job so I can pay Pearce off for fixing my truck, then maybe find somewhere else to go."

"Somewhere else? Like another town?" He asked with narrowed eyes.

"Another state."

Both kids were horrified. "Mom, please no!"

She held up her hands as though to ward off their accusing

looks. "I can't stay here where every time I turn around I'm being reminded of Pearce or Emily. Or," she blushed, "where I can run into Jack at any time."

Curly looked perplexed. "What's wrong with the preacher man?"

"Well," she paused, her eyebrows furrowed, "I didn't tell you, but when we went out to dinner, he asked me to marry him."

Jeff was the first to recover. "I guess he doesn't waste time, does he?"

"What do you mean?"

"One date and he's already asking you to marry him?" Jen finished for him, not in the least happy about not being informed earlier.

Becky couldn't help her grin. "We've known each other for years."

"Does anyone know about this?" Curly didn't bother hiding his displeasure about her news.

"You three are the only ones that I've told. Anyway, now you know why I can't stay here. I can't be with the one I love, and I will not marry anyone I don't. So, my hands are tied. When we move back into our house, I'll start looking around for another place to move to."

"So why did you come to tell me all this?" Curly asked after a moment's silence.

"I didn't think it would be right to leave without some sort of explanation. You've always been a good friend, and I don't want you to think ill of me. And," she paused, looking from one child to the other, "the kids love you to pieces."

"Well, gimme a hug before ya leave." He said gruffly, hugging both children to him at the same time, trying to hide his true feelings. "I've gotten used to you being here, and it's going to be difficult without you. *All* of you. Now, get so I can get my work done, or those horses are going to kick me."

"Goodbye, friend," Becky said quietly, turning her face toward the door so he wouldn't see her unhappiness.

"You do know that the boss man isn't going to take this very well," he said quietly, intending for Becky to be the only one to hear him. "I know this has been hard on you, but you've got to believe me when I say he really loves you. Not that *thing* in there. I think you're making a big mistake and you should tell him."

She wasn't convinced. "He'll be all right without us. Just take good care of him, you hear?" She admonished and shut the door, ushering the kids into the evening before anything else could be said. Or before more tears could fall.

"Why, how *are* you Susie?" Eva said swaggering into the kitchen after dinner that evening. Leaning on the counter, she watched as Becky diligently scrubbed the glass casserole dish.

Becky had been having second thoughts about leaving, but every time she saw Eva, it just made her more resolved to get away as fast as she possibly could. She had even considered telling Pearce her intentions, but when he wouldn't even look her way, she knew it would be useless.

Becky warily looked at her. "Okay…" Eva had a reason for coming into the kitchen, and she was pretty sure it wasn't to be friendly.

"You don't have to act so nasty to me," she smiled indulgently and flipped her hair over her shoulder. "I just wanted to tell you that I liked your, well," she screwed up her face as if she were trying to figure out what to call dinner, "whatever that thing was you made." She laughed merrily, her fake giggle resounding in the quiet room.

Becky looked at her as if she were a bug crawling on the floor and didn't give her the satisfaction of a reply.

"You know," Eva said, coming closer so she could talk more confidentially without the worry of being overheard from anyone who might happen to walk in on them. "When I first arrived, I had thought that maybe you and *my husband*," she paused for emphasis, "had something going on. In fact, to tell you the truth, I was just a tiny bit jealous." She held her finger and thumb close together just a fraction apart and a fraction away from Becky's nose. She resisted the urge to slap her hand away.

"But, as time progressed, I knew I didn't have to be worried. I mean, what would a rich man like Pearce want with just hired help? Anyway," she flipped her hair over her shoulder again, making sure to wave her hand in front of Becky's face. "The longer I was here, the more I realized that there never was anything between you two. So, do you forgive me?" She batted her eyelashes innocently and laid her long fingers on Becky's arm.

She looked down at the bony hand, intending to brush the nasty thing off when she realized what Eva was up to. A ring. On the third finger of her left hand. Her heart in her throat, it seemed time stood still, giving Becky ample opportunity to realize exactly what she was seeing. She swallowed hard and tried not to show any emotion when she saw the wedding ring, and it was the most difficult thing she'd ever done.

"Of course I forgive you," her voice sounded high-pitched and tinny, even to her own ears, and she wasn't sure the sweet smile she gave could be considered realistic, but the look on Eva's face told her she was completely surprised at her words. "What's there to forgive?"

With wooden movements, she managed to drain the sink and wash the soap down the drain before continuing. "And anyway, let me be the first to congratulate you both. I see," she pointed at Eva's hand, "that you're engaged. But let me ask you a question if you don't mind."

Eva glared, not bothering to give her the usual sticky sweet smile she used when being especially nasty. "Of course, Susie. What's your question?" She yawned and covered her mouth with her left hand.

Struggling against tears that burned the back of her throat and eyes, she kept her smile in place. "Do you realize what you have here? This isn't just a piece of property that you're marrying. This is an actual human being that has feelings."

"Oh trust me, I know what I have," she grinned wickedly as she brushed an imaginary piece of fluff off her designer shirt.

"I'm so glad to hear that, because I was afraid you were just using Pearce and Emily again. And speaking of Emily," she answered, rushing ahead, "I hope you realize that you didn't just have a baby when you had her. You gave birth to an eternal soul, a child that should be cherished and loved and taught, not a pawn you use to get what you want. But even more importantly, Eva," she looked squarely at her enemy, "do you have a personal relationship with Jesus?"

She flinched as though Becky had physically slapped her across the face. "A personal relationship with who? *Jesus?*" She sneered, her nostrils flaring as though she was having a tough time breathing. "Why would I want that? I mean," she added, collecting herself, "just look at you. You don't have any fun while I've done everything. I've been a model, an actress, and I've been with some of the most famous people you could imagine. What's *Jesus* done for you except give you a list of things you can't do?"

Suddenly, Becky was surprised to find she actually felt sorry for this wicked woman in front of her. "Just because I haven't been an actress or a model, doesn't mean that I haven't had my share of fun. God's been good to me and so what if I don't have everything this world has to offer? That doesn't mean he isn't taking care of me. In fact," she hesitated, "the best is yet to come for me because I've asked Him to forgive me of my sins. You? You don't have anything to look forward to except an eternity without God."

"I don't have anything to look forward to?" Eva hissed, glaring at her. "I look forward to taking Pearce away from *you!*"

"I hope that one day you'll ask Jesus to forgive you for your sins and save you," Becky answered, her face flushed in anger as she tried to ignore her last statement.

"If you're trying to convert me and make me a *Christian* you can forget it," she said angrily, clenching her fists, "and you're *fired!* So *get out!*"

With controlled effort, Becky calmly laid the washcloth over the sink divider and emptied the strainers into the garbage can. Quietly, she walked to the door, turned toward a seething Eva and said, "Well then, good luck to you. I'm sure you'll just *love* being a wife and mother again. Have a good evening."

Her heart broken and bleeding, she heard Eva cackle behind her, "And don't ever come back, Susie!"

It was a good thing she didn't need to think about putting one foot ahead of the other, or she would have never made it the small distance to the cabin. Her mind was numb and reeling from the news that she'd dreaded to hear. Pearce was engaged. To Eva.

With a shuffling gait, she made her way into the shadows of her front porch and dropped into the rocking chair, covering her face with her hands so she could cry without being seen.

Becky waited outside on the porch until she was almost sure her face didn't show signs of tears before letting herself in.

Judging by the look on Jen's face, she hadn't waited long enough. "When are we leaving?" she asked.

"I thought we'd leave after everyone in the ranch went to sleep."

"Do you want to play?" He asked innocently, holding out his hand of UNO cards towards her when she slumped into the chair next to him.

"I don't want to interrupt your game."

"Oh, you won't," he reassured her quickly, setting his cards down. "Jen's winning."

Jen scowled, then brightened with the thought of her mother joining them. "Yeah, of course he wants to quit this game. But that's okay. I'll just win the next game too!"

They sat at the table for a while, playing cards and having a good time being together when they heard a soft knock on the door. Quickly, Becky jumped up from the table, hoping it was Pearce coming to see why he hadn't seen her all evening. Throwing the door open, she endeavored to mask her disappointment and smiled at Curly who was twisting his cowboy hat in his gnarled hands.

"Come in."

"I just thought I'd stop in and say good-bye before y'all left."

"Well, we're glad you stopped by," Becky answered honestly, a lump in her throat. "I didn't see you tonight at dinner."

"I wasn't here," he answered quietly. "To tell you the truth," he looked her straight in the face. "I just don't have a desire to be inside that house with that woman. I like to stay as far away as possible from her."

"You know, as much as I hate to leave, I'm *not* going to miss her. Kids," she looked at the sleepy children, "why don't you go ahead and lay down until it's time to leave. I'll wake you up." Quietly they gave their goodnight kisses and went somewhat morosely to their bunks.

Curly sat in Jeff's recently vacated chair. "I still wish y'all weren't leaving. It's just not going to be the same when you're gone. You were the one who made this place run better."

"Oh stop," she smiled tiredly, the day's work frenzy catching up with her. "You did fine without me, and I'm sure you'll do fine after we're gone. Anyway," she lowered her voice confidentially. "I was told tonight that I wouldn't be needed here anymore. I was fired."

"I wouldn't believe anything Eva told you," he scoffed.

"Well," she hesitated and shifted uncomfortably in her seat. "What would you think if I told you that she was wearing a new wedding ring?" He stared at her dumbfounded.

"If it wasn't you telling me this, I'd think it was a lie. But," he scratched his head, "could it have been just an ordinary ring?"

"Nope," she sighed. "She made sure to flaunt it in front of my face, so I got a very close look at it. She was very proud of it, and I've never seen it on her before."

"Maybe it was her old one from when she and Pearce were married."

She brightened and hoped wildly he was right. It would be better to have Eva lie to her than it be true. "Do you remember what her old one looked like?"

"I remember, all right," he whistled with a shake of his head. "It was huge. I wondered how in the world he could have afforded a diamond that size."

"This wasn't it, then," she smiled ruefully. "This wasn't just one diamond, it was several smaller ones clustered around in a heart shape."

"Nope, that ain't it then, but I just don't understand why he'd ask her all over again, after all she's put him and Emily through. It just doesn't make sense."

She shrugged and gave him a sad smile. "I don't know why, but he seems to be taken with her, and there's nothing we can do about it."

"Well, I came over here tonight to ask you if there's anything that you needed help with before y'all left," he said finally, breaking the silence that had settled between them.

"I'm just going to wait until it's a little bit darker and then I'm going to put the stuff in the truck, and be gone. It won't take me long, there's not too much that I have to do. But thanks for the offer anyway, I appreciate it."

"Anytime you need something, give me a holler, and I'll be right there to help you," he stood to leave.

"I'm glad I got to know you. And if there's anything I can ever do for you, just let me know, okay?"

"I just might do that," he smiled, gave her a quick hug, and left.

Chapter 25

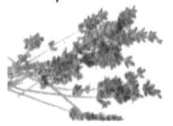

"Curly?" Pearce asked casually the next morning as he walked into the barn. "Where'd Becky go so early this morning?"

Curly kept shoveling hay into the stalls, not missing a beat. "I guess she went where she needed to be."

Pearce gave him an irritated frown, and Curly noticed he looked more disheveled than usual. "What does that mean?"

"She's gone." Stabbing the pitchfork into the ground, he leaned on it, swiped his hat off his head, and gave Pearce a stern stare.

"Gone? What do you mean 'gone'? Where'd she go?"

"Well," Curly stuck out his chin defiantly. "I guess maybe you should be asking your woman what she went and told Becky last night. Maybe then you'll figure it out."

The last thing he wanted to do was talk to Eva about Becky. "Why won't *you* tell me? You seem to know all the answers."

"Sorry, but you won't listen to anyone when we try to tell you something about Eva, so you're gonna have to go ask the one who caused all the ruckus." A staring contest ensued, and Pearce, aggravated to no end, was the first to look away. It was futile to argue or try to make Curly give him a direct answer when he was in this kind of mood. Giving the old man one last glare, he stormed out of the barn in search of his ex-wife.

He knew where to find her. It wasn't yet ten in the morning, and she never got out of bed earlier if she could help it. "Eva?" He switched on the light, irritated at her laziness. "Eva?" He said louder with a slap to the doorframe.

"What?" She snapped.

"Do you know why Becky left?"

"Susie's gone?" She asked a little too triumphantly for him not to notice her obvious pleasure. "Well, what do you think of that?"

Her smile sent him over the edge, and he trembled with rage as he stepped closer to her bed.

"Do you really want to know what I think? I think you're one of the meanest, laziest women I've ever met. I think you've been nothing but nasty and rude to Becky since the day you came here, I don't believe for a minute that you came back to get to know your daughter, and I think," he paused for breath, "it's high time you were getting your stuff together and leaving. Don't ever come back, because you're not welcome here!" His voice escalated at each sentence, finally ending in a shout. He was glad to see her wince with genuine fright at his tone.

"But that's *my* daughter too and I have a right to get to know her!" She spat hatefully as Emily came to stand in the doorway, rubbing her eyes.

"That's not your daughter. You only gave birth to her. Becky's the one who taught her, bathed her, loved her," his voice broke as he thought about all the things Becky had done that he'd just taken for granted. "*She's* more of a mother than you'll *ever* be. Now," he said as he scooped Emily up, and turned to face Eva again. "Get. Out. Of. My. HOUSE!"

"Well," she said with a mean smile. "I'm *glad* I'm leaving, and I'm *glad* I ruined your relationship with Becky. Oh yes," she said spitefully, narrowing her eyes until they were just tiny slits. "I'm pretty sure you have no chance with little Susie homemaker now. Especially," she looked at her nails and flicked a miniscule piece of dirt off the tip, "since I've heard through the grapevine that there's a certain little preacher boy who asked her to marry him. What do you think of *that,* lover boy?"

"What makes you think I'd believe *anything* you'd say? You're nothing but a liar and a cheat, and can't be trusted."

Her infuriating smile grew bigger, and he wondered if she could be right. "Fine. Don't believe me. Aren't you going to be surprised when you find out that I'm telling you the truth."

He stared at her for a moment, then, switching Emily to his other hip, he replied, "If Jack asked her to marry him, then I admire his taste. Get your stuff together, and leave. You're not welcome here anymore. I don't want to ever see or hear from you again, is that clear?" He turned and started to walk down the hallway, cuddling a crying Emily to comfort her.

"What makes you think I'd ever want to come back and see someone like *you*?" She spat maliciously, wrinkling her nose up in disgust. "I never loved you, and that goes for your brat too!"

"Eva," he said quietly, turning around to face her, "you make me sick. You better be gone in an hour."

"Trust me, it won't take me that long to get out of this *dump!*" She screamed at his retreating back as he took Emily outside to Curly, not paying any attention to her whatsoever.

They found Curly sitting in the chair in the office, relaxing for a minute between chores. Quietly, Pearce sat down opposite him in the empty chair and set Emily on his lap, gently wiping away her tears with a soft rag.

"I've made a mess of things, haven't I."

Curly chewed on a toothpick and gave a slight nod. "Yep."

"But why wouldn't she come talk to me?" He argued, not wanting to be the only one to blame.

"She tried," he answered flatly, looking directly at Pearce and held his gaze if not in a hostile stare, at the least a challenging one. "You weren't listening."

"Daddy," Emily said softly, interrupting them. "Is mommy leaving?"

He smoothed her bangs away from her face. "Yes sweetie, she is."

"She was mean to me."

"Mean to you? What did she do?"

Big, fat tears rolled down her chubby cheeks. "She would push me down and make me hit my head on the table."

"You told me it was Jen that pushed you," Pearce said sternly, upset that she had lied to him. "Why didn't you tell me the truth before?"

Reacting as she always had in the past, Emily leaned her head against his chest and stuck her thumb in her mouth. "Because I wanted her to love me."

"Emily," he tilted her face up to his, "you lied to me, and you're going to be punished. I also think you need to tell Miss Becky the truth." She nodded obediently then put her head back on his chest.

He looked helplessly at Curly. "What am I going to do?"

"Fix it," he answered simply, knowing that this was something Pearce had to figure out on his own.

"I think it might be too late."

"Why are we going this way? This isn't the way to church," Jeff asked, irritated again when Becky went in the opposite direction of what he affectionately called 'real church'. He was tired of trying new churches again, and got upset when she refused to tell him or his sister exactly why they didn't go to Jack's church anymore.

"Don't start," she answered shortly, unwilling to get into yet another argument with him. He'd been difficult to get along with since they'd left Pearce's place, and she was tired of having to explain her every move and decision.

"Why do we have to go somewhere else?" He grumbled, crossing his arms defiantly. Silently, Becky prayed for God's wisdom in how to handle his bad attitude.

Jen jabbed him in the ribs. "Why can't you be nice?" She asked severely in his ear so their mother wouldn't hear. "Don't you think mom's got enough to deal with? Why do you have to be a brat too?" Glumly, he looked out the window and pouted. Of course, he knew she was right, but there was no way he was going to admit that to his sister.

"Well," Becky said later as soon as they were in their truck heading home, "that was definitely uncomfortable." She grinned dolefully.

Jen nodded emphatically. "They were so unfriendly. Not one other kid in my class would talk to me."

Jeff, who was trying to get along better, piped, "It was like walking into an enemy camp."

"Yes it was," Becky and Jen both agreed, laughing. "Where do you two want to go now?"

"Home?" Jeff asked, surprised by the question. "We always go home after church."

"I don't want to go straight home today," Becky answered quietly. She had no desire to spend yet another afternoon alone with her thoughts and visions of Pearce and Eva. "I thought maybe we'd go to the diner for lunch. What do you think?" If she didn't want silence to rule the day, she'd succeeded as they both gave their assent. Loudly.

They chattered cheerfully all the way to the diner, and even until they were seated in a booth, oblivious to everyone around them. It wasn't until they were ordering their drinks that they noticed Jack sitting only a couple of tables away.

"Missed you at church this morning," he said casually, strolling over to their booth a few moments later.

"Mom made us go to a different church this morning," Jeff announced, clearly still aggravated about it.

"Is that right?" He asked, looking archly at a very red Becky. "And why is that?"

"I don't know, but I do know that we hated it." Jeff moved expertly aside as Jen aimed a swift kick at his shins.

Jack gave a good-natured laugh. "Well I guess that's good for me then, right?"

"Would you like to join us for dinner?" Becky invited, slightly uncomfortable as memories of their last evening together rushed at her. How did one go about forgetting that a man proposed and you'd refused him? She squirmed in her seat and felt her cheeks flame.

"No, I just thought I'd come over and make sure you were all right," he winked at Jen. "Pearce looked really bad this morning, and I noticed that Emily wouldn't go to her class because you weren't there, but that's about all that was new at church. I'll let you be." He turned to leave, then turned back toward them. "On second thought, why don't you all join me? They give me the big round table every time I come in here and I always feel like either a pig, or that they think they can bribe God and get to Heaven by being nice to the preacher." His look dared her to refuse.

"Sure," Jeff jumped up and grabbed his things, seating himself at Jack's table before his mother could say no.

"Oh my word, I'm gonna beat him yet!" Exasperated, Becky rolled her eyes. "I think we'll be happy to join you," she smiled apologetically as she and Jen followed Jeff's example.

They were just getting situated when the bell above the door tinkled merrily. Becky looked up and was horrified when her and Pearce's eyes instantly locked. Holding Emily on his hip, shock and longing flitted across his face which was finally replaced with a sadness that seemed to reach to his very core.

Becky tore her eyes from his when Jack called out, "Pearce! Why don't you join us? We seem to be having a church gathering here. We've got plenty of room." Smiling more wickedly then a preacher should, he leaned and whispered, "I hope that's all right with you."

"Well if it's not, I'll have to get over it, because here they come," she said through an artificial smile as they made their way over.

Pearce stared at Becky, and she once again caught a look of longing in his eyes when he said politely, "Becky."

Her neck warm, she looked away quickly and tried to smile, positive that someone had turned up the heat twenty degrees since he'd walked in. "Pearce."

"Miss Becky?" A small voice next to her elbow gave her something to concentrate on as Pearce sat directly in front of her. Now it was completely impossible to look up from the table at all.

She ran her hand over Emily's silken blond hair. "Yes sweetie?"

She shuffled her feet. "I'm sorry."

"What are you sorry for, baby doll?"

"Jen never pushed me down. I'm sorry I lied," she continued to look at the floor and stuck her thumb into her mouth. Surprised by the confession, Becky looked up at Pearce to find him staring at them.

With watering eyes, she turned away and planted a kiss on top of the child's head. "I already knew Jen didn't push you down, but I sure am glad you told me the truth, darling. Thank you."

Emily leaned up on her tippy toes and cupped her hand beside her mouth to whisper, "May I sit in your lap?" Becky nodded and helped her up. Almost at once, her eyes darted to Pearce to ask for permission, her conscience pricking her about the way she had left.

"Is this all right with you?" She half expected him to refuse, and wouldn't have blamed him if he had, when he nodded silently.

Jack cleared his throat, drawing attention to himself. "Well Pearce, how are you? You didn't look well this morning."

He looked down at the table and rubbed his hands down his tan dress slacks, evidently choosing his words carefully. "I'm *not* doing too well." Becky put her head down, afraid of what he was about to tell Jack. She knew she deserved his wrath, hatred even, but she didn't really want the whole story poured out at the dinner table in front of everyone.

"I could use a little good advice, if you wouldn't mind," Pearce continued evenly, making sure not to look Becky's way. "Do you remember my ex-wife?" Jack nodded. "Well, things got so bad I finally kicked her out and told her not to come back." Becky looked up, her mouth open slightly in surprise. "But, not before she came between me and my best friend."

His best friend? Curly? She took a bite of her non-descript food. "She and Scott ran off together, and she stole a bunch of stuff from me. But the worst part of it all," he turned red and glanced at Becky who was studiously eating, "was that I let her hurt the people that I care most about. I wouldn't listen when they tried to talk to me about the way she was treating them, and I always made excuses for her. I think what she did was wrong, but the fact that I let her get away with it was worse."

Now Jack understood why it had been so easy to call him over and get him to talk about his problems. He was really apologizing to Becky! Struggling against his own jealousy, he answered, "We all make mistakes, Pearce."

"I know we do, but I really want to fix this one. Before it's too late." He took a sip of his soda, his jaw working against some unknown emotion. Becky held her breath, not eating her food for fear that she would miss something.

"Excuse me," Jen said timidly, "but did you say that Scott's gone?"

"Yes, Scott went with her, wherever that may be. They drove off in his jeep the morning you all left." Jen looked crestfallen, and Becky felt sorry for her, knowing that she had really liked him.

"So, she took a bunch of stuff, and one of your workers," Jack prompted, leaning back in his chair.

"No," Pearce corrected immediately with a regretful smile, "she took a bunch of stuff and four of my workers. That's the problem." He cleared his throat and plunged ahead. "At first, I was hurt and more than a little angry when my workers left. I thought they were my friends, and I knew I would miss them terribly. But, as a little time went by, I thought about the situation. Well, to be honest, I never stopped thinking about it." He gave a humorless laugh.

"God kept reminding me about all the times they had tried to talk to me about what was really going on, and I didn't listen. No, that's not exactly correct. I *wouldn't* listen, even though I knew beyond a shadow of a doubt who was really to blame. I kept making excuses and I hid behind my Christianity and called it 'forgiving her' instead of stepping up and trying to protect those that meant the world to me. I had to lose it all before I really understood what was really at stake.

"Before she left, she told me something that I was sure was going to kill me if it were true, so I left the workers alone instead of trying to at least apologize. I just couldn't face them." He transferred his attention to Becky, and she couldn't tear her eyes away if her life had depended on it. "I was afraid to hear what was surely going to break my heart. So, after a little while of not hearing or seeing anything that would make me think she had told me the truth, I decided to go for broke. I made up my mind today. I'm going to fix this if it kills me."

Jack knew it was useless to hope Becky would ever change her mind about a relationship with him now. He gave it up as a lost cause and resolved to do the right thing, no matter how difficult it was going to be. "Is there something that I can do to help you?" He watched Becky shift a little out of the corner of his eye.

Pearce looked back at Jack, and Becky remained stone still, frozen to her chair as his words whirled around her mind. *He'd heard about Jack's proposal. How had Eva known about that?* she wondered, breathless. It took her a moment to gather her wits and tune into their conversation again.

"I need a new housekeeper," Pearce was saying, tapping his forefinger on the table.

"Is there something specific you're looking for?"

"Well, I'd like one that would love my child as if she were her own," Pearce started, ticking the qualifications off on his fingers. "I want someone that will teach Emily, because I really want her to be homeschooled, someone that will put up with me and let me tell them my thoughts, ambitions, and dreams, and someone who won't hold a grudge because of the many mistakes I make. A woman who will accept my humble apologies and will love me anyway. Even when I don't deserve it."

"Any kids?"

"Yes. She must have two, a girl and a boy. The girl has to love little Emily and never push her," he smiled brightly at Jen and Jeff who were watching him with undivided attention. "And the boy has to want to be a cowboy and be willing to help on the ranch."

"Anything else?"

"Oh yes," he scratched his chin thoughtfully, "she's got to make good apple pies!"

Jack laughed. "And is there a minimum time on how long this housekeeper has to stay with you?"

"For the rest of my life," Pearce said softly, staring at Becky's bent head as she quietly pushed her food around on her nearly full plate.

Jack whistled and leaned back in his chair. "You're still a young man and I bet you've got quite a few years left in you. She'd have to be someone pretty special, wouldn't she?"

"She is pretty special. In fact, I don't think I could live without her, and I know I don't want to try."

"Well, let's see," Jack said, stroking his chin, "why don't you come on over to the parsonage, and we'll have a cup of coffee as we get this thing written out and taken care of. What do you say?"

Becky didn't dare look up when Pearce stood and didn't see the determination etched in his handsome mouth. "Sounds like a good idea to me. Come on Emily, it's time to go." He held out his hand for his daughter, and watched Becky for a moment before leaving the restaurant.

They were barely outside the door when Jen shrilled, "Mom! Why are you letting him go? Didn't you hear what they were talking about?"

Jeff jumped to his feet and tried to pull his mother out of the chair toward the door. "Let's go."

"Sit down and let me think." Becky pulled her arm out of his grasp and tried to untangle the mess of emotions and desires that were currently attacking her.

Jen's anxiety turned to fidgeting while she looked out the window. "He was talking about us, mom. He wants you to be his wife."

Becky's heart leaped and her eyes twinkled with mischievous pleasure. "Are you sure?"

"Of course he was talking about us!" Jeff rolled his eyes impatiently.

"And this is something that you both think you want?"

"Yes!"

"Because," she said slowly, trying hard not to grin. "A lifetime is a long time at one job."

"Please!" They said agitatedly, ready to bounce out of their seats. "We'll help you."

She arched her eyebrows. "You're going to help with Emily? And never push her?"

"Yes, I'll help with Emily and never push her," Jen promised breathlessly, giddy with excitement.

"And," she turned an accusatory eye toward Jeff, "are you still going to be so difficult to live with and have a bad attitude?"

"No ma'am," he said staunchly, grinning from ear to ear. "I want to be a cowboy!"

Jen stood to her feet, unable to sit any longer. "But we better get going before he leaves the parsonage."

"Cool your heels, good things come to those who wait." Becky answered, gathering her things to leave just the same.

"Yeah, and you've been waiting nine years now," Jeff nudged her lightly through the door to their truck.

Chapter 26

Both kids were struggling not to scream in frustration while Becky made sure to take her time and drive carefully, obeying all traffic rules, including speed limits. Finally, she pulled into Jack's driveway and parked behind Pearce's truck. Their excitement brimming over, Jen and Jeff jumped out before they had completely stopped, and ran to ring the doorbell.

"Come in," Jack grinned and opened the door just in time for them to rush through. "Where's your mom?"

"She's getting out now," Jeff jogged toward Pearce, who was sitting on Jack's comfortable couch. Sipping a cup of coffee, he tried to look as relaxed as his restless nerves would allow while he anxiously looked for Becky.

"Hello Jeff," Pearce laughed and set the steaming mug down on the coffee table in front of him before the exuberant boy could topple it over. "What are you so excited about?"

Jeff came to a halt in front of him and stood as tall as he could. With his chest puffed out in front, and his chin tilted high, he said, "I want to be a cowboy."

"And I won't ever push Emily," Jen said solemnly when she came to stand next to her more lively brother.

"I'm sure you'll make a great cowboy, and I'm positive I don't have to worry about you hurting Emily. Have a seat!" He offered as they sat down to wait for their tardy mother who seemed to be in no big hurry.

The doorbell rang a few moments later, and they all sighed a breath of relief.

"Yes?" Jack opened the door to find a very embarrassed Becky standing on his porch.

"I heard that someone needed a housekeeper." She leaned around him and offered a small smile at Pearce who was coming toward her.

"Sorry," he said slowly, the tiniest of smiles playing at the corners of his mouth when her face fell, "but I changed my mind. I don't think you can be my housekeeper anymore. I want much more than that. I want someone who will belong to me and Emily. I want a wife."

She considered his proposal, her kids, Emily, and finally her heart. Taking his hands in her own, she squeezed them tightly and replied, "I've come to the right place because I want to be a wife."

He leaned his forehead against hers and whispered so only she could hear. "Who's wife?" Her eyes flitted toward her childhood friend for a moment, and she felt sad for him. He gave her a small smile and slight nod to let her know he'd be all right.

"Yours."

"Preacher man," Pearce hugged her to him and planted a slow kiss on her waiting lips. "Looks like we're gonna have a weddin'!"

"When?" Jack asked around the lump in his throat.

Pearce paused just mere inches away from Becky's delicious mouth. "Today."

"We can't today," she shook her head, surprised. "I don't have a ring for you."

Not to be deterred, he plunged his hands into her silky hair and let it fall through his fingers. "We can buy one after the wedding. I've got to buy you one anyway," he smiled at her tenderly. "That was one of the things Eva stole."

"What do you mean?"

"I had bought you a wedding ring right before she showed up, and it's missing. I'm positive she stole it."

"What did it look like?" She asked, remembering the ring Eva had been so careful for her to see.

"It had a bunch of diamonds in the shape of a heart, with a large diamond in the center. Why?"

"That was *my* ring?" She put a hand over her heart, and a glint of anger registered in her green eyes when she considered just how beautiful that ring had been. *Her* ring. "You bought that for me?"

"Yes I did. I knew I was going to marry you a long time ago.

From the moment you turned around to retrieve your pen. I knew you had to belong to no one but me." He kissed the tip of her nose, laughter making his eyes bright.

"Eva had it on the night before we left. She came into the kitchen and flaunted it all around, making sure I would see it. And all that time, it was really mine. She made me think you were going to remarry her." She looked up at him and lovingly caressed his cheek. "It about killed me."

"She told me the morning she left that you and Jack were going to get married. That's what took me so long to talk to you. When you didn't show up for church a couple of times, I figured she lied." He looked at Jack, laughing.

"Well," Jack smiled wistfully at the happy couple and shrugged, "she told me no again! But," he continued, seeing Pearce's discomfort, "You two belong together. My time will come. Let's have a wedding, shall we?"

"Now?" Becky turned her shining eyes on her husband-to-be.

"Now!" He grinned cheerily and took her hand in his own and promised before God and man to cherish her for better or for worse.

About the Author

Amanda Stephan is a Christian romance author and homeschooling mother that enjoys life to the fullest. Her first novel, The Price of Trust, was released in May 2010, and the keys have been smoking since! She emphatically believes in happy endings, and is living her real-life fairy tale with her husband in Columbia, TN, with their children, three cats, one dog, many chickens, and tons of laughs.

Visit Amanda Stephan:
Website: www.BooksByAmanda.com
Twitter: @amandastephan
Facebook: www.facebook.com/creativehomemomma
Blog: www.thepriceoftrust.com

The Price of Trust

Beaten and betrayed by the one
who was supposed to love her...

Carly Richards is on the run

Forced to live as a fugitive as her ex-fiance stalks her across country, she finds refuge in a small town in Montana. Her emotional scars are reluctant to heal, and Carly resists the friendliness of those around her ~ especially handsome farmer Joe Baird. Caught in the circumstances, the kind people around her begin to creep into her softening heart. God is at work, and she has to trust Him not only to take care of her, but care for the people she is learning to love.

Available at online booksellers and at
www.BooksByAmanda.com

What others are saying about
The Price of Trust

Well written, engaging, inspirational and a classically "good read". It was refreshing to read something I could pass to my 10 yr old and let her read with no fear of trashy content. ~ *Charmante Holden Isabell, homeschooling mother*

Great book, whenever I had to put it down I couldn't wait to get a chance to see what the characters were up to again. ~ *Sylvia Heim*

I loved the Price of Trust because it really hit home with me. I really liked that it is a clean read and inspirational. Carly reminds me of my sister, she is a very strong woman who can overcome any obstacle when she relies of her faith. ~ *Cathy Maynard McCully*

Well on her way to becoming one of this year's finest new Christian romance authors, Amanda Stephan has managed to take equal parts faith, intrigue, humor, and love and turn them into a delicious recipe called The Price of Trust. ~ *Aileen Stewart, author of Fern Valley*

An intricate tapestry of fear, faith, mystery, and down-home goodness, author Amanda Stephan has interwoven these elements and offers us The Price of Trust. ~ *Teric Darken, author of Wickflicker, Kill FM 100, and U-Turn Killur*